THE SMOKY QUARTZ CAPER

Janet McDermott

DEDICATION

The Smoky Quartz Caper is dedicated to Carol Farino. As my son said, "A larger than life lady who lived for adventure. "Hot dog!" she would declare with enthusiasm when we visited. To Jake's godmother, may you have united your mind and body once again. Your soul is now totally free.

CHAPTERS

ACKNOWLEDGMENTS

I fully declare that my writing is a fictitious collection of thoughts and feelings that I have absorbed and accumulated over my lifetime. From a writer scribbling thoughts on the computer, to the aspiring author finding a pathway to publishing, there is a multitude of friends and places to recognize. To my hiking buddies who respect and understand the majesty of the Rocky Mountains and to all the people who freely shared a facet of insights on the internet or in person, thank you. My places, events, people and incidents sift through my imagination then appear as fiction. I also need to thank Craig Ebel for designing the clever book cover after listening to my comments. Plus, of course, a loving scratch goes out to my stouthearted Schnoodle who slept through the entire book! Thanks all!

CHAPTER 1

FLOATER IN PARADISE

The nimbostratus clouds crashed together in rage like opposing boxers. Martin Keiser inspected the storm's turbulence with respect. 11,000 feet elevation always brought the ferocity of thunder and lightning as it spiraled through the atmosphere; it was chaotic and electric but exciting. Today was no exception. The weather forecast had said they'd get some much needed rain and it did look promising. Saddle Tree Gulch got wind mostly but this time the rains were coming. Probably one of the last rain storms before fall, Martin surmised as his intense hazel eyes scanned the pulsating sky.

He was a man of the mountains who always needed a hair cut and shave. His old cowboy attire was worn but clean in appearance. The light green color of his turquoise wedding ring fit his character well. Earth tones and facial wrinkles told the story of a man who loved the wind and sun. Keiser's Silverbelly Felt Stetson had molded to his head over the years. He was comfortable in his surroundings and his life; it complimented him. Martin's tall sinewy profile towered above the familiar high altitude terrain as he nudged the ground with his boot. Inspecting and prospecting was Martin's continual routine.

He began to wander along the bank of Saddle Tree Creek on his way back to their cabin. His eyes scanned the bygone tailings left behind after Freedom Mine had closed. He always searched for crystals here; it was his habit. 70 years of the same mien now brought Martin the reward of a Smoky Quartz Crystal. His cowboy boots gently overturned the sandy ground exposing this tiny lucid gem. Martin Keiser smiled as he leaned over and picked up his treasure. Emma would like it, he judged happily. As he placed the crystal in his pocket, the thunder rumbled; the storm was probably half a mile away crawling up Bross Mountain, he surmised.

Saddle Tree Creek was soon to fill up like an arroyo in New Mexico. The excess water would create a torrent of white caps hurling debris from higher terrain. The creeks would sweep and clean the land while the plant life hungrily drank their fill. Martin had always figured that rain was birth; a new beginning at least. It confirmed life, he comprehended.

His mind began to review his history. He figured when you hit your 70's, you should be allowed to savor old times. The Freedom Mine up the gulch had started it all for Saddle Tree Gulch. When the prospectors combed the Kansas Territory, it all changed. Hard to believe that this area was thought to be part of a huge parcel of Kansas. Not so at all. But then the exploration for ores was far more important than the integrity of the land back then. Hell, it still was, Martin assessed. Well, folks did finally realize that Colorado was a good moniker for the state. Times changed; scars remain.

Freedom Mine was a remaining dinosaur of past history. Back then dynamite had torn through the earth under the surface. The existing tunnels were like large wounds that bled toxic residue. Excess waters would force an unwelcome torrent to the surface. Rain storms like today, he thought. A hundred years later and still the prospector's poison seeped out. The toxic ooze would bleed into Saddle Tree Creek changing the color to an eerie orange shade. Martin would yell at the dogs not to drink the creek water for a couple days after a storm. Saddle Tree Creek would then clear again and life would go on.

He had to admit that the ore business had been good for Colorado. The 1860's brought gold fever and adventure. When Martin thought about the events, he did realize that Freedom Mine had added to the economy of Tiptop for a hundred years. It had belched out silver then moved onto the lesser economic boon of Rhodochrosite Crystal specimens. These magnificent red crystals were incredible. He had been fascinated when the Red King Crystal had been extracted and placed in the Natural Science Museum down in Denver. It was supposedly the largest Rhodochrosite specimen every found in the world. It now sat near Tom's

Baby, the giant gold nugget, found near Breckenridge. All good history, he thought.

So Freedom Mine had sustained an economy for one hundred years; he had to give it that. In the middle 1960's the mine was sealed. Now Martin would find an occasional Smoky Quartz Crystal but the Red Rhodos eluded him. His forte was Smoky Quartz; they would surface after a rain or by wind erosion. Nature's gift, he assessed.

He headed quickly now toward their cabin for cover. There was still some distance to hike; these storms were nothing to mess with. Lightning could take you out with no warning.

Martin Keiser became aware of a high pitched motor sound. It seemed to hover above him. He couldn't place the sound or worry about it now. A loud clasp of thunder suddenly threatened. Stopping to investigate wasn't a smart move at this point. He could come back later. Keiser decided to up the pace a bit and began to establish his familiar trot through the rough terrain. He concentrated on his pace and progress.

Suddenly, an immense pain shot through his upper torso. It was as if a bullet had entered his body. Keiser grabbed at his chest in shock. He sucked in air and let out a suffocating gag as if he was drowning. The only evidence of his death was a small stream of blood dribbling from his mouth.

The tall body toppled then slipped into Saddle Tree Creek without a sound. Martin Keiser's body submerged then blended into the sudden rush of orange water. His Stetson had caught on a branch of sage. It waved ominously as the storm gathered strength. The present volume of surplus water now testified that the higher biomes had been drenched. Martin Keiser's dead body twisted in the rapids; arms flailing, legs spread as it propelled toward a new destination.

***

Two weeks later the spheres of brilliant sunlight sparkled on the Blue River's surface. It was totally fall. The lazy current spoke of long gone rapids now waiting to replenish themselves during another inevitable winter. All creek tributaries had emptied their overflow water into the Blue; the journey to Dillon Reservoir was almost complete. Fall would bring a freeze then snow; this surrender was only weeks away. Frigid nights created ice crystals that glimmered during the mornings. These beautiful icicles disappeared with the afternoon's intense sun and blue skies. This cycle would repeat itself until fall was replaced by winter.

The Colorado Mountains were somewhat predictable and magnificent during the fall season. The weather was consistently mild during these sunny days. Brilliant yellow and orange aspen leaves shocked the mountain gulches as they became alive with the vibrant color. Was it the brilliant blue sky and intense sun at high altitude that made the environment so incredible or was it the anticipation of winter?

The wildlife was in a frenzy. Fall animal sightings were frequent during these constant days. It was like Mother Nature had intentionally paused in brilliant color for the food foragers. Squirrels began plucking and throwing green pinecones off of the trees with determined motivation as they stockpiled their food supply for the long arduous winter. Moose finished their grazing routes and revisited all the places where aspen branches still flourished. Bears ate everything and anything from disgusting to healthy; it didn't matter. The ground was searched for any remaining green sprouts by the deer. Bird nests were built and fortified for the hearty winter foul.

Locals started up chainsaws for cutting wood; cords got stacked and covered. The lawn furniture was put away and the snow throwers cleaned and oiled. Life moved through the season with purpose while everyone appreciated the remaining warm afternoons. Working people occasionally paused and turned their faces up into the sun; their eyes closed while absorbing the last fall rays.

Then the leaf gawkers from Denver migrated in car parades through the mountain passes completing their fall rituals. Pointing and stopping for occasional pictures before rushing back down to Denver was the norm. Urban sports and school now took priority over nature in most cases. It all fell into step.

One young couple had pulled off on Highway 9 to do some last minute fishing before they traveled back down to Denver. Fly-fishing was their passion. They decided to hike in on a trail that ended near the Blue River. Didn't take them long and the weather was simply beautiful. A couple hours of escape from their urban life was a great idea. The river waters peeked out from among the willows here. Could be good fishing, they thought.

Wading boots on, the couple quietly entered the water. Brown trout would hear your approach if they weren't careful. This location was somewhat off the trail so it offered them a quiet seclusion. It was possible that no one else had found this fishing place before. The Blue River contour was perfect. They waded out into the middle of the river. Their anticipation spiked.

Standing, facing opposite directions, the two began to flog the pools. Their rods skillfully threw a dry fly nymph out. It was time to wait and see if a brown trout would hit their line. It was the moment of truth when they hoped that this place was trout heaven.

The couple flogged the first small pool then moved on down toward the willows. The current was lazy as it drifted their fly toward shore. The second casts hovered around the same spots. Browns had to be enticed to strike. Both fly-fishers stood in the current using a slow concentrated technique as they reeled in. The willow branches stretched out over the Blue as far as nature would allow; the bank, itself, was in the shadows. A perfect hideout for the brown trout and the hand.

The bloated turquoise ringed hand waved passively in rhythm. The young woman abruptly stopped her second cast in midair. Her eyes riveted on the apparition. She first wondered if someone was swimming along the shore. Her mind dismissed that option as she comprehended the situation. The improvable specter initiated a ghastly scream exploding from her throat. Dropping her fly rod, the young lady ominously pointed! It was definitely an eerie sight that she would never forget. The hand beckoned!

Her scream had penetrated into the forest sending a chilling alarm throughout the biome. Even the wildlife stopped eating for a second, looked up and checked for danger then continued eating. It was a human cry for help; the animals were safe.

Bix and Bernie had just gotten out of their car when they heard the shriek. Both ladies looked around the trailhead then, without a word, decided the sound came from the river bank.

"I think it is maybe 300 feet or so ahead of us. Let's go," Bix Bixler waved her volunteer Forest Ranger badge at Bernie to illustrate her actual involvement. She had to wonder if someone was truly in trouble.

Bernie Holden was already running on the trail. She figured that someone needed help and that was all it took. They rushed with Simon Schnoodle leading the chase. His little black body became a streak as he ran the trail. The little dog knew it was trouble. Someone definitely needed a schnoodle's assistance. As they entered the clearing, the ladies saw two people out on the river. The couple didn't seem to be drowning or anything but something wasn't right.

Bix was the first to say something, "What's wrong? Do you need help?" she yelled between breaths.

The hiccupping young lady pointed down at the

moving hand. Obviously, shock had taken over. She croaked out a response, "My husband's calling 911. We were just fishing, that's all. Too horrible." Her pale face said it all.

"Here," Bernie murmured as she walked into the cold water and helped the lady back to the bank. Bix took off her jacket and put it around the shivering woman's shoulders. They watched her closely.

The man came over to them with thankful eyes. "The police are coming. Some unit called HAPT," he said. "Nice old guy on the phone. Hope he understood where we are," he stated then sat down next to his wife.

"Oh, he did. Frank Mason knows Summit County like the back of his hand," Bix Bixler stated confidently. Her stare now was drawn back to the willows. Bernie was getting the information that Bix would need for her report. "Thanks, Bernie," she said.

Bix's curiosity then brought her to the river bank above the hand. She lifted the branches to one side then verified that there was actually a body. Recognition hit like thunder when Bix saw the turquoise ring. She let out an audible gasp as she realized that Martin Keiser's body had been found. Two weeks later after a lot of dedicated people had searched, but here, by accident, poor old lost Martin had been found. Emma would be relieved, but the heartbreak was just beginning.

CHAPTER 2

FOUND YET LOST

Emma Keiser knocked timidly at Bix's door. Simon arrived at the door first. He wagged knowing that Emma wasn't exactly a stranger. Bix opened the door and gave Emma a warm hug before talking. Connection sometimes was so important; it could be far more important than words.

"Oh, Emma, I am so sorry. Come on in. You want some tea? I was just going to make some," Bix said leading Emma into the living room.

"You know, that does sound good. I was on my way into Breckenridge for groceries then I saw your turnoff and here I am." Emma Keiser was a tall slender woman. She had long grey hair gathered together at the nape of her neck. Her tanned weathered face spoke of the many years that she had spent outside with Martin. They were homesteaders in the true sense; salt of the earth and loving Colorado as much as life itself.

Bix began heating the water. She placed four tea bags of different variety on a plate along with some cookies. "You know, Emma, I sort of feel glad that I helped find Martin. He was found in the hands of friends. You know that?" Bix moved back into the living room again. Simon had jumped up on the couch next to Emma. She was petting him with a far away expression on her face as Bix returned with tea and cookies. Emma's focus came back to the present.

"Thank you, Bix, for the tea and for the thought. Martin was so lost," her words trailed off. Bix silently waited; Emma had come to talk. "I have to admit that losing Martin was bad enough and when no one could find him, I felt so helpless," Emma confessed. "That rain storm was something; he must have fallen into Saddle Tree Creek and drifted this way. You forget sometimes how all the water up here flows into the Blue River. Just hard to comprehend, you know."

"I know. Is there anything that I can do, Emma?" Bix asked as she handed Emma a tea cup. Bix's countenance of intense concern was framed by warm hazel eyes and short gray hair; she wisely listened to this old friend. Both ladies paused to toss a tea bag in and stir their cups thoughtfully. Bix sensed that there was more on Emma's mind; Simon snuggled closer, listening.

"Bix, there's something not right about all of this. The ME said Martin had a heart attack. Martin has never had heart trouble. He could still climb with the best of them. Then there was the hole in his back. Not a bullet, mind you. The ME said it had to be lightning but lightning comes in one side and out the other. There wasn't an exit wound. That's why I haven't cremated him yet." Emma's eyes welled up with tears. There was a stubborn look on her face; a look that just wasn't going away.

Bix assessed what Emma was saying and even more so, the emotion that she was feeling. The couple had never had children so Bix had to wonder if it was possible that this admission just became verbal for the first time. Emma's desperate look pretty well said it all. "Did the ME have any suggestions?" Bix asked.

"Willie Burnhart? No," Emma grumbled. "He just said that it wasn't normal but stranger things have happened. What the hell that means, I have no idea," Emma groused. She wasn't buying his conclusion Bix could tell.

"What did the HAPT team say?" Bix asked.

"They only took the body to Willie. Their part was over as far as I know."

"I can tell you that Officer Libby James and Detective Bill Smith did take pictures and investigate the scene on the Blue River. They are thorough and good. However, the body would go to Burnhart for examination." Her words trailed off as Bix reviewed the situation.

"Bix, I'm desperate. Do you know of anyone in crime forensics who would take a look just to put my mind at ease?" Emma stared intensely at Bix. Hope was so apparent; Emma held her breath.

"Well, I do know the Head of the Forensic Department at Colorado State University. He came to Summit last year and gave a lecture about how the human body is examined for evidence. The hospital opened up the lecture room for any locals who were interested and, of course, I was interested; you know, for my writing. Let's see, I should still have his card here somewhere." Bix got up and emptied a large bowl filled with business cards onto the table. Eyeglasses on, she fished half way down. "Yes, here it is. Dr. Harold Hastings. She handed the card to Emma Keiser. "He's a CSI Specialist. He mainly testifies in court as the definitive forensic ME. Expensive, I am sure."

"I have money, Bix. We've saved a lot over the years. Doesn't take money to make happiness, you know. Would you call him for me? Please?"

Bix inhaled quietly as she considered. Why not? What if Emma was right? Neither lady had said what the other option was but it was pretty obviously murder. Good Lord, Bix realized. "Are you sure you want to do this?" Bix asked just to make absolutely sure. The quiet hung in the air along with indecision.

Emma straightened her shoulders and replied, "Yes."

Bix got up and took the card with her. She found her smartphone in the kitchen and punched in the numbers. The chances that he would be there weren't good but who knew. Harold Hastings answered on the second ring.

"Hello, Dr. Hastings. How can I help you?"

***

Emma had left right after the appointment and

body transportation was organized. Bix was still in shock when Bernie got back from town.

Bernie Holden had gone over to the lumberyard returning with a truck load of 2 by 4's. They had decided to build a couple storage holders for firewood. "Hey honey, I have returned," Bernie exclaimed as she entered the front door. The tall speckled gray haired lady smiled when Simon immediately demanded attention. She bent down and picked him up for a hug. "What an ordeal. I think I got everything on our list." Bernie stopped in her tracks and stared at Bix. "What's up? Something has happened. I can tell by your face."

"Come sit down," Bix pulled her onto the couch. Simon had jumped down and wandered over to his food bowl just in case. Bix then began, "Emma Keiser just left. She doesn't think Martin was killed by lightning. She's thinking along the lines of murder."

Bernie eyes grew large as she processed that news. "You're kidding. Why? What's the motive? Who did it?"

"I didn't ask her any of those questions. She came to ask me if I knew of any ME specialist who could help her find out the answers. I happened to go to a great lecture by a guest speaker over at the hospital last year. We called Dr. Hastings at CSU and he'd like to examine the body. Emma made plans to have the body transported by hearse to him. She's paying for the whole examination."

"Whoa. I'm still back in 'the interesting lecture on dead bodies.' Sometimes, Bix, you shock the hell out of me."

16

"Well it was interesting. Sort of like listening to CSI on the TV only better because it was fact. Harold was really interesting. Don't look at me like that. It was interesting. It's kind of like me volunteering for Forest Service work."

"Yeah but that's because the Regime cut the EPA budget. You're now helping Smoky the Bear preserve the forests from the evil oil companies. I mean, that's a calling but a lecture on dead bodies?" Bernie's eyes held Bix captive for an answer.

"Okay, okay I admit it was curiosity. My writing, you know. We all do things for a reason and maybe my reason had to do with Emma."

Bernie leaned back and stared in amusement. "Do you buy what you just said?"

"Well no but it did sound good, didn't it?" Bix chuckled and smiled. "I do weird things sometimes. So there."

"And that's exactly why I love you. So are we going to CSU with Martin or with Emma Keiser?"

"With Emma after Dr. Hastings has a couple days to examine the body. Emma will then have it cremated up there in Fort Collins. Martin wanted his ashes thrown over their claim near the Freedom Mine. Sounds like she will have a Celebration of Life Ceremony the following week. We are, of course, invited. You'll like all the old prospectors and local folks who go. Not a fake one in the bunch, I would say."

"Well not exactly a party but it does sound interesting." Bernie leaned over and kissed Bix. "Never a dull moment, lady. So we're on another murder investigation?" she asked.

"Well, let's invite Captain Jen over tomorrow night and see what she has to say."

"Sounds like a plan," Bernie commented.

***

"She did what?" Jen Holly's fork stopped in midair. Her long brown ponytail swayed as she then turned and stared at Bix. Her brown eyes processed this new agenda. "And this Dr. Hastings is examining the body as we speak?"

"As far as I know," Bix answered while taking a sip of her wine. Her hazel eyes sparkled as she stared at Captain Jen Holly. Bix knew that she was relaxed enough this evening to listen and consider; it was a challenge when dealing with someone as busy as Jen.

The Captain's High Altitude Pursuit Team, had become swamped with cases since all the budget cuts had occurred. When the new Capital Regime Government removed all community grants, Jen had gone over Peak County and asked them to come into the three-county HAPT arrangement. 'It would be cheaper than having Park outsource and pay for special services,' she proposed. Peak County had agreed. HAPT now worked for four counties instead of three. Essentially, 25% more work for the same amount of money, but they had survived for now. It was the new way of life. Emma lived in Peak County so why not? It was worth the venture.

"Emma just wasn't satisfied with Burnhart's autopsy," Bix added.

Jen's large brown eyes stared at Bix then

Bernie. It definitely looked like this dinner had its own agenda, she assessed. She paused to consider.

The ladies' dinner preparations had been perfect. Bernie had barbequed a delicious chicken and it was served with a tasty bottle of wine. They were in the middle of the main course when Bix had brought up the subject. Bernie thought she might wait until dessert, but Bix had seen an opening and went for it.

"Good old Jerome Walker will not be happy," Jen mumbled. "He really doesn't take to someone working in his territory," Captain Jen said shaking her head. However, there was a hint of mischief in her eyes. "The man can literally be a monster," she admitted. "Retired sheriffs still wear the badge."

"I know but it is Emma's right to ask for assistance. We also talked about what if Dr. Hastings decided it was a heart attack. Emma felt that then she would be satisfied. She just needs a forensic expert to take a look." Bix lowered her wine glass and concentrated on her salad. "I didn't ask about motive or anything. It took us all afternoon to get the body released. Emma had to call over to Leadville to find a hearse that would make the trip. I didn't even ask what it would cost. What with the times the way they are, I'm pretty sure they were happy for the business," Bix said. "When you find people that still have cash, you go for it, right?"

"Right," echoed both Bernie and Jen together. They all concentrated on dinner for a few moments letting all the implications soak in.

Bernie glanced around the table, slipped Simon

some chicken then changed the subject. "So since I visited last, I hear that you have started dating. Is that delightful information correct? Bix also told me that Katie is a knockout."

"Well I think so," said Jen with a smile. Her face had turned into a giant blush as she hid behind a piece of homemade bread. "And yes, I am dating when my job allows free time which isn't very often."

"Congratulations."

"Thank you."

"Do I get to meet her?" Bernie ventured after a sip of wine.

"We could do dinner next week unless my schedule goes crazy?" Jen said confidently. "I have neglected my social obligations long enough. Bix hasn't even met her formally yet."

"No. I haven't. Don't get out quite as much as I used to though. Fortunately, I can still afford to eat out now and then," she added.

"So the Regime is still after social security?" Jen asked. "I was afraid of that, she sighed.

"Correct," Bix answered. Again, the silent implications settled. "Next week will be fine," Bix answered. "We will mark it on our calendar."

"So what happens if Martin Keiser was murdered?" Bernie asked changing the subject again.

"Well then I guess it could become a case for HAPT; we were called to pick up the body so it would make sense. I have to say, it does sound pretty fascinating. Dr. Howard Hastings, you say? Maybe I should give him a call just to let him know where to send a copy of the findings and of course meet him. Thanks for the heads up, ladies. Now, what's for dessert?"

***

The drive back from Fort Collins began quietly. There was a lot to process. Dr. Hasting's report was definitely meticulous and complete but produced so many questions, Bix concluded. When he had gone into his findings about a TMLR laser penetration, she couldn't believe it. Hastings had definitely ruled out lightning right away. 'No burn marks,' he had said. Plus, he hadn't found an exit wound either. So Willie Burnhart had gotten that right but a Full Spectrum Laser like the ones used in hospitals for heart surgery was the weapon? Unbelievable and so technical, she assessed. 'The beam was aimed right at Mr. Keiser's left atrium in his heart,' Hastings had said.

"A laser?" Bernie echoed out loud sensing Bix's thoughts. "How can that be? I mean he was at 11,000 feet in the mountains for heaven sakes during a rain storm. I may be a cowgirl in my thinking, but I sure as hell don't understand how that kind of specific laser got up there." She flipped on the car turn signal and entered the traffic on I-25. South they went. "It would take one of those expensive laser machines found in a hospital, right? I just don't get it."

"Neither do I," murmured Emma from the backseat. She and Simon were snuggled together. The miniature schnoodle always knew when someone needed to pet him. It was called dog therapy; Emma was a candidate.

"Glad it's not our job to figure that out," Bix said from the passenger seat. Her eyes scanned Hasting's forensic report. She could see Officer Libby James figuring out the technical stuff. The High Altitude Pursuit Team, known as HAPT, was definitely up to that challenge.

Bix did have a few questions for Emma Keiser at this point. "So, Emma, why Martin? Speaking of kind and well liked people; he was one of those. I am having trouble wrapping my mind around the concept of premeditated murder."

"Eminent Domain," Emma declared without hesitation. "That's why I needed a second opinion on Martin's death."

Both Bernie and Bix did a double take. The shock was that Emma hadn't even hesitated. She knew where to place the blame. It was astounding. The first actual threat of land grab in the Central Mountains as far as Bix Bixler knew. It was here and it was now.

Bernie Holden had already experienced the fracking land grabs in her home state of North Dakota. This grab didn't surprise her; it did depress her but it wasn't a surprise. Her family had survived the assault with their land intact, however, it had killed her father, Henry. Now, here it was again. She knew how this reality was impacting Bix. Land was so incredibly valuable and not always for the right reasons. Bernie felt Emma and Bix's pain; she knew the depth of their panic. It wasn't truly real until it happened in your own backyard.

Bix was definitely surprised that she knew nothing about the threat. Early in the summer Bix had contacted the Personal Property Coalition on line to make sure that there were no Eminent Domain cases in Summit County. After watching Bernie deal with a land grab, Bix had realized how vigilant one had to be during these times. The laws now wouldn't protect shit anymore: corporations could attack without any notice under the guise of Eminent Domain. It could come down to who had the most money and the best lawyers; the courts making the final decision. You didn't own your property anymore even though you had paid for it. The Personal Property Coalition had reported to her that Summit was clear. Of course that had been early summer.

It then dawned her that Emma and Martin Keiser owned property in Peak County. No wonder! She began to admonish herself for not going further into research on all four counties. Two of the counties, Lake and Peak Counties, were not as financially set as Summit County so they were fair game. Damn, she thought. Of course oil and uranium companies would go after them first. "Shit!" she murmured.

CHAPTER 3

THE CASE BEGINS

"So Martin Keiser was killed by a 3D laser?" Officer Libby James said as she munched on a muffin. Monday mornings were muffin day in the office. They divided up that duty. "I am hoping that you all will consider me for visiting Dr. Hastings in Fort Collins. Incredibly interesting, I think."

"I was hoping that you would volunteer for that duty. Thanks, Libby," Captain Jen said. "Bill, what do you want to do?"

Detective Bill Smith's body shifted in the chair as he considered. His eyes scanned the report on his ipad. He punched the screen and traveled through the report. "First, I am intrigued by the body's journey into the Blue River. Seems like we'd have to prove that the water flow could have naturally sent the body there. Weather and current would play into that path. Some idiot attorney could say it was picked up and brought there by car. I'd like to work with the Forest Service on the natural flow."

"You're right. If the courts could question the body destination then it could mess up the case. Good," Jen said. "Frank?"

Frank got up from the communication's board scratching his grey beard thoughtfully. He walked over and snatched a blueberry muffin then said, "I'd like to do locals and land investigating. See what Emma's neighbors know about this Eminent Domain land grab. Granted, some of those owners do live out of state. They still keep their land for sentimental reasons. Some of their ancestors were prospectors who worked the Freedom Mine. Hopefully, one of Emma's neighbors will have some names for us so I can contact them," Frank assessed. He then added, "If these people don't know about the land grab, they need to know. From what I hear, you can simply get a registered letter in the mail that says, 'Guess what? You lose and business wins.' Plus, the Tiptop Zoning Committee must know something. Any entity has to prove that their land grab benefits the public or so they say. The company would have to contact Planning and Zoning."

"Excellent. I think we need to get a list of all the individual property owners up there for sure," Captain Jen assessed. "For my part, I'll call Buena Vista and get Officer Neal to come on over and bring Tyler with him. A dog could sniff out something relevant near the actual crime scene. We haven't inspected that area yet since the body was found two weeks later and 20 miles away," Jen added. "Jerry and I can rope off the area and do a thorough search that is if Emma will take us up there. Hope she can pinpoint the actual murder scene. Come to think of it, that is going to be a hard one. The trouble is she wasn't there; I can't imagine her being involved in any way. Right, Frank?"

"Damn straight," he answered.

"Anything else for the good of the order?" Jen asked. Her question was met with silence. The meeting was adjourned.

***

Libby was about five miles from Fort Collins. She was going to be right on time it looked like. She and Marshall had argued about who showered first this morning so they both lathered up together. However, that always made both of them run late. Delayed by sex was so wonderful, she sighed, then smiled. Her red hair was still damp but her body sure was warm and content. They had moved in together right away after Marshall Tate had gotten the Frisco Sheriff's position.

When November came and the national election had changed everything, they had been so thankful that Marshall had resigned from the FBI. The Capital Regime had created a nightmare at the national level. His friends called once in awhile to vent. Marshall just listened and smiled at her. They really were so happy; their romance took Libby's breath away. Both police officers were building their own careers and experiencing their new relationship. Every day now, life was so incredible.

She had made up some time on I-25. The traffic wasn't bumper-to-bumper this morning. Libby turned off on the exit and then flipped on her smartphone for driving instructions. Dr. Hastings office was on campus and easy to find. She glanced around the university. Pedestrian traffic was high; Libby figured they were between classes at this time. A new year had started and so many of the students looked so incredibly young.

Universities were experiencing less enrollment now, Libby calculated. A college education was almost unaffordable for the middle class at this point. Even scholarships were drying up. Many parents were looking more seriously at the offshore schools for price and safety.

Health insurance and education would become offshore commodities soon, Libby concluded. That was the price tag for a corrupt government who took away all benefits. The educated population would be looking for employment in countries with health care benefits if the next election didn't swing things back to democracy. This country would experience a brain drain if things didn't change period. "Ouch," Libby mumbled as she parked her car.

Libby rushed up two flights of stairs and knocked on Suite 222. "Come in," said a cheery voice. He was a friendly and accessible teacher, Libby surmised. The office was warm and inviting. Dr. Hastings came out from behind his desk and gestured toward two well worn comfortable chairs. Hand shakes and introductions out of the way, they settled. He handed her a rather small folder of data.

Libby looked up and asked, "So I can get on line and find out the specific details?"

"Correct. Didn't want to kill all those poor trees so you will find it all on that website," he added. "Could you tell me what has occurred so far in this case?" he inquired leaning back ready to listen.

"Well, the body was discovered a couple days ago and my team got assigned the case."

"You are the HAPT group correct? What does that indicate?"

The High Altitude Pursuit Team's purpose is to rescue and find individuals. We also have been known to take on cases that require special investigations. Martin Keiser's case falls under that description. It requires a technical piece plus high altitude investigation," Libby stated.

"You know now that you mention it, I have heard of your team. The McPherson Case with all kinds of international implications comes to mind. That one was yours, right?"

"Yes. We tackled that one last spring."

"Hmmmmm. Yes, it had quite a few interesting components, the avalanche and big business. I can see how this case would end up on your table. Mint?" he asked offering a small bowl full of green mints to Libby.

"Thanks," Libby popped a mint in her mouth, got out her ipad for notes and then continued, "So Dr. Hastings, my assignment is to figure out how Keiser was murdered. 11,000 feet makes the crime scene extremely unique. How in the world did a 3D laser get up there and cause a direct hit on Martin Keiser's heart?"

"Easy. The instructions are on YouTube. An assassin could buy the stuff at a lumber yard and make his own weapon. Actually let me grab my computer and send you the instructions." Hastings fetched his laptop and did a quick search. He got Libby's email address and sent her the website.

Her eyes grew large as she examined YouTube. "So anyone with any science background could create this laser?" she asked after a few moments. "This DIY Laser could be built from scratch. All you need is listed right here, right? Is glass tubing hard to find?" she asked.

"No."

"Washers, shellac, JB Weld and masking tape are the major components?"

"Yep," he nodded and smiled. His brown eyes sparkled as he watched Libby realize how convenient a weapon the laser was.

"Would you need a degree in chemistry or anything?" Libby asked. "You know, because of the helium, nitrogen and CO_2 in the mixture?"

"Nope," Harold Hastings replied folding his hands in his lap and waiting for the rest of the inevitable questions. "*Scientific American* would have an article on what you need to know. Although, you would need to be able to read," he added.

Libby was processing quickly. "How about the transport of this weapon?" she asked.

"Go to Walmart."

"What?'

"Oh, I'd go to Walmart and purchase a Swift Stream 2-9 Remote Drone for about 90 bucks then connect it to a smartphone for the firing piece. The assassin could be 500 feet away from the target.

That drone will carry almost a hundred pounds so there you go, windy or not. Attach the laser to the drone and let it talk with your smartphone. All set and lethal."

Libby sat back and tried to comprehend what she had just learned. So simple yet so deadly, Libby assessed. "Unbelievable," she murmured. "Then I would need to create this weapon for the case. My glass tubing would be mm size to keep the weight down. The laser could be less than 20 pounds?" she calculated and verified.

"Yep. You would be in business and a lethal assassin at any altitude. I'd say your laser would mount on the drone easily and your accuracy would be better than with a rifle scope."

"Have you run across any laser weapons like this before?" Libby asked leaning up in her chair.

"Actually no. This is my first one, but there are other cases out there. Want me to send you what I can find on our forensic websites?" Libby looked shocked, so he verified, "Easily done. Sounds intriguing to me. Plus, I sure did like Emma Keiser and her gang of friends. A breath of fresh air on this old stuffy campus," Hastings admitted. "I will, of course, aide you in anyway that I can. Emma has hired me and I'll go to court for her any day. You and I can meet again before the trial and get our act together. I am assuming that you are the tech person and will need to testify. If you have any questions on the building of your laser weapon, let me know. I am generally available when I'm not grading papers or lecturing."

"Thank you, sir. You have been incredibly

helpful. I probably will need some help with my invention so I do appreciate your aide in advance. Love a good challenge and I have one now. So for less than 200 bucks, I can build a laser weapon? Amazing."

"Racked and loaded, young lady."

"Need to ask if you have any clues on when the murder took place." Libby asked.

Dr. Hastings scanned his notes quickly then said, "I would testify that the murder occurred between 4 and 6:00 PM the day Keiser didn't return home, September 15th. The body was fairly well decomposed but there was enough left for analysis. Laser holes don't destroy the internal organs like a cartridge would. Cause and time was easier to determine. I'm not sure that criminals know that information yet. Could be interesting if we need to process any more of these types of cases."

"Wow, thank you Dr. Hastings. I'm sure that will be of help. All that information is in your report?" she asked to make sure.

"Of course. Anything else we need to cover, Officer James?" Dr. Hastings asked with a twinkle in his eye as he cleaned his round glasses.

"No. I think you have been very thorough. Thank you again."

Libby closed her ipad and got ready to leave when Dr. Hastings totally changed the subject and inquired, "So…Officer James, if you ever want to get a degree focusing on forensic science and computers, let me know. You're quick. I like that." Dr. Harold Hastings stood up and shook Libby's hand again. He stared into her eyes and searched for any interest that might be there. "We're always looking for good candidates," he added.

The 'interest' was there, Libby knew. She could see starting a specific degree from here. Right now there was a lot on her plate but a few hours at a time certainly wasn't a bad thing at all. "So I could take a few credits at a time and keep my job?" Libby ventured.

"Yep. Call me, Libby James, when you're ready." Hastings released her hand and wished her a safe drive home.

Libby could feel a definite attraction to forensic science. Her thoughts were spinning as she drove south on I-25. Maybe late winter she could start; it was another one of those life altering surprises for Libby. Another positive event. Marshall Tate had been quite a surprise this last year and now Libby was suddenly thinking about a degree. Her resolve formed as the miles flew by. She couldn't wait to talk with Marshall. Maybe she could find a course from Dr. Hastings online? Yep. Start small and work your way up, she thought.

Officer Libby James then began processing what she had learned today within a short hour's time. Martin Keiser's case was definitely going to be interesting and probably dangerous when you have to deal with an assassin this clever. Guns were obvious but lasers brought a whole new dangerous dimension into the pursuit. "Oh boy," Libby whispered as she exchanged 1-25 for I-70, west.

***

Officer Frank Mason drove up to the Freedom Mine Lode. It just seemed like a good place to start, he thought. Frank had taken his old truck instead of a cop car and changed into his weekend clothes. All was quiet here except the usual wind that swayed Frank's walrus mustache slightly. His appearance fit perfectly into Freedom Mine's past; he looked like a miner reporting to work. Actually, all the authentic employees had left by the 1960's. They had simply moved on or had retired in Tiptop. The mine was said to be tapped out according to the last company, Rhodo Gems. They had finally sealed the entrance after extracting the Red King Rhodochrosite Crystal. Even the precious gems were tapped out so they said.

Frank rolled down his truck window and now scanned the quiet claim. He wanted to get a feel for the land's importance. Mountain cops assumed that murder up here just might involve land value in some 'way, shape or form.' It was the new trend taking place with corporations moving in on unsuspecting locals. Was Emma Keiser right about the possibility of Eminent Domain? That was the million dollar question. Sometimes, people had no choice in the matter. They could try and keep their lives peaceful but then here came the outside forces.

Quiet little towns like Tiptop tried to maintain their isolation; they didn't vote to expand. Tiptop had chosen to let their wealthy neighbor, Breckenridge, take all the notoriety. The locals, however, did welcome the employment opportunities of a ski area. They also liked coming home to the quiet. It was a balancing act to maintain a living and keep their precious isolation.

Tiptop locals didn't take to uniforms and cop drama . The town was quiet by design; the early prospecting had always dictated the town's profile of independence. Gold rush to silver claims and then crystals had been in its history. Now, the only new businesses were a couple marijuana shops. They did keep up with the Colorado opportunities and had added tourist shops over the years. If one looked closely the gems and mineral samples were still present in novelty merchandise. Not a lot of silver though but the past wasn't totally forgotten.

Back in the 1870's silver had motivated prospectors to a small town named Silver City. Silver City's town limits had been built above where Tiptop was now. Some 5000 men rushed in to operate the claims. A smelter was built by a man named Meyer and the silver industry took off. Colorado's famous gold millionaire, Horace Tabor, had even been in on the discoveries back then. Eventually, the silver vein disappeared and they all moved toward Leadville leaving Silver City abandoned. Since then the authentic ghost town had been bought twice and moved twice. A large part of Tiptop's identity was gone. Sold. The recent rich owner kept Silver City hostage on his own large estate. Private property. Silver City now had no roots; it had been separated from Freedom Mine and Tiptop. The history was completely erased as far as Frank was concerned.

Frank sighed as he shut the truck door and wandered up to the sign announcing Freedom Mine's closure. He pulled out the land map copy that he had gotten from the Tiptop Court House this morning. There seemed to be a vortex of four land claims in the gulch. One of them was, of course, Martin Keiser's North Star Mining Claim. The one characteristic of all claims was that Saddle Tree Creek ran through them. The Freedom Mine claim ran horizontally along the top then the four other claims were surveyed and drawn below that mine like table legs. So five property claims in all constituted the Freedom Mine Lode located in Saddle Tree Gulch. All were owned separately.

Frank figured that North Sage Claim was owned by a family located over in Leadville. That was close. Also, Nathan Abel still owned Smoky Quartz Mining Claim, He still lived in Tiptop. Nate Abel would be the only prospector still in this area now that Martin Keiser was gone. Abel's ancestors had come from Kansas if Frank remembered correctly. They had worked Freedom Mine in the silver era. The other claim, Saddle Tree Creek Mining, was a mystery to Frank. That one would take some investigation. Nate Abel, however, was the place to start.

Frank began to walk through the gulch hoping to find some of the metal stakes that would designate the surveyed claims. Sometimes, these old surveyors would indicate a point by saying that they marked it by chopping into a six inch diameter tree. Hell, that was nonsense. A hundred years later who knew if the tree was a monster or gone. Railroad ties were far more sensible, Frank reconnoitered.

He spent a couple hours searching and was successful in finding two stakes that proved the claims were probably normal surveyed size, 100 feet by 5000 feet; long and narrow was the norm. They weren't for building but for tracking veins of precious metals. Frank was able to find the corners of Smoky Quartz Mining Claim and the North Star Mining Claim. Saddle Tree Creek Mining Claim was still a mystery.

Frank wandered back to his truck and decided to see if he could find Nathan Abel who might be able to locate the other survey corners up here. He figured that it was lunch time and maybe Nate would be hungry. Food and conversation just might be of great value today.

He drove down the old rutted road. There was a small cattle herd grazing on Nate's claim, Frank observed. As he went lower in elevation, the grass had become greener. Nate was still making a little cash off of his claim. Not as spectacular as mining but financially helpful, Frank assessed. He had checked out the address in Tiptop for Nate Abel's cabin before leaving the office this morning. Gold Miner's Road was his destination. Seemed like a pretty appropriate address, Frank Mason thought.

CHAPTER 4

WATER GIST

"It looks like the pending Eminent Domain dispute is about water," Melanie Camp of the Personal Property Coalition said as she examined her computer monitor screen.

"What? I thought it would be Freedom Mine originated? No uranium or silver? Water?" Bix exclaimed. Her hazel eyes registered shock as she shifted in her chair. Emma's comments now made sense.

"Actually, thank you for bringing your concerns to the Coalition. The Regime is up to something and you can be sure that it is not for the benefit of the public. Quite frankly, I hadn't seen this case before; obviously, it was hidden on purpose. Hmmm. I need to get this information to our central office immediately and have them research what's going on," Melanie stated then looked up at Bernie and Bix. "Yes, ladies, it is of concern." She then handed an informational sheet to them. It was entitled *Ten Steps to Protesting against Eminent Domain.*

"So these steps should be taken before the lawyers come in, right?" Bernie Holden asked sending a hand through her graying red hair. She listened intently.

"Correct. You have to set the stage with paper trails including letters to your Zoning Committee. And if need be, protest their conclusions. Postcards will help; it all becomes effective. These steps should have started months ago. You need to take a close look at the Zoning Committee also. Could any of these people be bought or of the wrong political persuasion? Everything concerning the area's politics will now come into play."

"Well, I guess we'll start to dig when we get back up the hill," Bernie said. It occurred to her that Melanie was incredibly organized. Much more organized than in North Dakota, she concluded. These folks would learn how to deal with corruption quickly, thank heavens.

Melanie then asked, "Are you organized or at least have a group of people who are willing to work on this situation?" Her eyes searched for answers as she looked at Bernie and Bix again.

Their mouths were open and nothing was coming out. Neither lady had understood what part the community needed to play in this water grab. Bix was at a loss. Bernie realized that the opposition against corporations and government had become much more sophisticated. It wasn't simply a legal matter that ran over you. The public needed to contest all takeover actions.

"You know, I could talk with Emma Keiser and see if she would set up a community meeting. Hopefully, Tiptop would come out and give a listen to this approach. Don't get me wrong, I see the need but if we can't get the public to buy in then it simply happens, right? The government wins, right?"

"Exactly, it could be difficult to get these people motivated into action," Melanie assessed. "Tiptop would have to protest in a loud voice. It's got to get in the Denver papers and other small towns need to see what opposition looks like. This water grab has to be exposed. You have to reveal the Regime's motives for what they are, political corruption."

Melanie leaned back in her chair and remembered a piece of history, "Did I hear years ago that Tiptop's ghost town, left town? I mean, letting your history be sold is definitely not responsible citizenship. Hope the town has changed somewhat since then. When you consider that maybe even Freedom Mine could have become a tourist site instead of being patched shut with cement. I mean, I don't know but getting them to respond may take a miracle. Having said that, I do want you to know that if you can get the people interested, I will come and help. Lawyers don't just jump out of woods by the way. They have to be enticed by an interesting case. You want them to volunteer their services then see that the media will follow your rally."

"Then you almost have to have a large protest, don't you? We're actually revolting, aren't we?"

Bernie concluded.

"Correct," Melanie answered. She took a sip of coffee and began to think out loud again. "Tiptop and Freedom Mine, you say? The area has symbolism written all over it. People wanting freedom at the top. Solitude can mean freedom, you know. Have you talked with any of the environmental groups yet? They should be interested."

"This is our first stop. Have you got any suggestions on who might be a good source?" Bix asked.

Melanie hit her computer keyboard quickly. She brought up a list of contacts then hit print. A full sheet of possibilities was in Bix's hand within minutes.

Melanie's expression now formed into a smile. She cocked her head to the side and raised her eyebrows. "I have a feeling that you two are going to get this done. Have no fear, you have absolutely nothing to lose. The Regime just doesn't like to be in the media eye when it comes to this kind of takeover. You two could very well be their worst nightmare. I just have a feeling." Melanie's smile was infectious; her freckles surfaced from underneath her tan face. "Just keep in mind that we could win one little town at a time. Good luck, ladies. Talk to people and organize." Melanie walked them out of her office to the elevator. "Trust me," she said, "all things are possible. In the meantime, I'll work on the Capital Regime motives. We'll get them."

As Bix and Bernie left Denver, they began to

realize what it took to contest an Eminent Domain case. There was no time to spare. The ladies decided to drive back through Placer City then Tiptop.

Bix called Emma and asked to stop by with the information that they had gotten. It became pretty obvious to them that if they didn't have Emma's support then there was no need to go any farther.

They arrived at her door two hours later after a good Schnoodle sleep. Simon was ready to get out of the backseat of Bernie's Subaru. It was nice to have this new car to ride in, but Denver and back was enough. As they parked, Simon shot out of the car. He peed several times in relief.

Emma ignored the ladies and yelled for Simon who rushed through her front door quickly. Her two Border Collies were friends of his. They went into a sniffing frenzy while the humans got comfortable.

"So the Personal Property Coalition is willing to help us?" Emma repeated. "That is wonderful news I think. I guess we have no choice. The fear has gotten stronger since Martin's murder. The town has been awfully quiet; I know they are thinking and talking. It's funny when you know that life just might have to change. I guess we've reached the old 'put up or shut up time.'" Emma got up out of her rocker and stared out her window, thinking.... The quiet seemed endless to Bix at this vortex.

She slowly turned around and faced them with a new idea. "How about getting the food that people brought in memory of Martin out of the freezer and organizing a meeting? I haven't been able to eat period," Emma confessed. "We could get it defrosted and set up a meeting right here. I could put up signs around town. Will you help me write the announcement? Could you come over on Thursday of this week?" Emma asked tentatively.

"I think that would work," Bix said and waited for a nod from Bernie. She got it. "Okay, we're in."

"Now what should the announcement say?" Emma asked poised with pen and paper.

Bernie thought for a moment then said, " Please come to share my food and thoughts. Come to eat and save our Tiptop. Lets make Martin proud. Thursday at six; please bring silverware." Emma copied the words and smiled. "That's exactly what needs to be said. Thanks, Bernie."

"Shall we come over at five and help set up?" Bix asked.

"Thank you. I hope people do come," Emma said thoughtfully.

"I have a suspicion that they will," Bix said. She could feel the wheels of progress rolling.

***

The locals of Tiptop started arriving at 5:00. Many of the women came first to help set up. Some people unloaded tables in Emma's front yard. Chairs mysteriously appeared and many packs of paper plates piled up. More food arrived. The place was a beehive of energy. It was obvious by 5:30 that this little town of 500 population, not including dogs, was here to help and listen.

Bernie glanced around and was totally shocked

by the amount of energy. The folks had come with a purpose she could tell. Martin's death was to be honored in more ways than one; Tiptop had responded. She had been shaking hands since 5:00. It was obvious that Emma had also been spreading the word in more ways than one.

People began loading their plates exactly at 6:00. The kids began to turn the ice cream churns about ten minutes later in their own circle of tables. The adults now began to focus on Emma and Bix who were seated up front. Emma got up out of her chair at 6:45 and stood quietly waiting for the noise to subside. A couple of the women went over to the kid tables and stood, keeping quiet order.

"Thank you all for coming. I think Martin is here in spirit; he knows," Emma said. "He knows how important our meeting truly is. My good friends, Bix and Bernie from over in Summit, have some information about this here Eminent Domain thing. Kindly give them a listen." She promptly sat down.

Bix was a bit shocked to realize that the meeting was now focusing on her. She got up slowly and began, "I truly want to thank you for coming. I have been watching our mountain counties for any type of land grab situations since we learned what the political tone was going to be. Make no mistake that national and international corporations are viewing our land and have incredible power thanks to the government."

Carefully clarifying the topic, Bix stated, "With the attack on the EPA, it leaves no support for your community other than the courts. What the Regime doesn't have, thankfully, is public support. The courts are ruling in favor of the public in many cases. We, the people, must remain vigilant in all cases." Her eyes scanned the audience to see if she could sense the tone before she continued, "How many of you are willing to become involved in a campaign to protect Tiptop?" she asked and waited for the raised hands. It was unanimous. Bix let out a breath and felt one hundred percent better. "All right then, let me tell you what I know and then we can go from there." And so she did. Their meeting with the Personal Property Coalition was covered along with what happened over in Summit when Johnny McPherson's land had been threatened by large companies for his uranium and/or ski area potential.

Bernie finally was asked by Bix to tell the crowd her North Dakota fracking story, and what needed to be done there. Bernie then sensed that it was time to move on into the present. "You need a slogan to unite all the people. A phrase that can be chanted and published in the papers," Bernie stated. "Any suggestions?" she asked looking around the crowd.

A man in the far back row yelled, "How about 'Tip the Top for Justice." The crowd roared! The decision was made."

Bix then asked everyone to divide into various committees: publicity, environment, Personal Property Coalition and lawyer liaisons, Zoning Committee monitoring, and the rally organization.

About that time Melanie Camp drove up and was delighted with all the newly formed groups.

After taking notes, she began, "My news is that the Coalition is here to help in anyway that we can. We have contacted a couple of the law firms that specialize in Eminent Domain cases and should hear back from them soon. The bad news is that the Regime has become aware that Colorado is the water capital of the western United States. To divert the water from the Colorado River is something they are investigating. I don't have to tell you what effect diversion of a river could have. It starts right here, right now in Tiptop. Their plan is horrifying. It includes cutting water off to any state opposing their views."

The silence that fell on the gathering was incredible and then from the back of the meeting came one voice, "Tip the Top for Justice!" The chant was then echoed throughout the mountains. The locals stood and Melanie Camp smiled. It did look like a strong beginning for an arduous fight.

Bix and Bernie decided to go with the Publicity Committee since their work could be done from Summit. The task forces decided to meet again on Thursday of the following week to report progress. Melanie was satisfied with the local efforts and the chairpersons were chosen.

It was organized and motivated. Bix felt a chill go down her back as she clasp Bernie's hand. The resistance had begun.

***

Detective Bill Smith of HAPT had begun investigating the approximate location of Martin

Keiser's murder. He had then taken a map and traced the water flow as best he could following the creeks with wider and stronger currents. He now found himself in John Bend's office at one of the last remaining Forest Service Centers in Summit County. John's salary was now paid by Summit so that he could try and keep all the volunteers in place. The man was overwhelmed with work. His wife, Janice, had come in today to help sort some paperwork.

"So you're trying to trace the body's route from Saddle Tree Creek to the Blue River above the Tarn, right?"

"That is correct. We just figured that the path would need to be established for the Martin Keiser Murder Case."

"Well, let's see how much territory we're talking about. You say it happened during the last rain storm in Saddle Tree Gulch?" John walked over to a pile of weather related papers. His brown eyes scanned the reports. "Here we go. Yep, that was quite a gulley washer. The force could have definitely sent the body on down into the 'y' just above Tiptop. The Three Creek River would then have taken the body over Hoosier and into Summit County. Two weeks travel might be in the realm of reality. It would probably get stuck now and then on the way. Hmmm." John pondered the journey for a few seconds. He sat back down and thought. "I would say that a court would have to see photos of the creeks more than the rivers. You would have to prove that there are no culverts stopping the flow."

"I'll probably have to hike it tomorrow. John,

could I get copies of any maps that would help convince a jury?"

"Sure. Janice and I can get that official information for you. It will take us about a week longer than expected. Budget crunch of course." John did a hand motion that took in the entire office which had been transformed into mounds of paper that might never be filed. "I wish that I could go with you and do a journal of the hike but getting out of here is almost impossible anymore."

"Honey, why don't you go?" Janice urged. "What have you got to do except keep an eye on me so that I don't take some time off," Janice giggled. "I don't get paid anyway, so why worry. Your volunteers do the best they can, thank heavens. Go. Do something you like. You've been cooped up in this ugly office far too long."

"Sure would be interesting," he said while rubbing his chin. "That way you'd have a witness if an unemployed Ranger is any good. Might do my morale some good actually."

"We might also keep a log of the distances and later I could figure out what properties these creeks go through," Bill said studying the maps. He then eyed John cautiously before continuing, "You know, Tiptop is about to get tangled up in an Eminent Domain case with the Regime? The Personal Property Coalition has been contacted, and Emma Keiser just hired a forensic specialist from CSU to examine the body. It was murder by laser. Sounds like the Regime just might have had a hand in his murder.

"Oh my gosh," Janice Bend murmured and

shook her head. "How awful. So this is definitely important to the mountain communities. Well there you go, John. Maybe your help will keep the county happy," she added.

"Could be," John answer. He began to check out the maps more thoroughly now. "My guess would be mostly forest service lands on the Summit side," John speculated as he placed the maps next to each other. "Of course that ain't good for the Tiptop locals. On the Tiptop side the land is mostly privately owned which can be bought or forced into Eminent Domain. The new government will simply come right through our forest service land of course. It's theirs according to our federal laws. Summit's Open Space Association is the only thing that can stop them. Open space designates public domain already and, therefore, could protect the property from other entities. There's a parcel under consideration right here in Summit." He pointed at an area below the peak of Hoosier Pass. If Summit purchases that property, then that could slow down the government progress. I'm all for that, trust me."

"So you're coming with me tomorrow?"

"Sounds like a plan," John Bend said. Janice nodded in agreement. "Janice," Ranger John Bend ordered, "set up a meeting with Summit Open Space immediately so that I can get them going on the purchase of that Hoosier Parcel. We need to get that done this week. Signed, sealed and delivered." Janice smiled and saluted.

Bill stared at John for a second. He could see that John now understood what was happening in Tiptop. Bill's murder case had greater implications than HAPT had thought. Mountain development was center stage as a motive. He'd tell his wife, Bonnie, tonight about the open space meeting and get her to go. Possibly take their interested friends along. The more the merrier. It was time for action.

CHAPTER 5

SMOKY QUARTZ BOUNTY

Captain Jen Holly from HAPT and Detective Jerry Neal from Buena Vista Police arrived in Tiptop early morning. They had contacted Emma Keiser who was expecting them. Jen turned onto the back gravel road toward the Keiser home. Tyler the K-9 German Shepherd, was in the cab of the Ford Interceptor and hoping that today would bring him a hike.

"So these folks are getting ready to fight Eminent Domain?" Jerry Neal commented. "I hear there was quite a meeting last night in Tiptop with the Property Coalition people present. It's got the Buena Vista locals talking for sure. Pretty scary stuff," he admitted. "That kind of shit can wake up a 'sleepy hollow town' pretty damn quick."

"Probably the norm for this new political environment; the lawsuits flow. The news coming over the wires now takes on a whole new scope," Captain Jen added.

"Well, it's probably good that Buena Vista is waking up to what is happening. Sometimes you have to shake up any belief that the mountains protect locals from world events. Not true. The domino effect is starting to tumble sooner than I would have expected."

"Why, Jerry, do I hear a little political activism coming from your lips?" Jen smiled as she probed.

"In my spare time, you bet." Jerry's intense blue eyes twinkled. "Sure am glad that the police are on the same side as the population in our counties. I can't image…." His voice trailed off into silence as they both processed what could have been. Jerry turned his neck to one side to relieve any tension present. He was of medium height with curly brown hair; his soft voice enhanced his professional tracker mystique.

Jerry was a tracker machine, Captain Jen acknowledged. "Bix is on one of the Tiptop committees so I am getting the lowdown on what is happening ," Jen said. "She and Bernie said that the meeting didn't deal with negatives but just got everyone busy. Sounds pretty healthy to me," Captain Jen assessed as she turned onto Emma Keiser's driveway. They slowly drove the Ford Interceptor down the narrow road. Emma was outside sitting on the deck waiting for them. She waved as the SUV pulled up.

"Emma Keiser?" Captain Jen asked closing her car door.

"I am. Glad that you have come to investigate Martin's murder. 'Murder.' I'm just getting used to saying that word. It's hard, you know." Emma came down off the deck and shook their hands. Her eyes spotted Tyler in the back of the Interceptor. "Can the dog come out?" she asked both of the officers.

"If you wouldn't mind," Jerry said. "I'm sure he'd like a break." He walked back and opened the door. Tyler flew out and quickly rushed up to Emma. It had looked like he would tackle her but instead he sat down right in front of her waiting for recognition. Tyler knew a friend when he saw one.

She reached down with no hesitation and petted him gently. Tyler was putty in her hands from that moment on; his tan tail wagged happily. "I have a dog treat in my pocket. Can I give it to him?" she asked Jerry first.

Detective Neal then couldn't help but like Emma. She had asked before handing the treat and that was important. K-9s were trained to not be impulsive; Emma understood. Jerry nodded. "His name is Tyler by the way," Jerry Neal said.

The treat came out, Tyler looked at Jerry who signaled the dog, okay. Tyler was now in heaven. "Nice to meet you, Tyler," Emma said never taking her eyes off the dog in appreciation. "He is a magnificent fellow, I can tell. Now how can I help you all today? Come on up, let's sit for a spell. Coffee?" Emma asked before she sat back down in her rocker.

"No thanks, Emma," Captain Jen said as she settled into a deck chair. "First of all, thank you so much for making sure that Dr. Hastings faxed us his autopsy report. I am so sorry for your loss, Emma. It was an incredible tragedy. HAPT will do everything in our power to help you through this time."

"Well, that's sweet of you. Thank you. Martin was my whole life," Emma admitted then sighed. "Life does change doesn't it? I need to resolve what happened for me and for Martin; he, especially, would have wanted that. Dr. Hastings is a good man, and I will put a lot of trust in his opinion. The whole concept of murder seems so far from reality for me though. I can't imagine."

"Neither can we, Emma. We are researching the computer technical piece by the way. Officer Libby James is meeting with Dr. Hastings and will be able to shed light on the specific murder weapon soon. Detective Neal and I are here to see if we can find the actual murder site. We're hoping that you can direct us to a possible location," Jen said.

Emma rocked for a few moments and thought. "I haven't dealt with that fact that we really don't know where Martin died. It all seemed to center around Blue River and finding him." She rocked some more while thinking. Tyler got up and put his head in her lap to help with the process. She petted him thoughtfully. "You know, I just might have an idea of where to start. Wait a minute."

With that comment, Tyler and Emma got up and went inside the house for a few moments. When they returned, she carefully placed a Smoky Quartz Crystal in Captain Jen's hand. Jerry leaned in to take a look. Both officers silently inspected it then turned to Emma for an explanation.

"This gemstone was found in Martin's pocket at the morgue. Bless his heart, Martin always searched for crystal; it was his gift to me, you know. I have saved all of them over the years; they're lined up on my window sills in the house. You can tell our living history by those precious gems. Forty years of Smoky Quartz Crystal; I wouldn't have changed a moment."

The very core of this marriage struck Jen with profound cognizance; it was both powerful and breathtaking. Emma and Martin had been a team to cherish and that was a fact. The Smoky Quartz Crystal had more value than money in their home.

Emma rocked again then declared, "Martin deserves your help, officers, and so do I. I can't tell you how much I appreciate you coming."

Jerry leaned forward and stared out at the panoramic view. "Emma, I know this would be hard but could you take us out where you think Martin was hiking?"

A sigh escaped from Emma as she considered. "The murder site, right?"

"I am afraid so," murmured Captain Jen carefully. "I hate to ask but could Tyler have something of Martin's for the scent? He might be able to lead us to the very spot."

"Of course," Emma disappeared back into the house for a moment. She came back carrying a red bandana. She gave it to Jerry carefully. "I'm ready anytime that you are," she said. "We can drive a ways then it will be on foot." Emma leaned over and pulled on a pair of old boots.

Detective Neal and Tyler sat in the back while the ladies occupied the front of the Interceptor. They maneuvered through the sage and cactus in a pasture. A few old cows owned this space; they munched and watched the intrusion. It didn't seem to bother them much. When the SUV came to Saddle Tree Creek, Emma said, "We best walk from here." They followed a cow path to a small rickety bridge over the narrow creek. It swayed in the soft wind but held them. Emma then walked down near a rather steep gulley and stopped.

"You'll need to go over on the other side and follow the creek bed that-a-way," Emma pointed then said, "Martin always hiked that same route home so he could find crystal. I can't go any farther at this time. Give me a couple of months to heal. Will you stake the area for me if you find the place where it happened?" They nodded in agreement. "Freedom Mine is up over the top of that hill by the way," she added.

"Thanks, Emma," said Jen. "This will be fine. You want me to drive you back?"

"No. The walk will do me good. I'm going to herd those lazy old cows back to the barn for feed. Poor old ladies haven't had any attention for a couple of days. Please stop back at the house when you finish. I would like to know what you find."

"We will," Captain Jen said as she watched Jerry give Tyler the scent.

Emma turned then and went back to find the cattle. In the distance they could hear her directing the 'old ladies' home. The officers then went down into the gulley and onto the other side. Tyler circled them and set out toward where Emma had pointed. He seemed to have the scent; they followed.

Both officers spread out and inspected the property on Saddle Tree Creek banks. Essentially, they combed the land while moving in Tyler's direction. Their eyes flashed from one side to the other. In places one could jump the creek today so both sides got inspected.

Captain Jen Holly stopped after a mile and asked, "What do you think? Are we on the track?"

"From the way Tyler's moving, I think so," Jerry said. He stopped then leaned down and picked up a tiny gemstone. "Whoa, I might have found my first crystal," he said. "Don't think I will ever hike the same way again after listening to Emma. Crystals are pretty impressive," he held it up to the sun and smiled then placed it in his pocket for safe keeping.

Tyler let off a bark that brought their attention back to the task at hand. He was some 50 feet ahead of them. His tail was waging. As they approached, Jen could make out an old hat caught on a sage bush. "Must be Martin's," she said taking pictures before approaching. Tyler sat down at attention. Jerry circled the area inspecting the ground carefully.

"Foot prints over here," he shouted some ten feet back from the hat. They took pictures of the tracks that they found. Unfortunately, because of the rain storm there were only a few tracks left. Jerry had found the prints under a tree on higher ground. They kept combing the area as best they could.

Tyler then let out another bark and sat down again. He was some fifteen feet back from the hat and pointing. Jen got there first and saw a small piece of masking tape about three inches long nestled in between two rocks. Captain Jen had no idea if the tape was of importance or not as she placed it in a separate evidence bag. Who knew? Jerry came over and inspected the find.

"Hard to tell," he murmured then yelled for Tyler. "Let's try this tape out on Tyler. Maybe he can lead us to something else. Worth a try."

"Yep," Jen added.

Tyler sniffed the evidence bag thoroughly then took off at a fairly fast clip. They followed slowly watching for anything else. They came upon a pile of trash that Tyler had ignored. It could have been a campsite from tourists and not related to the case. At least that's what Tyler thought. He was nowhere to be seen.

"Let's do some quick pictures here then bring Tyler back around this area on our way back to Emma's," Jerry suggested.

"Good plan. Tyler sure dismissed this site though," Jen added as she took numerous pictures and then marked the area. Some of the trash seemed to be fairly old. Water stains were on the small food containers; rust was on some of the cans. It really didn't look too promising. Then, Jen began to sense the silence. All of sudden it didn't feel like there were three of them. Tyler was missing, she realized. "Hey, Jerry, have you heard Tyler lately," she asked.

Jerry's head popped up from the campsite debris quickly. "Tyler, Tyler," he called. His eyes scanned the horizon. Nothing. Not a sound came back to them. His voice had echoed back without a response. No dog just voice.

They quickly glanced at each other. Nothing had to be said. The search would begin. Both officers moved a little faster scanning a larger area. Jen had moved away from Jerry to focus on the south while Jerry went southwest.

Their calling of Tyler's name was syncopated. A call, then both of them would stop to listen. The wind had begun to pick up slightly sending the sound of sage and brush swaying. It collected loose dirt then swirled it into miniature tornados before their eyes.

Awareness of any and all movement became their focus as they searched for the next half hour. Their hunt seemed almost inept. Jen began to realize that intuition began moving them aimlessly forward. She sensed an emptiness permeating throughout the terrain. She glanced across the way at Jerry. His anxiety was increasing and apparent as the silence loomed. Where? How? Questions that they couldn't answer. Her eyes jumped from one plateau to the next always hoping, always searching.

"Let's go up on that ridge over there," Jerry said. "Maybe we'll hear something from there. Right now it is dead silent and pretty alarming."

They both ran up the ridge. At the top, one could see for miles, sage and bush but no dog. Jerry fished around in his small pack and brought out a whistle. He blew it and then waited. They strained their hearing into the distance; their eyes raced along the vista.

Where was Tyler, Jen thought? He couldn't have just disappeared or could he; she began to

panic. Her body was about to go into a fast run in
all directions until she looked over at Jerry who was
now a silent statue. His tracker training had kicked
in. 'Stop,' Jen demanded of herself. She watched
the intense calm taking over Jerry's countenance.
He was in the moment and nowhere else. Aware.
Intense.

Jerry whistled again and turned slowly in a 360.
His breath was soft and there was such a strong
focus radiating from his body that she could
actually feel his intense concentration. He had gone
within not out in panic. He listened. The wind
whispered in a small gust then became calm
allowing them to hear the distance coming to them.

"Did you hear that?" Jerry whispered.

There was a pause as Jen closed her eyes and
saw through her ears. "Yes," she murmured. In the
far distance there was a muffled, barely audible,
bark. It was a soft howl traveling on the wind. They
were a party of three again!

Now there was elation as they ran in Tyler's
direction. The officers literally flew over the
distance. The barking became louder as they moved
forward. Jerry would occasionally stop and whistle
to make sure about the direction. It was a solid lead!

Tyler had gone at least a half mile farther than
their last meeting, Jen realized. He had gotten
carried away with the scent from the masking tape.
Jen adjusted her pace to running distance. Their
boots were in rhythm pounding the dirt in unison.
The two officers covered the distance with ease;
both were trained in endurance.

Jen could feel the sweat trickling down her

back. The perspiration on her face disappeared quickly with the breeze. The bark kept increasing in volume motivating them to go faster.

Jerry suddenly halted and stared ahead. The sound was maybe 25 feet in the distance. "We should be able to see him now. What the hell?" he said trying to comprehend.

"There," Jen pointed. "See that old mining tunnel?"

"Of course. No wonder we couldn't hear him," Jerry said taking off in a fast sprint.

They came to the small entrance of the mine and peeked into the darkness. Tyler was back in the tunnel. Of course, Jen concluded. Tyler had been trained to stay with the evidence. No wonder he hadn't come to them. Jen and Jerry both knew who would fit in that small opening; it had Captain Holly's name all over it. She dropped her police equipment belt and got ready to crawl into the tunnel. The entrance hole was going to be a snug fit even for her, she calculated. Her flashlight was in hand. Jerry placed a rope around Jen's waist and got ready.

"Be careful, Jen. Make sure that you don't start any cave ins. Watch the ceiling. Stand down, Tyler," he ordered. There was silence.

Jen felt the coolness of the shade and damp floor of the old mine as she crawled. Some 15 feet in, Jen was met by two intense brown eyes. Tyler was panting but quietly seated in a small cavity. Tyler had organized the evidence that he had found. He quickly licked Jen's face but didn't move his torso; Tyler was in stand down mode.

"Good boy. You had us worried," Jen admitted as she petted him. So lost, fuzzy buddy; it's all good now," she reassured him.

Jen began to inspect the narrow cavity with her flashlight. The old shaft had dried up during the summer but there were still a few puddles of stagnant water on the floor. Old decayed boards were holding the ceiling for now. Good, she thought. Next to Tyler was an object with broken plastic propellers. "Hey Jerry, I do believe I just spotted the remains of a drone," she yelled. "We have evidence!" Tyler looked at her happily. "Yes Tyler, you did good. We would never have found this evidence without you, buddy. Scary as hell in here but all good," she murmured. Jen then tied the drone onto the rope. "Pull the rope slowly, Jerry; I'll guide," she directed.

The dog crept after Jen patiently. It was a bizarre parade exiting the mining shaft. The cool stale air hovered around them as they crawled. The drone stuck occasionally on a rock but did lead the parade willingly. Finally, Captain Jen crawled out into the sunlight. Tyler, emerged last, unscathed and wagging.

"So whoever had thrown the drone into the mining shaft decided to get the hell out of here after killing Martin Keiser. The perp just didn't want to carry all that shit back to his car would be my guess," Jerry said. "Man, if we hadn't found that tape, Tyler wouldn't have had the scent. Amazing," Jerry processed. "How did the drone get so far into the tunnel?" Jerry asked Tyler and Jen.

"Good question. If the assassin had pitched it

into the tunnel on his way out, then I don't know. He sure as hell didn't crawl into the space that I did," she offered. "Unless he's a midget," Jen quipped. "I've got no idea but Tyler found it."

"We'll leave it at that," Jerry concluded.

The officers then stored away their evidence and went to find Emma. On the drive out, Jerry's hand held the Smoky Quartz Crystal. He began to wonder, just maybe, if that the crystal had brought them to the old mine. You never know, he speculated.

CHAPTER 6

MOUNTAIN DATA

Officer Frank Mason drove into Tiptop slowly looking for Gold Miner's Road. It was the next right. Nathan Abel's house was at the end of the row. The rustic log cabin was compact in size and built a century ago. The sagging green shingled roof illustrated that maintenance wasn't a priority for good old Nate.

A knock at the door brought an immediate response. Nate Abel was older than Frank by ten years and four inches taller. His grey beard and mustache reminded Frank of a skinny Santa Claus. No rosy nose or twinkly eyes but accurate in beard color. Nathan inspected Officer Mason silently. Frank figured that Nathan Abel did, indeed, know why he was here. The murder of Martin Keiser was common knowledge.

"So what brings you over this way?" Nate asked.

"Martin Keiser's murder. Seems like you have a mining claim next to his up in Saddle Tree Gulch?"

Frank stated casually. He was rather surprised that Nathan Abel was playing the 'uninformed card' even though he lived right here in Tiptop. Oh well.

"Are you officially here as a police officer? It don't look like it," Abel commented checking out Frank's casual attire. Another interesting comment, Frank assessed.

"Well, I am on official police business, yes. I was just up walking around in the gulch checking out the claims near Freedom Mine. Figured I could stay comfortable for that work. Was wondering if you'd like to get some lunch downtown and give me some location tips to where the corner markers are for North Star and Saddle Tree Creek Claims. I found the stakes for the bottom corners of your claim and Martin's, I think," Frank ventured.

"You buying?" Abel ventured.

"I could be persuaded," Frank said. "Yep, lunch would be on me even though I'm on official cop business."

Without another comment or look back for anything, Nate Abel shut the door of his cabin and followed Frank to his truck.

***

"Thanks for coming," said Detective Bill Smith to Ranger John Bend who was the last surviving Forest Service Representative in Summit County. John still wore his uniform and badges proudly. His short stature was highlighted by his brilliant blond hair. His blue eyes began to scan the streamflow chart that he had brought with him. He glanced up at Bill and nodded then smiled a greeting. Bill couldn't help but admire the guy's abundance of hair; Bill was completely bald. The good news was that he didn't have to worry about gray hair. Detective Smith's body was muscular and ready for team rescues but his head always needed a hat. Sunburn was to be avoided at all cost.

"What have you learned, John?" Bill asked while staring over Ranger Bend's shoulder.

"Well, I have located where we want to start. Saddle Tree Creek is famous for becoming an arroyo during these gulley-washer rain storms. The specific beginning would be above Freedom Mine then weave through the claims below there. The last one of those claims is Martin Keiser's."

Ranger Bend pointed on a small map at Keiser's claim then continued, "I think we start above Freedom Mine so we can document the streamflow specifically and measure the bank width all the way down. That information will validate our log of findings. I checked out the water flow chart report for the day when Martin was murdered so we're set to go. Sound good?" he asked Bill Smith. "I can also approximate at what time Saddle Tree Creek would have had enough water flow to move a body. Will that be of help?"

"Definitely. That is exactly the informational data that I would need in court. Thank you," Bill added. They checked their packs for the second time then began the hike heading above Freedom Mine. The climb was moderate in elevation increase.

Ranger Bend then continued his information as

they walked, "The relevant water flow would start at the conversion of the two streams, Hanging Tree and Miner's Boot right above Freedom Mine. These streams collect the majority of water descending from Brose Mountain. The two combined streams were then split again by the miners so that half the streamflow was diverted into the Freedom Mine shaft for cleaning the ore. One of the first man-made diversions back in the 1860's that I know of," he added and looked at Bill who nodded. "We can't examine the underground tunnel because most of the mine is sealed off," John stated. "However, the evidence of that water diversion appears during storms. Freedom Mine will still spill out a toxic orange ooze when the extreme rain storms come. Saddle Tree Creek takes on an orange glow until the water has traveled far enough to become clear again."

"That's a problem in a lot of high altitude old mines, right?" Bill asked.

"A terrific form of pollution that just keeps giving as industry contaminates more waterways," John added. "These new oil pipelines will also pollute for decades after they are destroyed. People just don't get it." The men silently processed that potential disaster as they climbed.

John's needed equipment of test tubes for water samples, depth monitor, width and current measurement tools, maps plus a GPS monitor for coordinates. This equipment did add to their pack load as they climbed. Bill could tell that today was going to be long and involved but incredibly interesting.

***

So, you think that Andrew Hall's immediate family still owns the North Sage Claim?" Officer Frank Mason restated for clarification as he watched Nate Abel generously salt his fries. Frank was just a little jealous. The doctor had warned him about salt too many times to count. Damn. They had picked a small café on the main street in Tiptop for lunch. The place was filled with locals and tourists so the food had to be pretty good, Frank assessed.

"Yep, and they're still living in Leadville. Their granddad followed the silver from Silver City to Leadville way back when. I heard he lost his fortune playing poker over there so his family had to stay put. I hear the family just don't want to sell that claim because it's all they got of their grandfather's legacy. The grandson owns the Rusty Bucket Restaurant over in Leadville. Should be doing pretty good these days. Plenty of damn tourists, you know?" Nathan said then gulped the last half of his beer. Frank had noticed that Nathan was becoming more talkative as he drank.

"Want another beer, Nate?"

"Sure."

"So what's your take on this Eminent Domain stuff?" Frank asked casually as he motion for another round.

"I think it's a bunch of crap. The government will damn well take what it wants and that's a fact. These snoopy locals who got a burr up their asses aren't going to do anything but get the Capital

Regime to attack the town. I can fucking see it now. Humvees will be coming down the damn street. People couldn't stop the state from digging the Dillon Reservoir. Hell, the town of Dillon was moved three times. Bulldozers just rolled through in the 60's. Give me a break; it ain't going to make one fucking bit of difference."

"So you don't think that the Personal Property Coalition can stop it?" Frank Mason ventured.

"Hell, no. Those outsiders are just looking for headlines and money. 'Much ado about nothing,' is what I say."

"So what are you going to do?" Frank asked with interest hoping he could get an answer.

"Sell first and get the best price," Nathan Abel shot back.

***

Ranger John and Detective Bill Smith now had moved down past the Freedom Mine and were beginning to follow Saddle Tree Creek. They had hiked onto Saddle Tree Creek Claim. Each half mile the men stopped for their calculations. Measuring the bank had become Detective Bill Smith's job for Ranger Bend. He took two measurements. Where the base water was and then where high water had left evidence of the flow. To Bill, it looked like the creek filled up about two feet higher on an average during a storm. "So the force of this streamflow would be how much?" he asked.

Bend pulled out a chart report. "Well at 4:00 PM the day of Keiser's murder the water flow was at 2.81 stage which produced 43 cubic feet per second or .332 gallons. Meant that 289,000 gallons of water went by in 15 minutes. That's the base flow of Saddle Tree Creek that day." John Bend checked his test tube of water then continued, "Then at 4:16 PM that same day when the rain storm began the creek stage increased to 17.33 or 6,630 cubic feet per second. That makes 49, 600 gallons per second which would translate into 44.6 million gallons of flow per 15 minutes. Martin Keiser's body would have been sailing down the creek with considerable speed. It also would mean that nature could time Martin's demise between 4:16 PM and when the storm was over for Peak County. That time was 4:48 PM. Now Keiser would have drifted into the Blue River by 4:48 where it wouldn't matter if it was a storm or not. The water base there would keep the body moving.

Detective Smith stared down at the lazy creek. It was hard to imagine the cubic amounts of water flow that John was describing, he confessed. However, these facts were extremely helpful for the case. This hike had proved to be much more important than Bill had considered.

John then placed his test tube of water in his pack and prepared to move on. He had a thought that he wanted to share so he turned back toward Bill. "You know, this creek isn't just the water you see on the surface. It goes below ground also. There's water flow under these dry banks. It is wider than what you see. Scientists can determine how much bigger the creek is by the water flow quantity. You need those facts? I didn't bring them but I'll email them to you when we get back."

"Sure wouldn't hurt. Thanks, John," Bill said as they entered Martin Keiser's property. Using the GPS coordinates, John Bend then found the corner marker for Keiser's claim.

As they hiked down the creek bed on the claim, they came upon Captain Jen Holly's murder scene markers. John dropped his pack and began taking extensive measurements of the exact area. They designated the actual GPS location in their log. Half an hour later, they had finished their examination of the specific area.

"Anything else we need to document up here?" Ranger Bend asked.

"Well, I might need us to find the old mine where the assassin trashed his drone. It could be important, I guess."

John rustled through his maps to see if the Forest Service had ever marked this specific location. Sure enough, there it was marked with an 'X.' "You know, I do have the coordinates for that location. It would add to our forest data if I reported the water table level for that mine this time of year. I could justify going there to collect information. Who knows maybe some day all this data will be deemed relevant again," John said with a shrug.

It took them only ten minutes to find the old mine entrance with the GPS help. John peered in then hammered a pipe into the entrance base recording when he did hit water. "Water is 1.45 feet below surface here. My bet would have been that eventually the storm would have flooded this mine and the drone would have drifted either out or farther back into that tunnel. Probably hard to prove at trial though," John calculated.

"Agreed," Bill mumbled as he measured the diameter.

"How did HAPT find this mine by the way?" asked John.

"Poor old Tyler the K-9 dog found the mine. Of course that was after he'd climbed in and found the drone. The good news was that Tyler could howl loud enough until they found him."

"Yep. Lots of old relics up here from the mining days. There's even an old cistern somewhere near here. Glad that dog didn't jump in there. You got to be careful what you investigate up here," John added. "You can get trapped or hide stuff that stays hidden forever. Miners were really messy."

Three hours later, the men had arrived at the body retrieval site on the Blue River. It could now be proven in court where the actual murder scene was and how Martin Keiser had been delivered into Summit County. Mother Nature had simply offered Martin Keiser a ride.

***

As Officer Frank Mason paid the lunch bill, he asked Nate, "So what do you think you could get for that old mining claim?" There was pause in the conversation until the two men walked out of the restaurant and opened the truck doors.

"I got to ask a favor of you," Nate said. "My son would be furious at me for telling you about selling. That information could get me killed here in Tiptop," he confessed. His anxious eyes scanned the town. "Too much beer got my big mouth running. What I told you could cause me big trouble; I need you to keep the 'selling thing' under raps."

"Hell, not your neighbors? You're not serious?" Frank inquired a bit shocked.

"Yeah, my neighbors. The sentiment is running high. My son is in the process of finding out what the claim just might be worth. Might be better than gold. If you know what I mean?"

Frank Mason did know exactly what Nate meant. If a speculator got hold of the claim, they could then turn around and sell it at an exorbitant price to the government. Sell it and then get the hell out of Tiptop, Frank speculated.

Nate continued, "You see, my son's a lawyer and he's investigating what we want to do. I wouldn't mind spending my last days somewhere warm all year round. My bones are beginning to ache. Plus, I wouldn't mind some cash to spend now and then. It's fucking tight living up here in Tiptop. I ain't got no cushion for my old age since this Capital Regime Government got around to stealing from my retirement accounts. They owe me big time. I'd like to get the hell out before my roof falls in," Nate grumbled.

"Well, I understand what you're saying. Anyone over sixty knows exactly what happened to retirement funds and who's to blame. Yeah, and I did notice the roof. You sure there isn't another option here for at least the roof? Maybe you could sell your claim to the Leadville guy at Rusty Bucket Restaurant?" Frank offered.

Nathan Abel looked at him for a few moments then said with determination, "I want more than a damn roof and beer money. I want a life. End of story," he nodded.

"Okay. I hear you. Still…" then Frank thought better of it and stopped. Better to not go any farther with that concept, he realized. "So Nathan, you still haven't told me about the two other claim locations?"

"Simple," he groused. "Go a hundred feet horizontal from my corner and you got North Star Claim. The stake used to be on top of a stone ledge. Saddle Tree Creek Claims is another 100 feet and marked with a stone cairn. That claim was the earliest surveyed. Hasn't been touched for years. It was there last time I checked. Got to admit that's been awhile," Nathan admitted. "Damn hikers had left it alone but they don't always understand what a pile of rocks means."

Frank pulled up in front of Nathan Abel's cabin and stopped. He now ventured to ask, "So, Nathan, what your son's name and law firm? I'll find out. You could make it easier for me, you know." Frank confessed as he shifted the truck into first gear.

"Ain't saying. I've said enough," Nate Abel huffed.

"You know, Nate, there might come a time pretty soon when you just might need to contact me for protection. That is, if you're so sure about your neighbors; my phone number might be good to keep handy. Favors go a long way, you know,"

Frank leaned up on his steering wheel waiting to see if Nate would budge. He waited not looking at Nathan.

"Jackson Abel and that's all I'm saying." Nate got quickly out of the truck, he slammed the door and disappeared into his cabin. Pretty damn quick for an old guy," Frank Mason assessed as he watched Abel escape.

So the witnesses or suspects were starting to line up and Jackson Abel was definitely on the list. And speaking of suspects, Nathan Abel was right to worry about how the town would take his defection. Tempers were obviously running high. Abel's decision to most folks would be interpreted as selling out Tiptop. Frank had to wonder if Capital Regime had talked with Martin and Emma? Looked like Nathan Abel had been contacted. That left the other two claims out there.

Frank figured that his next stop might be back over to Placer City. He wondered where the property ledger was for The Freedom Mine Lode. The old titles had been shuffled around over the years. Some were even down in Denver and many had disappeared due to floods, fires and computer transfers. One thing was for sure, however, someone had paid Peak County Property Taxes on these claims. Or, had they?

Frank pulled out of Nathan Abel's driveway and headed back over to Placer City. It would be good to be able to find more answers about Saddle Tree Creek Claim. And, he assessed that the tax histories were very important to this whole case. Might open up a Pandora's box but that was okay.

CHAPTER 7

A CHESS GAME

"Okay then, I would say the amount of investigative information uncovered since our last meeting is a super start! Good job, officers," Captain Jen Holly declared as she stirred her coffee. The office was fairly warm due to the sunlight coming in the large windows. They had waited until afternoon to meet so that everyone could read all the long email reports. All eyes finally looked up from their ipad screens. The HAPT meeting could begin.

"So, Bill, what is going to be your next step?" Captain Jen asked in her usual meeting fashion.

"Since we were able to get confirmation of the murder time plus body movement from the actual murder scene to discovery on the Blue River, my preliminary investigation is complete," Detective Bill Smith stated. "Ranger John Bend would testify to 4:16 through 4:45 for the body drift and Dr.

Hastings said…" Bill checked Libby's report and then verified, "that the murder occurred on September 15 between 4:00 and 6:00 pm. It all fits nicely. Now I would like to change my direction and work the suspects to investigate motives. I'd like to investigate Jackson Abel and his law firm plus the proprietor of the Rusty Bucket Restaurant in Leadville. If you're okay with that, Frank?" Bill watched Officer Mason closely.

"Hey, I'm fine with that," Frank said. "Tiptop Court House had closed by the time I got there yesterday. I'm thinking that I'd like to dig into the old dusty mining claims and property taxes. There's a history out there just waiting for me to investigate. North Star Mining and Saddle Tree Creek Claims are of particular interest to me at this point. Those claims will be my priority at this time. And, I might add, that Nathan Abel is either a suspect or a witness. Extra surveillance on him might be in order." He looked at Captain Jen for confirmation of his suggestion.

"I think you're right. How about you and I heading over to Peak County tomorrow and chat with retired Chief Jerome Walker, Frank? Maybe he could swing by Abel's cabin now and then in his spare time. Retirement does have its benefits. Time being one."

Frank nodded with interest then added, "Seems like the other corners of the claims could be of importance for the case also. Don't get me wrong, I definitely like working communications but getting out once in awhile does help. You suppose we could also go find those survey corners tomorrow?" he ventured hopefully.

"I think that's an excellent idea. Maybe while I'm talking with Chief Walker, you could search the Clerk and Recorders Office files on property taxes?"

"That could work," Frank's enthusiasm had now peaked.

"Libby, could you work on your mad science project here in the office tomorrow morning and take on the communication board for a few hours?" Jen asked with a smile. "I rather like Frank's new sunburned face. It does keep him dapper and handsome if we actually let him out of the office now and then," Jen quipped.

There was a chuckle from everyone except Frank who was a bit embarrassed. "Can I take that as a compliment, Captain?" he asked shifting in his chair.

"You bet. So, Libby, does that work for you?"

"It should," Libby said. "I'm not welding or cutting any of my laser parts tomorrow. It's a fitting and calculating sort of day. I have to tell you that I am totally fascinated by the complexity of building a laser." Libby's blue eyes twinkled; she was excited and content to be the office nerd for now. "Complex, but easy if you follow the instructions," she admitted. "I've only had to call Dr. Hastings once so far. No problem, Frank, I could take your place tomorrow for sure." Libby really did like the way Captain Jen Holly gave orders. She didn't exactly order; she offered suggestions slash 'orders' and, somehow, her style made you think that it was your own idea.

"So Libby, how soon until your laser will be ready? I am all excited to actually experience the 'how' of this murder. It's like the unveiling of an art project," Jen admitted, not hiding her enthusiasm.

"Give me two more days, ladies and gentlemen," Libby said happily. "I am sure that we can actually have an reenactment by then."

"Let me know what time, Libby," Detective Jerry Neal said. "I want to be here. Make sure you give me a couple hours of heads up. I'll make sure that I can schedule myself away from Buena Vista. Now, let me direct your attention to the center table." Jerry then uncovered the actual drone and the other evidence found in Saddle Tree Gulch for their presentation. He whipped the cloth off and they all leaned up and inspected.

"Oh, wow, it's a drone from Walmart just like Dr. Hastings had guessed!" Libby exclaimed. "It's not exactly the one he thought but it is damn close. Wow. Can I research this model for us since I'll be in the office tomorrow?" she asked.

"Absolutely," Captain Jen said. Jen then checked out her notes and added, "I think our report is self-explanatory. Martin's hat helped identify the murder scene location and the drone may help identify our assassin. The tape, I don't know."

Libby offered another piece of information. "The tape could very possibly be from the laser assembly. I am using masking tape like the 'you tube' internet site says."

"Ah then, there you have it," Jen commented. "Make sure that you all give Tyler a pet when he wakes up out of his bed before you get busy today.

Without his incredible nose, we would not be examining the drone or the tape. He is our K-9 extraordinaire," she pronounced proudly.

The meeting was then adjourned.

***

"The government is trying to purchase much of the water tributaries that flow into the Colorado River at this time. It is no longer conjecture but a fact. The scam has been revealed." Melanie Camp took a deep breath before she continued, "As you know, Capital Regime is now fighting with California; water control would be a huge bargaining chit for them. These Eminent Domain goals are small steps toward public consumption control and water utilization for fossil fuels. The larger picture is to divert all waters for national control." Melanie shook her head in disgust. "These bastards like to come into small communities and spin fear first. If the people coward, they take control. "

Bernie could tell that it was an emotional issue for Melanie who then paused to maintain, "The bottom line is that all state water supplies will become quite the commodity soon. Colorado waters will be a huge target. We have to stop their scam right here, right now," she finished. "It is a very dangerous and ugly scheme."

"Unbelievable," Bernie said as she sipped her water. They had ordered at the hamburger restaurant in Breckenridge minutes before. Melanie Camp from Personal Property Coalition had joined them.

It was an early dinner before the first rally in Tiptop at 7:00 pm.

Bix had contacted the media stations in Denver plus local reporters in the hope that they could get the coverage needed for the rally. She had also contacted the Western Slope TV stations. Water rights were always a huge issue for the agricultural communities. It boiled down to state rights versus Capital Regime, she now concluded. You would think that the state had the upper hand but who knew? Politicians did what was best for them these days. Yes, it was scary, she considered. Bix took a deep breath and calmed down. 'One small step at a time,' she preached to herself.

Their food arrived; dinner began. Bernie had a question before she could take her first bite. "Melanie, do you think that our rally is too little too late?"

"The people must start somewhere so my answer is, no," Melanie said with conviction. "The government's scheme will be exposed as the protests grow, and they will. The public voice is the only way," Melanie stated as she piled the condiments on her burger. "However, you do realize that some media station employees have been ordered to not even mention global warming on air these days. Some CEO's are trying to shut us down. All information needs to get out, one voice at a time. Fortunately, Capital Regime has to prove to the courts that their reason for grabbing the land, benefits the whole country. And, Tiptop just happens to be part of the country. There will need to be a substantial reason created for Tiptop's case.

Let the legal minds work on that one . Our job is
Tiptop's Eminent Domain rally and no more. One
step at a time."

The three ladies all munched and considered.
Bernie then needed to ask, "So which 'big guy' law
firm is volunteering to help Tiptop?"

Melanie popped a fry in her mouth before
answering, "Freedom Water Foundation's Branch in
Denver will be helping another local team at this
time. The State knows exactly what this 'little land
grab' is all about. Believe me, it's one thing to
supply water and, totally another thing, to have
Capital Regime control your quantity. Colorado will
be involved, I have no doubt."

"So where's the main office for Freedom Water
Foundation?" Bix asked between bites.

Melanie smiled as she glanced at Bix. These
ladies were sharp no doubt about it. "New York."

Bernie and Bix then realized the ramifications
of this small town case. Tiptop was only the
beginning. This little town was secretly being
protected by two very powerful entities; Personal
Property Coalition and Freedom Water Foundation.
It was a chess game, Bix calculated. Tiptop was
playing the part of the pawn while the queen
maneuvered her knights to guard and protect.

As Melanie Camp finished her dinner, she
looked at these two smart women with interest. Bix
could tell she had something else on her mind. "You
two do know that the Tiptop's Zoning Committee
will be a huge factor in what happens in the next
week. If they vote to allow the government to take
control, then the fight is very much over. We hope

that the locals can give united support and positive media coverage," she added. "Having this committee come out for Eminent Domain would be a huge blow to our campaign."

Bix suddenly got an idea, "Do you suppose Emma Keiser and the other landowners could talk with the Zoning Committee privately? It could be very hush-hush. Better that no one knows at this point. At least find out what these representatives think then we would know how they planned to vote."

Bernie looked at Bix and asked, "Well can you and Emma organize that meeting?"

Bix was speechless. It did make a hell of a lot of sense. Bernie was right. Bix looked directly at Melanie to see what she thought. "Should I get that involved, Melanie?"

"Can you work miracles, Bix?" Melanie asked with a twinkle in her brown eyes as she grabbed the check. "I will consider this meal business. And, my answer to your question is, do you drink water?" Melanie quipped while placing her credit card on the bill. "Who knows? Maybe someone needs to tell the committee what is at stake." Her eyes explored Bix's face as she added, "They just might need a negotiator, you know."

How did Melanie know that Bix had been a negotiator and president of her teacher's union years ago? Yep, she had been investigated. Fair enough, she thought. This event was far larger than she had ever imagined. So be it. "I'll talk with Emma tonight. We'll put together a game plan. Do you want to know what happens , Melanie?"

"Absolutely. Every twist and turn. Keep talking, Bix. Remember that the first answer may not be the final answer."

"Okay. Well, Tiptop does have a team investigating the Zoning Committee. We'll talk before the rally tonight. Looks like we'll be pretty busy behind the scene, Bernie."

"Does look that way, doesn't it? We'll say good bye then, Melanie. Hope you have a good week," Bernie added sheepishly as she pulled her almost six foot body out of the small chairs.

"Actually, I'll be in New York for the next couple of days. My part of this event is now to chat with the lawyers and maybe ACLU," Melanie added.

"What's the best thing that can happen with the locals?" Bernie asked as she put on her jacket.

"Total town commitment to rally and to protect what they have. When you find out anything from Zoning, call me immediately on my cell. Everyone will want to know what is the situation."

As Bix and Bernie walked to their car, they were quietly processing . "I'm going to go grab a sign when we get to Tiptop and protest while you spin the web with Emma Keiser. Sure got complicated, didn't it?" Bernie added as she drove her car out of Breckenridge.

Bix placed her hand on Bernie's leg for warmth and support. She knew that Melanie had handed her quite a job. "No pressure, right?" She mumbled. Pressure yes, she admitted to herself.

"Well, good luck, kiddo. You can only do the best you can," Bernie murmured. "It is their decision; you can only suggest so much," Bernie's blue eyes glanced at Bix thoughtfully. She was so proud of Bix and had no doubt that Bix would make a difference. Bix always made a difference. " I love you," Bernie said softly.

"Thank God. I love you too." Bix leaned over and kissed her cheek then curled Bernie's red hair back behind her ear like Bernie would do. For Bix, the gesture brought warmth. Their silence then became perfect.

***

Officer Frank Mason and Captain Jen Holly drove to Tiptop early the next morning. Frank closed the passenger door and headed into the courthouse to research Freedom Mine Lode. The courthouse had just opened. The Clerk and Recorder's Office was downstairs. He followed the signs until he entered Millie Jean Marvel's domain. Her office was lined with floor-to-ceiling shelves of dusty old property claim books. These 'dinosaur books' measured 12 by 18 inches. When the office was renovated in the early 90's, they began to keep the newer records on computers. Frank was destined to research the old books.

"So, Millie Jean, my lady, I need to research the Freedom Mine Lode way back in the 1800's on. You got any idea where I might look?" Frank asked with a smile. He combed his mustache with his fingers as he waited for Millie Jean to respond. She was staring at her computer. Frank speculated that she just might be reading her email. Who knew?

She finally glanced up, sighed and pointed to the top shelf some six feet above the floor. "On the end over there. Those are busy records these days. The Regime lawyers were in here last month and then here came Jackson Abel from down in Denver. Busy. Busy," she added then looked at Frank for an answer that she had already suspected.

Frank knew that not much got passed Millie Jean. Forty years she had watched over the property lives of Peak County in one capacity or another. No one ever fired Millie Jean. She either was the recorder or worked for another recorder. Millie was there to stay.

"I figure you know about Martin Keiser's murder? I'm here on official business and then some," Frank answered.

"What's the 'then some' on this case?" Millie Jean inquired briskly.

Frank figured to just come clean so he could get some help, "Eminent Domain is part of the inquiry and who is involved and why is also important. I'm here for more than just names and dates. Family history actions and reactions," he speculated.

"Third book over ain't been touched, research Volume 6. You'll be the first to have a 'look-see' at that information. Nobody asked and I sure as hell didn't offer," she stated, then, went back to her email.

"Thanks, I'll do that," Frank said and dragged the sliding ladder over to get the recorded documents. He dived in with interest. Millie Jean Marvel knew something that she wasn't telling to just anyone. Cool, Frank thought. He was motivated to say the least. Officer Frank Mason started to hum softly as his mustache twitched.

CHAPTER 8

STEP-BY-STEP

Officer Libby James discovered two screw holes on the recovered drone as she dusted for fingerprints the next morning. Before starting the print examination, she tested the entire surface for DNA and sent a couple swabs down to Denver. Now she worked on the prints. They were partials, smudged by weather and time. Damn.

Her green eyes now peered closely into the two holes on the drone surface. As she used a magnifying glass, Libby could see screw threads. The assassin had attached something to the drone other than just the laser and screwed it down. Whatever it was, had come off when the laser was removed.

Could it have been some apparatus to support the laser? Maybe that was the answer; who knew at this point? She decided to move on.

First, Libby found the exact model of drone used on the Walmart shopping site. She made copies for their evidence file. It was a Swift Stream Z-9 Remote Drone that could be controlled by a smartphone. Wow, she thought. The assassin could have been 300 feet away and if he had smartphone service, he could maneuver it then detonate the laser from his device. Incredible, she thought.

Libby's red curls bounced as she got up and walked over to the counter for more coffee. The sheer idea of this deadly weapon made her extremely nervous or was it the coffee? It didn't matter either way. The assassin had to be very intelligent and on top of his technology game. In fact, he didn't even have to be a marksman at all. Fly the drone and aim the laser. Maybe the assassin could be a gamer instead of a sharpshooter? That sure opened up the field of suspects, Libby reconnoitered. She then stopped herself and came back to the job at hand.

She was on step five of her *Scientific American* magazine instructions for the DIY Laser. She had just finished making the list of chemicals needed: helium, nitrogen, CO_2 gas. She now picked up the JB Weld sealant and sealed her glass tubing. The washers were to be arranged into pairs which meant flat sides facing.

Libby would have to wait 24 hours for the curing process now. Pretty well done for today so she read on for general information. The whole laser would weigh approximately 70 pounds; the drone could carry 100 pounds. It all fit. She would end up with a 3D lethal weapon. She couldn't wait to try out her invention! It was sort of like purchasing a new rifle but not quite. The skill level here was in the creation not the target practice or was it? Would she have to practice just like the accuracy in a computer game? The odds were good, she assessed.

There was a knock at the door as Chief Marshall Tate of the Frisco Police Department walked in carrying their lunch pizza. He immediately came over and gave Libby a kiss. His blond hair was wind messed and he smelled like the outdoors, she noticed.

His blue eyes inspected her face closely to interpret the mood. "I see that there has been successful progress on your creation, Dr. Jekyll." Marshall's smile spread over his entire face. He inspected the glass tubing closely without touching anything. "I wondered how you were going to use the washers. Interesting. What's that stinking smell?" he asked turning his focus on Libby.

"JB Weld. It now cures for 24 hours. Probably should open some windows." Libby got up and headed for the window expanse. Her short 5'4" was in direct contrast to Marshall's 6'4". Still, it was obvious that they were a 'pair.'

"Ready for pizza, my lady?" he asked opening the box that then filled the room with a flood of cheese and triple meat smells. They both settled as far away as they could from the curing laser and pulled out slices of the delectable pizza.

"Hmmm," murmured Libby. "Delicious," she said.

"It hits the spot," Marshall said.

Libby then smiled and whispered, "I wasn't talking about the pizza, honey." Her eyes took in all of Marshall with intense hunger.

"Ooooh, I like the sound of that. I don't suppose we'd have some extra time here for a trip to the house, would we?" he asked hopefully.

"Sorry no. I'm tied to the communication board today. Frank is out gallivanting with Captain Jen over in Placer City and Tiptop. I figure they'll go up on the Freedom Mine Lode and establish the locations of the corner stones. The North Star Claim is still a mystery. Frank is heading into the courthouse to research and Capt. Jen is going to go talk with Chief Walker. She'll inform him that his town will be the focus of this murder investigation. I never quite understood why the acting police have to inform him of anything since he's retired What's that all about?"

"Well, the gossip among the Chiefs is that he has never recognized his forced retirement. Placer City simply leaves him alone. The word is that if you are dealing with Peak County, other than Tiptop, you contact Chief Leonard Jones in Placer City first. If it's Tiptop specific, inform Walker. Make sense?"

"No, but that's okay. So, Marshall, you got any internet games hoarded away?" Libby asked.

"Well yeah. In that box in the living room closet. Why?" he questioned.

"I have a feeling that I am going to need to practice with the laser after I finish. It dawned on me this morning that the assassin needed computer gaming skills. Since I've never played computer games much, I just might be at a disadvantage."

"We could get them out tonight and play

around if you want. Might be kind of fun," Marshall added as he reached for his third piece of pizza.

"That would be after we satisfy other needs," she said then eyed him closely.

"I was hoping that you would say that. See you tonight for an evening of fun and games, Libby. I can't wait." Marshall got up, gave Libby a kiss and secured another piece of pizza. He was out the door and back to being Chief Tate of the Frisco Police Department.

Libby smiled. Her body was experiencing a warm arousal between her legs that was hard to control. Libby crossed her legs and stared out the window. She found herself lost in the sun's warmth and thought of what waited for her after work. Step-by-step, Marshall Tate was becoming an incredible lover and friend. "I can't wait either, Marshall," she whispered. A sigh escaped from Libby's mouth just as the communication board had an incoming call.

***

"Just reporting that I'm in Denver and outside of Jackson Abel's law firm office," Detective Bill Smith stated. "He's not making lots of bucks from the look of the Double A Law Firm location. It's a tan one story stucco on Downing Street.

"10-4, Bill," Libby said. "You made good time getting there. Congratulations."

"Am planning on getting over to Leadville at lunch time. Hope the Rusty Bucket has decent food. The owner's name is Wally Hall by the way. He apparently inherited the North Sage Claim 12` years ago so he's been paying his taxes but that's for after lunch. Will call in again when I reach the restaurant."

"All is quiet here. No rescues and everyone is busy. Talk with you later then. 10-4." Libby then switched the intercom off.

Bill was thankful that the law office did have a small parking lot. He locked the SUV Interceptor and went over to the door. The lettering on the door was ornate in design with their hours printed clearly. The office was decorated with live plants and antique furniture. It was friendly, Bill assessed, but rather sparse. He found the one secretary seated behind a well oiled oak desk. The surface was immaculately tidy. She was surrounded by succulent potted plants of all kinds. The windows were spotlessly clean, Bill noticed.

"Good morning," she said in a perky tone. "Do you have an appointment?"

"Actually no. I am Detective Bill Smith from Summit County. Does Jackson Abel have a few moments to talk with me?"

"May I tell him what this meeting will be about, Detective?" Miss Perky got up out of her chair to greet him.

"His father's land in Saddle Tree Gulch should get his attention."

She smiled politely, went over and knocked quietly on one of the closed doors then disappeared inside. Bill promptly sat down and waited. Some five minutes later, he was ushered into Jackson Abel's office.

The young lawyer certainly needed his

secretary's help in organizing his office. His desk
was covered with piles of paper. The book shelves
behind his desk were dusky from lack of use and
care. His suit was wrinkled but clean, Bill noticed.
Jackson Abel did, however, have an expensive
computer perched in the center of his chaos.

"Detective, what can I do for you?" Abel asked
as he offered his hand to Bill. He smiled as they
made contact. There was a gleam in his eyes that
said he was interested or at least intrigued by the
visit.

"I am assuming that you have heard about
Martin Keiser's murder?'

"Indeed I have. What a tragedy. We always feel
that the times won't involve us until they do," he
commented thoughtfully. "When my dad told me
about it, I was shocked. Tiptop is such a sleepy little
town." Jackson shook his head to emphasize his
disbelief. "Well, sit down, Detective…?"

"Bill Smith," Bill clarified. "As you know or
not, Keiser's body drifted into Summit County this
last week and things have developed from there.
We, of course, have been researching the properties
involved because of the Eminent Domain
controversy. You have heard about that, I assume?"

"Yes, my father keeps me informed. I hear the
town is all upset?" Jackson Abel studied Bill's face
closely for a reaction.

"So I hear. Our job, of course, is concerning the
murder. Obviously, the motive might be tangled in
Capital Regime's interest. Did I hear correctly that
you are advising your father to sell to Capital
Regime as soon as possible?" Bill ventured.

"Well, I wouldn't say immediately. I do think we need to see what's being offered and try to negotiate for the best price. Looks to me like the government will either take it out right or force the community. There's not a lot of money invested in Tiptop; the selling is obviously a sure thing."

"So you are advising your father to sell?" Bill pressed.

"Okay, yes. Hell, as Capital Regime threatens to cut the senior citizen's health care benefits and attack their Social Security, I need to get my father out of the United States as soon as possible. We've been talking about a location off shore in some warm climate where health care is way less expensive and let's face it, just as good nowadays. We can thank the government's meddling in the medical market crisis for that. Dad's okay with that plan. Just one more citizen getting the hell out of here, I'd say."

Bill could understand Jackson Abel's sentiments. Anyone who hadn't considered leaving wasn't thinking straight; it was an option. "So how much do you think the land would sell for?" Smith asked.

"Well right outside Tiptop an acre of mountain vacant land sells for about $30,000. Now Dad's land is 5 acres with Saddle Tree Creek running through it. Like to get Dad $500,000 because of the Eminent Domain markup. Probably wishful thinking but why not try. The community can't afford that much so his property might be considered the tip of the iceberg for these crooks. Anyone who knows Emma Keiser knows she will be the last to sell. Dad, however, has no loyalty to his neighbors and neither do I. This is his retirement. It's either the claim or it's from my pocket at this point. Common sense says, sell." Jackson shifted his weight in the office chair waiting for Bill to deny what he was saying.

Unfortunately, Abel was right from what Detective Smith knew. Jackson Abel was a young lawyer trying to get a practice up and running and now this burden beckoned. Bill and his wife had just had this discussion a few days ago. Their parents, on both sides of the family, were feeling the government threats over their benefits. It was scary times. Bill then pulled himself back into the case again, "Have you been contacted by anyone about selling?"

"Actually no," Jackson stated. "I've been just sitting around lately wondering if these protest people are going to help or hinder. The Regime hasn't played its hand yet. I brought this topic up with the state politicians the other day. No one knows exactly what the Eminent Domain case is all about yet. The fuckers are playing a 'wait and see.' And yes, I've thought about offering the state the chance to buy the property. Highest bidder is the way I see it."

"So, Jackson, I have to ask. Where were you on September 15th ?" Bill inquired carefully.

Abel checked his calendar on the computer quickly then leaned back in his chair. "I was in court on an inheritance case. Have Ellen verify that as you go out," he added.

"Thanks for your cooperation. I always have to

ask." Jackson nodded as Bill continued his interview, "Do you know of anyone who would have taken Martin Keiser's life for any reason," Bill pressed.

"That guy was a nice old prospector. I can't think of anyone who disliked him. And, like I said, anyone who knows Emma, would bet that she'd stay in Tiptop after his death. They never did have any kids as far as I know. It's still her home."

"Did the Keisers have any financial problems that you know of?" Bill asked.

"None. In fact I heard that they had a little mining fortune to live on. Martin was always careful about finances. He was a sharp old guy."

"I hadn't heard that so that's interesting."

"Yeah, Dad was always a little jealous about that. He'd grouse about their good fortune now and then. Usually when he would borrow money from me,'" Jackson remarked sheepishly.

"You know of any other neighbors that might have been jealous?"

"Probably most of the town. But hell why wait until now to take him out. They've had plenty of years to plan. Just doesn't fit."

As Bill got up to leave, he asked, "How's business here in Denver proper? You have a good location to say the least."

"It's a 'step-by-step process' here for new lawyers. Lots of competition in the Denver area as you well know. I bought this office two years ago. I'm keeping my head above water. Inheritance cases and divorces seem to be on the rise. Bad times create more family problems, you know. I've even gotten some cases from Peak County recently. I am still considered a hometown boy by some people. You have any more questions? I do have an appointment downtown in 20 minutes," Jackson said as he checked the time on his smartphone.

"No. I'm good for now. I may need to come back later, but it's all good for now. Thanks," Bill said.

"No problem," Jackson Abel replied.

CHAPTER 9

TARGETS

Frank was now hunting in Volume 6 when he found it. "Holy shit," he whispered. Frank glanced up at Millie Jean who smiled over the top of her monitor screen in the Clerk and Recorder's Office. Frank read the passage again just to make sure that he understood what had occurred.

The Saddle Tree Creek Mining Claim had been traded to Donner for property in the Donner Ranch State Wildlife Area by the county. Saddle Tree had been a target of delinquent taxes back in the early 1900s. Colorado traded it in 1965 to Edward Donner in exchange for the last piece of property to complete the Park Wildlife Area. Simply said, it was an exchange of five acres for five acres. This was the high and mighty Edward Donner who established Donner Realty, one of the oldest and respected real estate companies in Denver. Edward Donner had died around 1990 and his son, Kevin, inherited the business plus properties. The prestigious company still sold homes and businesses in Colorado. Big realty with huge money, Frank assessed, and Kevin Donner was a trust fund baby. 'Holy shit," he mumbled again. Frank searched his memory about the land trade. Nothing came to mind. "So Millie Jean, you remember anything about this property quit claim?"

"Well, I can remember seeing Kevin Donner's lawyers come marching in here to check on the papers once in 2000. They paid the remaining fees and left with zero fanfare. I kind of got the idea that I shouldn't make any big deal about it so I didn't," Millie Jean replied. "Ain't been anything to talk about since then. Until now," Millie Jean's eyebrows went up and down as she stared at Frank. "What do you think? We keep it under raps until someone finds out or what?" she asked.

Frank leaned back in his chair and gave it some thought. "Yeah, let's keep quiet," he said, then thought some more. He stared at Millie Jean for a few moments before continuing, "I just might know who would be interested, and who should have first crack at this information."

"Who?" Millie Jean asked with interest. She peered over the top of her computer monitor again.

"You know Bix Bixler?" Frank waited until Millie Jean nodded. "Bix is trying to help Tiptop. Maybe I could sort of mention it to her quietly. Maybe just mention it in passing and say nothing else. Let fate do its' work."

"You do that, Frank. Me? Just another day of checking my email and serving the public. Nothing new except a cop from Summit came by to look at property claims. Same old; same old," she sighed staring at him above her half glasses now. It was all up to Frank at this point was her intended message.

"Yep. Well, I best put the books up and find Captain Jen. She's over talking with Jerome on police business." Frank then said, "Didn't find anything much in Volume 6 though, Millie Jean. Don't think that you would have to recommend it to any strangers if you know what I mean."

"I know what you mean. Of course if someone would come in and ask to see Volume 6, I would indicate where the volume was. That's my job," Millie Jean mumbled half-heartedly.

"Of course. Well, thanks for your help, Millie Jean." Frank then trotted out of the office feeling pretty damn successful.

***

Captain Jen and Frank found themselves hiking down from the Freedom Mine Lode that evening. There still was enough light to search for the property corner markers if they hurried. Jen put the coordinates that Frank gave her from the Clerk and Recorder's Office into her GPS gadget. They now found themselves staring down at the stone cairn of the Saddle Tree Creek Mining Claim.

Frank had found this marker with ease. "Looks like the area does take on a little more elevation as we go west here," Frank said. His eyes drew a horizontal line in front of them. The terrain now formed into a steep cliff. The backside descended into a valley. They hiked along the ridge until he saw the first ledge. "What's the GPS reading, Captain Jen?"

She stopped and checked. "I would say that maybe 20 more feet and down a little would bring us right to the coordinate. Does the terrain check out with what Nathan Abel described?"

"Yep. According to good old Abel, I would say right over there would be a good area to inspect," Frank said as he pointed at the granite ledge some forty feet down from their position.

They descended carefully holding onto the rocks and bushes for support; the grade was straight down at a 60 degrees decline. As they rested on the ledge, Captain Jen checked the GPS again. "Should be right here if this thing was getting any service. She glanced back and realized that they could no longer see north at all. The ridge was now some 40 feet above them blocking the GPS service. "Damn. No service, Frank." Jen groused.
"From what you said last time we checked, we should be pretty close. We got maybe 20 minutes more of light before dusk. Let's check this area real close," Frank said. Both officers spread out and began looking under bushes and in crevices.

"Bingo!" Jen yelled five minutes later. Hidden near a healthy wild raspberry bush, she found it. The location brought renewed activity from them. They began to clear the area for further investigation. Jen finally stood up with her hands on her hips and inspected their handy work with satisfaction.

Abruptly, from the blocked northern view came a horrific boom. It was deafening as it pierced their ears with extreme pain. Then a monstrous shadow fell upon them, black and evil. They could almost touch the huge Black Hawk Helicopter's nose as it cleared the ridge. The pilot, in black goggles paused to inspect Frank and Jen's surprising position; his stare sent them into their own private terror.

The huge rotors began to pull them upward with a powerful suction. Jen grabbed the raspberry bush; Frank hugged a stump for life. Finally the pilot's decision was made. The Black Hawk left with a fury of power that sucked up mountain dust and uprooted sage in its path. As suddenly as it had arrived, the Black Hawk now was merely a spot on the horizon. Their world was shocked to absolute silence.

Nothing could have stopped that beast, Jen realized. They had been caught like prey! The fright had left her body shaking as she now could remember to breathe.

Frank's ears were still ringing as he watched the predator head south. It made their little Summit Rescue Copter look like a defenseless baby, he assessed. "That thing was a monster," Frank murmured. "My God, what was that all about?"

"Well if it was sent to cause fear, it accomplished the goal," Captain Jen Holly confessed.

"That's for sure," Frank admitted. Suddenly, the changing and potential threat of the government, took on a whole new meaning for Frank. He had pretty much stuck his head in the sand about politics and such. His life was good and he was busy. That approach now seemed like an absurd excuse. If a person valued their life, then they needed to fight for it. The wake-up call had sounded loud and clear and boy had it! "We weren't his target, were we?" Frank asked then answered his own question. "Naw, it's got to be something else," he mumbled. "Holy shit. Friggin unbelievable."

They both sat on the ledge now and stared at the empty sky in front of them. It was like it had never happened. Almost. Their calm somehow felt different though. "You know, Frank, you asked me about letting Bix know what you found in Volume 6? Well, I've got an answer for you now. Tell her immediately."

CHAPTER 10

THE FEAR FACTOR

"Then what you're saying is that there is a one-to-four split on the Zoning Committee? Four are voting with Capital Regime and one for Tiptop, is that correct?"

"Yep," Emma Keiser said. Our team has one member for support"

"Do we have any reason why the four feel the way they do?" Bix asked with concern.

"Three are of the political persuasion that agrees with what's going on; they won't move until hell freezes over which could happen. The chairwoman wants to protect the locals from any Regime action and, also, sees value in economic growth. She feels it's better to raise the white flag than fight. She's a coward as far as I am concerned," Emma stated with defiance.

"Not so fast, Emma. I have a feeling that there's always hope. Let's have a conversation with the chairwoman of the committee and see if we can arrange a meeting with the landowners. Better that it's from one of the members not us," Bix said.

Bernie Holden nodded to add her two cents in the conversation. They were now at the rally grounds waiting for it all to get started. Emma considered what Bix had suggested. "Well, the chairwoman's name is Betsy Jonquin and her husband ain't on our side from what the gossip says. He's one of those realty know-it-alls that wants economic growth which is also her position at this time."

"Still…." Bix studied Emma's expression then held her hand for a moment. "We have to try. Can you introduce me to her?"

"Sure. She's right over there," Emma motion with her head trying not to be too obvious.

"Come on then. Let's meet her. I'll see you later, Bernie. I'll come find you."

"See you later then. I just know there's a sign over there in the pile that's got my name on it." Bernie Holden moved off into the crowd now inspecting the signs. She shuffled through the options and made her choice.

Bernie wanted to blend in and support the environment; that would be a safe move for an outsider. Her North Dakota roots could easily be represented in that tone. God knows her brother, Billy who was a state senator, was fighting tooth-and-nail for the protection of the land. He might be in the minority but his message was loud and clear with the farmers and ranchers. The public voice was growing with concern even in North Dakota. "Thank you, God," she whispered.

Bernie then watched the media people who were setting up their equipment some twenty feet away. A few interviews were being conducted. Bernie figured that was a pretty good place to take a listen. Who knew what the various media channels view points were. Obviously, the politics of the CEOs' were going to slant the news no matter what. Her choice of the signs was, 'Tip your vote for the land.' It was fairly innocuous with a universal plea, she felt; not just Tiptop but environmental.

"Betsy, this is Bix Bixler from over in Summit County. She's here representing the local views over that-a-way," Emma stated as she watched Bix offer her hand to shake. Betsy looked at it, hesitated then shook it.

"I guess you people do have a stake in what happens over here," Betsy conceded reluctantly.

That statement was a good sign as far as Bix was concerned. Betsy was at least open to alternative views. Didn't mean a damn thing except that she might listen. "Summit County would be the next environment changed if Tiptop allows the government's Eminent Domain case to stand. Sort of like the domino effect, don't you think?"

"I suppose so," Betsy Jonquin allowed as she stared at Bix and considered. "Nevertheless, it is the actual government that has come to our doorstep."

"That is exactly right," Bix said with a slight smile on her face. Her negotiation training dictated that she agree when she could to get things rolling. "I guess the major question becomes should the town and the state approve?"

"No. It's more than that," Betsy said quickly. "It

is also a show of force. We have been ordered by the government to approve their Eminent Domain case. I think the word, 'ordered' carries more power than just 'choice.' There really isn't a choice; it's concede or take the consequences. I'm not sure that this little town understands what those consequences might be." Betsy folded her arms across her ample chest and stood her ground.

Bix then moved into the 'question mode.' "Then you feel that the consequences of resisting this order would hurt the town?"

"Of course it would," Betsy laughed. "Are you really so naïve that you can't see that? These people are in danger and they are putting everyone in danger even the group that doesn't agree with them. Even Summit County would be in danger. It's not a pretty picture," she stated defiantly.

"Then Tiptop should not have a voice in the outcome here?" Bix ventured. "Do you really think that Summit County, whose major business is tourist orientated, would be in favor of the Regime's directive?" Bix then continued building her case, "Do you think that the State of Colorado, including Denver, would be in favor of this directive? I assume that the government's Eminent Domain case deals with water control? Is that correct?"

"I believe so. We haven't actually seen the case arguments yet. It should be coming in the next couple of weeks," Betsy confessed.

"Can I then say that this unfounded threat is only a fear tactic at this time?" Bix asked staring Betsy directly in the face; they were both short in stature.

Betsy ignored Bix's question and continued her argument, "Buck thinks it could add jobs to Tiptop and boost the economy. Maybe the locals wouldn't have to travel to Summit County for work. They could stay home in Peak County and work in their own community. Tiptop could grow and become a city with actual stores and a growing population. No. There's nothing wrong with that," Betsy declared. Her countenance sparked with belligerent enthusiasm.

"May I ask who Buck is?" Bix inquired quietly. Her tone was soft; it definitely contrasted Betsy's last outburst.

"He's my husband," she said gathering strength but lowering her voice also.

"Is he on the board?" Box asked blandly without emotion.

"No. Buck owns a successful real estate business in town. He does have quite a voice in our community and is well liked," she added for her own effect.

That remained to be seen, Bix thought. So Buck was the guiding light behind her decision. "You mentioned the consequences in your answers. Has the Zoning Committee had any contact with Capital Regime yet?"

"A written letter that introduced their intentions," Betsy Jonquin confessed.

Bix could sense that it had been more a preliminary letter with no details just demands. The Regime had said that they were going to take the properties that the Eminent Domain case was coming in the mail. In other words, it was entirely possible that this little Zoning Committee had been told and not asked for their help. Interesting development, she thought. "Has the Zoning Committee met with the landowners of the claims yet?" Bix asked.

"Well, no. The committee has studied the economy of Peak County and believes their decision would benefit not only Tiptop but the entire county," she added strongly. "We have been analyzing the county's future."

"May I ask why this decision is being discussed without the property owners' input and Tiptop's? What if Tiptop decides not to grow into a large city? Maybe they have watched Leadville be manipulated over the years by industry promises and have learned a lesson. If all the promises of growth had come true for Leadville, the town would be thriving. Industries move on: people don't," Bix said.

"Well, you have to take chances in this world," Betsy Jonquin huffed.

"How is it going to look in the eyes of the media when they ask your committee if you have met with and have the support of the landowners?" Bix torpedoed across Betsy's bow. "Right now you have the people of Tiptop protesting. How many more do you think might show up if you totally ignore the public voice?"

"I...." Betsy snapped her mouth shut wisely and considered. "What do you want, Bix?"

"Could you meet quietly with the landowners sometime soon? Somewhere that won't be picked up by the media? Give the people who own the properties an opportunity to tell you how they feel. I think it would help your case down the road when you make your decision."

Betsy Jonquin considered. Her husband, Buck, would not like it but she saw the merit in the meeting. Didn't mean they would change their vote, but it did look better to Colorado. Then there was also an election coming up; she did like having some town input all of her own, not Buck's. Plus, maybe if all hell broke loose, the Zoning Committee could stay safe and neutral. She figured that she could sell that argument not to Buck, but the committee. Betsy could take care of Buck in other ways.... "All right, I will take the idea of a meeting to the other people on the committee and let you know tomorrow what we decide."

"Here's my business card," Bix offered. "Thank you for listening."

Betsy's eyes sparked as she said hesitantly, "You're welcome." With that, she turned and walked off.

"Whew," Bix mumbled as Betsy Jonquin disappeared into the courthouse.

"Tip the Top for Justice" came the voice of the protesters promptly at 7:30. The cameras began to roll as the locals marched down main street! It was a determined and fairly impressive show of resolve, Bix assessed, as she searched for Emma and Bernie. They were on the back end of the protest march. Bix moved into rank quickly and added her voice, "Tip the Top for Justice."

"Well?" Emma Keiser asked before any greeting.

"She'll call me tomorrow with the Zoning Committee's decision. I think they'll want to meet to protect their own asses."

"Makes sense," Bernie Holden added. "You like my sign?" She waved it at Bix.

"Nice pick," Bix said as she assessed the crowd. "Looks like the whole town is here. What do you think, Emma?"

"Most of the town but I don't see Nathan Abel nowhere. What's his problem?" Emma questioned.

Bix and Bernie remained silent; it was curious to say the least, Bix thought. She wondered what that old prospector was thinking. Was he with Tiptop in defying the government: it was the million dollar question.

"Wonder if he's in town?" Emma continued. "Visits his son quite often down in Denver. Oh well, I'm sure I'll learn what's happening. Small towns know everything about everybody sooner or later," Emma stated while hoisting her sign in protest. "Tip the Top for Justice!" she shrilled. In her heart Emma knew that Martin was there in soul tonight. She screamed again, for him, "Tip the Top for Justice and Martin!" The folks gathered around them, joined Emma's call 'for Martin'. The voices grew in resolve as they got carried away with their plea! **"Tip the Top for Justice and Martin!"**

Bix, however, began focusing on someone else. She grasped Bernie's hand and pointed in the direction of an old prospector in a big hat motioning to them. Bix grabbed Bernie's arm pulling them toward the old guy. There was something familiar about that mustache, Bernie realized. Bix knew it was Frank.

The human mass of Tiptop grasped the moment

and marched forward leaving Bix and Bernie. The people were strong. Confident. The crowd then turned the corner and headed toward the courthouse. It was the final piece of defiance against anyone who dared try to take their land. They stormed together and taunted the old brick building as if it was the symbol of tyranny.

Then in the distance a hum began to grow in volume. The black dot became larger then immense. The noise overpowered Tiptop's voice as the Black Hawk approached. The roar of whirling blades and military strength swooped down pulling posters and dust into the sky. The Black Hawk descended its' angry face staring down at the courthouse. The mounted machine guns were aimed at their heart. Nevertheless, there was no firing or destruction as its dark shadow hovered above the courthouse. The fear factor was enough. The people scattered helplessly hiding behind trees, buildings, and cars. Their chorus had become screams for survival!

The immense noise beat at them and spun the fear. Partners held each other for support. Children hid behind their parents. The scepter of evil spread a dark ominous cloud over them. This powerful intervention threatened; it was a symbol of the new reality, The Regime.

As if following instructions, the large military copter then pulled up and headed south. It flew away as quickly as it had come leaving everyone wondering if the event had been real. The people felt their escalated hearts pounding yet the sky was now empty and night was settling in silently. The silence perched.

A hesitant voice whispered from the TV anchor, "Did you get it?" All eyes riveted on the camera man. "Yes," he whispered. The threat had been filmed! The media camera staged outside of the courthouse for the finale of the march had been filming the entire time and as fate would have it, it was the one free station from Denver. The one station that was not afraid of the words, 'Climate Change or treason!' It was a defining moment. No chastisement of the media tonight; tonight, they were the angels of fact. It had been recorded!

The people, hesitantly, began to appear once again out in the open. The empty sky spoke of the evil that they had just experienced. It was a reminder that the word, 'calm,' would be changed forever.

Then, one small voice, calmly intoned, "Tip the Top for Justice." The adults stared at the beautiful little girl for a moment; her blue eyes began to search into the heart of her parents. Her father and mother reached down for her hands and began the rage, **"Tip the Top for Justice Now."** The crowd roared in resolve, "Tip the Top for Justice," then, **"TIP THE TOP FOR JUSTICE NOW!"**

CHAPTER 11

WAVES

The High Altitude Pursuit Team's meeting
started right on time. There was so much to process
this morning; the Black Hawk Helicopter threat,
what part HAPT would play in the protest events,
Franks information, Libby's drone presentation at
the meeting's conclusion. The room was electric
with anticipation. Even Detective Jerry Neal from
Buena Vista with Tyler his K-9 dog was present.
All eyes were riveted on Captain Jen at the moment.

"Okay, let's get started. As you know the stakes
in this case have really escalated. I have been
informed by the Denver Police Department that the
news stations will be sending media teams into our
vicinity around noon today. This is the peace before
the storm, officers."

"I want to quickly review our policy on media
for you. Remember, be polite and refer them to me,
and /or, the Frisco or Breckenridge Police Chiefs.
No slipups, Officers. Chief Josh Anderson and
Chief Marshall Tate will help me buffer the

inquiries. It is our hope that you all will be left alone to do your job. Understood?" The heads nodded.

"The assaults, and I will refer to the events last night as actual assaults. However, that description is for our ears only at this time. Our specific police description for the public is 'that these events seemed like potential threats.'

Captain Jen shifted her position slightly and continued, "I was up all night with our four county police departments discussing policy and our approach to keeping these assaults under control. It won't be totally under control obviously. The people of Tiptop will get interviewed and rightfully so. We have no control over their observations. The bottom line is that their voice must be heard; it is the process of democracy, as you well know, so keep that in mind at all times."

Captain Jen then paused before continuing, "Having said that, the first sighting by Frank and I will not be mentioned to the press at this time. That sighting has everything to do with our murder case and not the protest specifically. The copter could have been simply traveling to their destination, the protest. We will assume that scenario until we prove something else. The military has no comment at this time by the way. They are saying that it was totally an accidental military maneuver that had nothing to do with the protests." The officers mumbled skeptically amongst themselves.

"What will you, officially, call the sighting at the protest ?" Libby asked. She moved nervously in her chair wondering. The answer would affect all of them as they investigated this case. It had already affected Libby's home life. Marshall had been called out of bed from ten on. The shock waves had started to roll.

"We will call it 'The Sighting' and when pushed as will happen, the phrase 'Potential Harassment' will be added." Captain Jen looked around the room as she enlightened her officers about the Summit County Police policies. Retired Chief Jerome Walker in Peak County had decided to go with no comment when he was called last night. We will honor his decision." Jen didn't agree with his decision but that was okay. One had to assume that he knew his community well enough to go with that answer. She knew that there were people in Peak County who thought the government action was perfectly okay. It had to be a difficult situation.

"Then what will be the definition of harassment for Summit County?" Detective Jerry Neal asked. He knew his boss in Buena Vista would want to know that information. Policy would need to spread throughout the police units in the high country. It was best to inform all the leaders.

Captain Jen then took a deep breath and continued, "Harassment of any kind is defined as an assault even when the only punch thrown is fear. The news stations have been showing the video on TV both last night and this morning. The public now knows so I have a feeling that not only the media but other entities will be up here by afternoon. All officers in Summit are to say, no comment then politely refer the public to the Chiefs and me. Clear?"

"Yes, Captain," the officers said.

"Who else are you expecting in the county?" Frank asked. He knew the answer but he wanted to make sure that everyone was on the same page. Government entities wouldn't be mentioned but he knew.

"Chief Tate believes that he will be contacted by the FBI today. It is not out of the question that Capital Regime Representatives will appear. Again, it will be up to our Administrative Team to deal with them."

"Will we cooperate?" Detective Bill Smith asked. He had spent a sleepless night thinking about how large this type of protest had become and sure enough, the morning news from the major national medias had shown the video. The nation was involved, both sides.

Captain Jen inhaled and then continued, "It is the decision of your Administrative Team that you will take direct orders only from us. We are the law in this jurisdiction for Summit County in the state of Colorado. Rest assured, that the state is now aware and will be working with us. Nevertheless make no mistake, it will be an incredibly difficult tightrope for all of us. It is our hope to keep the murder case separated from the Eminent Domain protest. But as they say, 'the cat is out of the bag.'"

The meeting then covered the murder case. Bill talked about his interview with Jackson Abel. Frank talked about Nathan Abel and their findings including the mention of real estate mogul Kevin Donner's ownership of Saddle Tree Creek Claim. Captain Jen covered the claim location and assault.

Now it was Officer Libby James' turn. She could hardly wait for her contribution, the demonstration.

The group moved outside and into the back parking lot. Earlier, Libby and roped off a section of the lot for her demonstration. There, sitting on an old tree stump about 100 yards away was the murder victim, Mr. Green Watermelon, weighing in at a stately 10 pounds. Libby had drawn a bright red heart on his front. The stage was set; the officers began relaxing. They were definitely ready to enjoy Libby's presentation.

Captain Jen decided it was time for fun so she challenged, "I've got ten bucks that says, Libby is going to miss Mr. Melon here. Any takers?"

The pot grew quickly. The rest of the officers formed behind Libby of course so Jen stood to lose $50.00. Tyler, the wonder dog, was even in for ten. How he got money, Jen had no idea.

Libby moved over to her SUV and pulled out her project. "Whooooo," came the encouraging voices from the crowd. Chief Marshall Tate had driven up and was now helping Libby get the laser and drone ready. The officers all gathered around totally amazed. It did look deadly.

"How far away can you be from the suspect, Mr. Melon?" asked Bill with a grin on his face.

"I'd bet you 300 yards with accuracy of course," Libby stated proudly.

"Woah!" the crowd murmured.

Libby looked at Jen for the go-ahead.

"Carry on, Officer James," Captain Jen ordered.

Libby cleared her throat nervously then placed the drone on another stump and pulled out her smartphone. She stood back with all the other officers behind her.

"So how many melons you gone through, Chief Tate?" Frank asked the tall blond Frisco Police Chief.

"Well, I'd say Safeway is down at least a dozen but you can eat the remains which has been nice. Can say I am getting tired of watermelon already, however." Marshall reached in his car and brought out plates and forks.

"Woot" came the yell from the crowd; their eyes darted from Libby then to the drone then back to Libby who now was furiously programing her smartphone. With the final tap, Libby then waited for the drone to liftoff. There was a long pause at this time as the drone stood silent.

Of course, all eyes went back to Libby for explanation, "Hey," she said defensively, "you know how slow internet can be up here. Give me a break!"

Then, finally on command, the drone's propellers began to turn. The drone motor slowly lifted the laser off the stump. It moved some ten feet closer toward Melon Man as it stalked his green body. The drone then ascended 20 feet in the air so that the lethal shot would be angled down.

When a slight breeze moved the trees around them the officers began to voice anxiety. Captain Jen then said, "Anyone want to change their choice now? Going…going?"

"Ah, hell, Frank mumbled. "I'll change mine just to make things interesting."

"Frank! How could you?" Libby looked

wounded but smiling.

"I'm in," Marshall said waving another ten. This machine is damn straight," he whooped.

Then the laser, on cue, came to life with an audible click; it rotated and eyed melon man with a deadly stare. Suddenly, with no warming, the accurate ray hit with a splat! Melon Man exploded sending chunks flying twenty feet in the air! Libby had hit the melon right on the heart target! The breeze had made no difference whatsoever.

"Woot!" yelled the team.

"Hot damn!" Frank added in support.

The team then happily waited for melon and money! Forks ready.

***

Detective Bill Smith hit the road to Leadville after the meeting and melon murder. Yesterday, he had been ordered back to Summit because of the Tiptop Protest so he had cancelled his trip to find Wally Hall at the Rusty Bucket Restaurant. When the helicopter's assault happened, it was clear to him that the Team had to be on alert and in Summit. Escalation was always a factor that had to be taken into account. Peak County would deal with the Tiptop Protest in their own way. Actually, Wally could have been over in Tiptop. If it had been Bill's land, he would have protested for sure. Priorities were front and center right now.

Bill considered how hard it was for everyone to separate the Keiser murder from the protest, however. The events seemed to be on a collision course. It had been interesting to find out this morning that Kevin Donner was one of the claim owners. What persuasion was Donner's politics, Bill wondered? The guy owned a lot of Denver realty and was powerful. Kevin Donner's attitude would make quite a difference. Bill had been ordered not to meet with Donner until after Bix's Zoning Committee and owners' meeting. Once again, the murder and the protest were automatically linked; Bix would be the liaison between the events, he assessed.

Maybe the Administrative Chiefs' separation of events was simply good politics. He could see the merit in only having to comment about the murder case. It made sense since the body had been found in Summit; the protest was in Peak County. What if the Regime had taken an obvious part in Keiser's murder, Bill thought suddenly? Then all bets were off. Can you say, 'media explosion'; what chaos would that be?

The Rusty Bucket Restaurant was located not too far down Main Street in Leadville. Bill found it easily; great location, he surmised. It also had a nice ample parking lot that was half full between breakfast and lunch. The food and conversation had to be pretty good, Bill concluded. He parked and then entered by the front door.

The ambience was miners' décor. A row of old style boots were placed to the side of the front entrance. Prospector mining helmets, pick axes and gold pans adorned the walls. Old pictures of prospectors standing outside of working mines hung between the rusty antiques. The salad bar was loaded in replica ore cars with railroad tracks underneath. It was clever to say the least, Bill thought. He scanned the kitchen entrance and counter for signs of an owner.

Finally, Bill asked one of the waitresses behind the counter, "I am looking for Wally Hall?" Bill pulled out his badge. "Is he around?"

"Head through the swinging doors back there. He's outback trading jokes with the meat man," the waitress said then continued brewing more coffee. As Bill entered the kitchen, he could hear loud laughter coming from the open back door.

"So then the guy said, 'My wife ain't home.'" Both men howled in laughter. Wally was, obviously, the large older man enjoying a laugh with the meat distributor. He glanced over at Bill then and waited.

"Wally Hall?" Bill asked the obvious.

"Back at you," Wally said warmly.

"Detective Bill Smith from over in Summit County. May I talk with you for a few moments?"

"Sure."

"Gotta head out, Wally. Got at least five more deliveries today," with that said, 'Mr. Meat Unlimited' disappeared into his truck and left.

"Now what can I do for ya?" Wally asked.

"I assume you've heard about Martin Keiser's murder?" Bill inquired.

"Sure as hell have. Damn, he was a good man. How's Emma doing?"

"We had officers out there this week. She's doing as well as possible," Bill said watching Wally Hall's reaction.

"I called her first thing when I heard," Wally said. "I did know them personally; they were damn good locals. Emma sure got more than she deserved what with it being murder. Have you found the motherfucker who killed him yet?"

"We're working on it. My job is to investigate the people and history of Saddle Tree Creek Gulch. You own North Sage Claim?"

"Yup, I have ever since my father died; his father, Andrew Hall, was the prospector who filed the claim in the 1800's. Ya want coffee? Let's go sit down and I'll brew a new pot. It's quite a story, Detective Smith. Be glad to bend your ear. I love talking about the old times," Wally said then patted Bill on his back as they walked through the kitchen and into the restaurant seating.

They landed in a comfortable booth near the kitchen swinging doors. It was obviously Wally's office during the day. Order receipts were piled up next to a laptop. Wally had been totaling up the breakfast tally. He moved his work aside and concentrated on Bill. "So how can I help you?"

"Did you participate in the protest last night in Tiptop?" Bill asked.

"No sir, I did not. This restaurant was packed due to our prime rib special but I sure as hell heard about it. That Black Hawk Copter was really something. If I can have an opinion, I'd say pretty damn stupid. There's a philosophy that says don't tip your hand. The Regime did and it was stupid. Tiptop is damn angry now. You don't mess with mountain folks like that," Wally stated.

Wally Hall was angry, Bill observed. It was

easy to see how he would vote on the land issue. Wally pulled himself up and got two large mugs filled with new coffee. As he came back his temper was under control again. "I'm sorry, Detective, but it pisses me off. A man's land is his heart and soul. If a guy is lucky, he's owned by a good woman, and they own some land. That's the way I feel. Always have. Detective?"

"Call me Bill, Wally. Off the record, I agree with you. I really do feel for Tiptop. Then I can assume that you aren't going to sell happily to the government, and that question is on the record?"

"You fucking got that right. Martin Keiser and I have both been here all our lives and we were of the same mind about not selling ever. You can quote me on that, Bill. My grandfather's legacy is worth far more than any business deal. Plus, taking water control away from the public just ain't right. Tiptop don't need the government to own that water; hell, it's perfect the way it is. Tiptop cleans it a little and takes a little. That's how it has always been. Capital Regime wants control over all our freedoms. They want to strangle us into submission." Wally eyed Bill closely then added, "I have a feeling that I don't need to tell you that." He tasted his coffee and waited for Bill's nod.

Even this interrogation was hard to do without personal opinions, Bill conceded. Nevertheless, he continued in police mode, "I have to ask the next question; it is police protocol. Where were you on September 15th, the day Martin Keiser was murdered?" Bill asked.

"Hell, right here as always. Probably sitting at

this table. What time?"

"Around 4 to 7."

Wally pulled out his wallet and extracted a small calendar for the day of the week verification. "Wednesday. We were doing the preparation for our Italian dinner that night. I end up cooking a shitload of lasagna until 5 when the dinner starts. Ask anyone of the five cooks back there," he said pointing his thumb in the kitchen direction.

"Thanks," Bill said then continued, "I wonder if you know who owns the Saddle Tree Creek Claim since your family has been here for so long?"

"Andrew Donner got it years ago in some trade with Colorado. The state was making a deal to enlarge the Wilderness Area. I remember my dad telling me about it. The state wanted another piece of that wildlife area so they traded him years ago. I suppose he's dead now and it belongs to his family. Think he had a son? Not sure of his name but I bet I'll meet him, or his representative, when we all get together with the Tiptop Zoning Committee tomorrow."

"So you're going to the meeting?"

"Yep. Pretty hush-hush from what I can gather, Bix called me this morning and told me. We're meeting in the gulch right at the Freedom Mine entrance so the media folks don't catch wind of it. Nice of the Zoning Committee to finally get around to asking us how we feel," Wally groused then took a sip of coffee to wash his disgust down. "Bix said that they was having trouble getting hold of good old Nathan Abel though. He's a prospector from way back. I figure he doesn't want to sell like the rest of us. At least that's the way I figure it. Haven't seen him in years though; he don't get over this way very often," Wally said.

"You then have no idea where he might be?" Bill ventured.

"Nope. All I know is that he still prospects some. Could be out in the field."

Bill hesitated for a moment. He kind of wanted to tell Wally what he had heard from Abel's son that they were ready to negotiate for the most money and not keep the claim. Bill stopped himself, however. That information might be better to not repeat this early in the investigation.

"You got any more questions to ask? If not, I probably need to get into the kitchen and start dinner prep."

"One more question before I go. Can you think of anyone who might want to kill Martin Keiser? Maybe someone who just plain had a grudge against him. Someone who would profit in some way from him being gone?" Bill asked.

"Hell, no. Look, Bill, if it had been a local they wouldn't have waited so damn long to knock him off. Most of these old timers up here have known each other all their lives. We're talking 40 years or more. And please don't try and tell me that there was a love triangle. Emma Keiser is the salt of the earth; she loved that man and stayed with him all these years. I'd stake my life on that. No, I'd bet that Martin Keiser was killed by the shock waves of the times through no fault of his own or Emma's. You can take that to the bank."

CHAPTER 12

TWIST OF FATE

"I want to know what took you so damn long to finally ask us claim owners how we felt about this Eminent Domain?" Wally retorted. His arms were crossed in front of his chest. His eyes sparkled as he looked directly at Betsy Jonquin who was the designated speaker for the Zoning Committee. The meeting had started precisely on time which was pretty incredible for mountain people. Kevin Donner was there with a lawyer in brand new hiking boots; the guy looked totally out of place. Emma had brought Bix. Noticeably absent was Nathan Abel.

The Zoning Committee's representatives were standing in their voting clusters; 1 for Tiptop; 4 for Capital Regime. Betsy Jonquin, of course, was in the cluster of 4. She stepped forward as she attempted to answer Wally Hall's question. "It was the decision of our committee to first investigate how Peak County would view this acquisition."

"It ain't no 'acquisition' until the community and the owners have their say," Emma Keiser corrected Betsy. She wanted to add her two cents worth quickly. If anyone of these Zoning members thought she'd sell the Keiser claim to the government, she wanted to squelch that gossip right away. Emma moved closer to Wally Hall.

"Who you talking about, Betsy? Some damn high rollers out of the Urban league who are greedy sons-of-bitches?" Wally spat. "The town ain't for it."

"Do you speak for everyone, Mr. Hall?" Betsy ventured forward like a shot. Their eyes met in total disgust. There was a pause as all the folks processed the obvious split.

Bix then saw an opening and suggested, "Maybe it would be wise to first off go around the circle here and have introductions before we venture into statements of position?" All eyes fell on Betsy Jonquin to acquiesce. She did and the tone became somewhat civil.

The final introduction landed on Kevin Donner and his lawyer; the eyes of the Zoning Committee became intense. Obviously, they knew that this man was going to play a pivotal role in politics from this moment on. The group was ready to find out just what Donner was thinking. He was big business so 'the 4' assumed and hoped.

Bix then suggested that statements of position might start with Mr. Kevin Donner. All heads nodded in agreement and focused on him.

"My family has owned this claim ever since my father traded away our wilderness area in the sixties. It was his intent to preserve the open space in Peak County. It was his philosophy and my grandfather's philosophy, that Denver needed a place to recreate. Grandad wasn't a skier like the 10th Mountain Division boys over in Summit," Donner said glancing at Bix while acknowledging her residency. "Starting ski resorts and courting tourists wasn't in his future. No, the Donner Clan fished and hunted, not often but now and then. Andrew Donner II wanted his wilderness area to be left alone and remain open space. My family brought me up here and taught me about respecting the land."

Kevin Donner now stared directly at Wally Hall and Emma Keiser. "My reaction to this government takeover is nothing short of outrage. It goes against the grain of Colorado. My lawyers have been appraised of my position and will work with the state and other entities."

His announcement was met with stoic silence as the Zoning Committee comprehended the implications of Donner's position. It was a total shock to find out that this real estate mogul was now their opposition. 'The 4,' who advocated for growth and government control, began to twitch nervously. Today they had lost a big chunk of their power; bullies hate that position. The vote had become 4 to 4 with Tiptop standing tall. Nathan Abel's vote suddenly loomed large; they needed to find that old geezer and quickly.

"Where is Nathan Abel?" asked Betsy Jonquin defiantly. "I heard that he is going to sell. Yes, sir, that is what I heard; that's what his son said." 'The

4' nodded their heads in unison gathering some dominance back.

"I wouldn't be so sure," said Howie Page the '1' Zoning Committee member for Tiptop. He spit on the ground to establish his presence. The old geologist rocked back and forth. He wasn't going to say another damn thing but Betsy's attitude bugged the shit out of him. These people were so stupid. As soon as the Regime stirred up this area, toxic chemicals would surface. Hell, they had no idea. It wasn't fucking politics, it was common sense. He'd spent twenty years surveying the area and studying the county's mountains. These stupid idiots would destroy the area for greed. Howie spoke defiantly, "Nathan might be damn hungry to get out of the mountains but he does have a brain. It is entirely possible that he just might use it." With that comment, Howie Page was done.

Donner's lawyer quickly invited Howie and Emma Keiser to go have lunch. The lawyer whisked them away immediately depositing them in his car. They disappeared before the crowd could react. Obviously, the meeting had been adjourned.

The car dust hadn't settled yet when Kevin Donner, ignoring 'the 4 Regime allies', turned to Bix and Wally Hall asking them to promptly show him his claim.

Donner had heard enough of this group's agenda and wasn't buying it. He knew that the Eminent Domain case would explode next week. At least that's what his Colorado sources had told him. His time in Tiptop was limited; he needed to use it wisely.

Bix and Wally began to lead the way down the slope toward Saddle Tree Creek Mining Claim. The 4 'no-budge' committee members were left with their mouths open, Bix observed. They would have to lick their wounds and spin the events into positive gossip somehow, she assessed. Bix now had to admit that Donner's moves were well orchestrated. He had turned the tables efficiently. This was a man used to making the deal, she concluded.

"Well, Mr. Donner, I sure as hell appreciate your position," Wally Hall stated after they were out of earshot. In fact, Wally even felt more confident about the whole damn mess now that Donner was on the scene. Their pace slowed as they began to talk.

Kevin knew where the claim was but his intent, all along, was to have a private conversation with these two. "And I certainly was glad to find out that I wasn't going to be fighting this group of greedy crooks by myself," Kevin answered. "Oh, and why don't you two call me Kevin, since we're going to be business buddies."

"I can do that," Wally Hall happily answered. The day had taken on a whole new perspective, he reconnoitered. Kevin Donner had been a fucking surprise. Hot damn, he thought!

"And Bix," Kevin said, "We're not alone in this fight, are we?" He stopped walking and looked directly at her. Kevin Donner was of slight build and average appearance. He blended well in any group and used his appearance for advantage. Bix knew immediately that he was aware of the

Coalition's involvement and probably much more. "Tell Wally and me about the Personal Property Coalition and one Melanie Camp. And are we going to see the ACLU in Tiptop by the way?"

Bix now realized the extent of Kevin Donner's research. The man had investigated the case thoroughly; he knew what was coming. Lordy, Bix realized; Donner was the political link to the State Capitol! Oh, wow, that was excellent news! The powers that be were now set in this drama. Her mind began to sense more hope. How incredible was that?

The threesome began to relax somewhat; mountain hikes had a way of doing that. They now had time to process all the events and organize their united front. Bix began to explain how the Coalition was involved. She mapped out how the protest had been orchestrated and her part in the situation.

As Donner listened, his attention was routinely drawn to the ground; he found himself hiking and searching for crystal; it was his childhood habit . His grandfather had always reminded him to watch for a gem. No matter where they were in Peak County, the search for quartz crystal was a family tradition. He had stored his collection in a soft marble bag and kept it in his sock drawer for over twenty years; it was priceless.

To Kevin's surprise, his eyes actually spotted a creditable glint of color. Oddly enough, the location was on Martin Keiser's claim. As he leaned down to surface the gem, he realized that it wasn't a crystal. Damn, a new crystal would allude him today. One had to work for those gems, he concluded. Kevin rubbed his thumb over the rock cleaning it. His inspection had altered his forward movement as the rifle shot sought him as a target. It was an unforeseen twist of fate that had interrupted the assassin's aim.

***

"I need to talk with Captain Holly now!" Jackson Abel bellowed into the phone. Libby shot out of her chair as Frank pulled the phone piece away from his ear. He immediately put the phone on speaker so Officer Libby James could hear Nathan Abel's son also. They starred at each other for a few moments. The wakeup call had happened bright and early. The lawyer sounded really pissed at something or someone. Wow!

Libby, immediately, talked into the speaker, "Mr. Abel, this is Officer Libby James. Captain Holly will be in the office within the next hour. Can I help you until she is available? Rest assured that the High Altitude Pursuit Team will help you in any way that we can. What seems to be the problem, sir?"

Jackson Abel's volume came down a few decibels. He continued, "I just got off the phone with that old retired cop in Tiptop. I informed him that my father is missing. I haven't been able to find my father for 24 hours. It just isn't like him, at his age, to simply disappear."

Frank then entered the conversation, "I know that times right now are really stressed, but has your father ever taken off before without telling you, sir?"

"Well, when he was younger maybe a prospecting trip in the back country but not in the last couple of years. That old fart in Tiptop tried to tell me that my father was off drinking with some of his old buddies."

Libby and Frank rolled their eyes and figured that Jerome Walker probably felt that his answer would have been helpful; it wasn't. The current events merited far more attention. Nathan Abel's furlough might indicate something much more sinister. Frank now remembered Nathan's fear of retaliation for wanting to sell.

"We understand your concern, sir," Libby responded warmly. "As soon as we disconnect from this call, we will contact Captain Holly. My instinct tells me that she and I will then head over to Tiptop and investigate your father's disappearance. We will contact you today with what we find out. Is that arrangement acceptable?"

"Then you will call me later, Officer James?" Jackson Abel verified.

"Definitely," Libby said. Frank nodded his support of her decision.

"Very well then, I leave the situation in your hands. Thank you," he said and hung up.

Frank and Libby both blew out a sigh of relief as they recuperated.

***

Captain Jen Holly and Officer Libby James raced over Hoosier Pass on their way to Tiptop.

Libby had pulled up in front of Jen's condo some 30 minutes after Jackson Abel's call.

Jen had been trying to get a few hours sleep after the protest events. Forget that, she thought. This case was coming at them fast and furiously. She had talked with Bix on her cell last night before the morning landowner meeting at Freedom Mine. Bix had promised to get back with her after that meeting; it was still too early for Bix to call back. Now, Nathan Abel was missing, and who knew what that meant?

"I can honestly say that Abel's son is definitely concerned. I hope Nathan is at home by now," Libby said then checked her rearview mirror as she drove. They had the lights on but no siren.

"We can hope that maybe he left the phone off the hook because the media has been harassing him. Certainly won't hurt to do a welfare check," Captain Holly said. "We're 15 minutes out at this point. Surveillance of the bars and restaurant would be our second action later. So Jackson had no idea where his father might be?" Captain Jen asked.

"I'm sorry, Captain, but Frank and I were trying to calm the guy down and didn't go much further with him. He seemed offended by Chief Warren's suggestions. We didn't want to aggravate the situation anymore. The man was lawyer-mad and frustrated."

"Well, we'll check the cabin then general areas in Tiptop. Hopefully, Nathan can be found. Wonder if he ended up going to the land meeting about the claims after all?" Captain Jen then called Bix's cell to check, no service. "If need be, we'll drive up to

Freedom Mine today. Make sure that we covered all bases including informing Jerome Warren's answering machine about our findings or lack of findings. Jerome doesn't answer his phone, you know, he is retired sort of," she added.

They knocked on the cabin door; there was no answer. Libby moved around back and tried that door. The cabin was locked up tight. Both officers peered in the small windows on all sides. It definitely appeared empty. As Libby came around front she asked Jen, "Wonder if Abel always locks his doors? Lots of folks over here don't if they're in town. What do you think?"

"I'd say that's one question we need to ask. Let's check all the usual haunts for Nathan. We should start with the local restaurant and see what we can find out," Jen said.

The locals were happy to supply Nathan Abel's daily routine to them. It became apparent that Nathan wasn't in town. No one seemed on high alert yet but there was concern brewing, Jen noticed. Two hours later she leaned back in the SUV seat and considered their remaining options. "I'm thinking that we have one more stop before we put an BOLO out on Abel. Let's head over to the courthouse. Frank got quite a bit of information from Millie Jean Marvel, the Court Registrar. Let me contact Frank and have him smooth the way for us with a quick call. Millie Jean has been in Tiptop for decades. Maybe, just maybe, she can help us."

The sunlight dimmed as they opened the courthouse entrance doors five minutes later. The old building's atmosphere smelled of wood and polish. The well-worn oriental rugs softened their footsteps as they proceeded toward Millie Jean's office. Small town libraries and courthouses went hand-in-hand in atmosphere; they demanded respect. Most adults were suddenly reduced to childhood memories as they entered these buildings of historic data. It was a gut reaction, Jen surmised.

Libby tiptoed over and opened the office door for the Captain. "Miss Marvel?" Jen inquired of the ancient lady sitting near the back of the office staring over her half rim glasses at their approach.

"That would be Millie Jean and, yes, Frank just called. How can I help you, officers?"

"I'm Jen Holly and this is Libby James," Jen offered with a wave of her hand. "I'm sure that Frank told you about Nathan Abel being missing. Millie Jean, we are now at a dead end on where to look other than walking up to his claim. Do you have any suggestions?"

"Sit," Millie directed as she began to consider Nathan Abel. "That man don't take much stock in letting people know his whereabouts. He has always liked being free and unaccountable to everyone. Nathan did marry and was accountable to one lady for twenty years. After Nell died, he went back to being a loner. He is in the true sense a prospector."

"What does that really mean?" asked Libby.

"It means, young lady, that the mountain minerals are more important than people to these old geezers. Nathan is getting old, but his spirit will always be out there searching for some kind of treasure. Don't matter what mineral anymore just so it gets found," Millie Jean answered.

"If you were looking for him, what would be your most important premise?" Jen asked sitting back in the old wooden captain's chair.

"I'd move away fromTiptop and check out all his old haunts in the mountains. He knows a lot of miners from all over the state but he is especially drawn to the high country. It's a big area. Go where the prospectors migrated would be my guess, if you ask me and you're asking," Millie Jean finished with a nod.

"Does he have many friends left that you can think of?" Libby asked leaning up in her chair. Her laptop poised to receive any names.

"Let's see…." Millie Jean went deep into her memory. The woman was definitely a wealth of history; you had to respect that concept, Jen assessed. "If I was really determined to find him, I'd head over Leadville way," Millie Jean proclaimed. "Chief Carl Hagen is fairly reliable on prospector history. He'd be able to help you with Abel's social list of old men. Send Frank to break the social barriers with those old guys."

Frank was a good suggestion, Jen realized. He talked prospector language. Maybe not with Chief Carl Hagen though; those two men had ego trouble. Still, Frank would go on that investigation, Jen decided. She'd call Chief Carl Hagen in Leadville immediately and let him know, however.

Captain Jen Holly now probed Millie Jean in another direction. "One thing that bothers me though," Jen interjected, "is that Nathan Abel would choose this time to be missing? His son is quite concerned. It just seems odd to me that Nathan would not think that he should be here watching what happens in Tiptop. I don't get it," she confessed.

"Well, that's cause you don't know Nathan. His son, Jackson, has always been concerned. He don't understand his father any better than you do. Once a prospector, always a prospector. These old men don't think nothing about obligations. It is an addiction just like gambling, ladies. If someone called him and said that there was a vein of gold that needed to be checked out, Nathan Abel would go. He wasn't here for Jackson's birth and never considered that as a bad thing. Nope, he'd go," Millie Jean admitted and then moved on into another tangent.

"However, having said that, I shouldn't and wouldn't, assume anything in these times," Millie Jean wisely added. She moved slightly in her chair and speculated while placing her hand on her cheek in 'thinking mode.' "Nevertheless, I wouldn't have assumed that Martin Keiser could be killed by a laser carried on a drone. I wouldn't have assumed that Tiptop would be protesting Eminent Domain. These are new times and I haven't quite wrapped my head around what is happening," she admitted.

"Neither have I, Millie Jean," Captain Jen agreed. "It seems like one just gets used to the world when the rules are suddenly up and changed. Trust me, we're as baffled as you are over in Summit. I used to think that the mountains could buffer the ugliness from the nation. Now, I know how ridiculous that concept is. Life does strange things," Jen confessed.

"Find him, Captain Holly," Millie Jean commanded. "Find that old coot; I have to admit that I would really miss him."

"We'll do our best, Millie Jean," Captain Jen said.

They all were abruptly interrupted by Jen's cell ring. "Hello, Captain Jen here." Her body suddenly jolted out of the chair. "What? Where? We're on our way! ETA, ten minutes. 10-4. We'll let you know," she shot back at Millie Jean as they ran from the courthouse. Their police car flew out of Tiptop with siren and lights on!

CHAPTER 13

DAY OF SURPRISES

Detective Bill Smith had gotten the alert from Frank to escort the ambulance over the pass. Fortunately, the traffic hadn't been too extreme today. The envoy, with sirens and lights, was able to force most vehicles off and onto the roadside. Bill felt somewhat impatient as the medical vehicle slowly lumbered up to the summit; it was almost unbearable.

He still hadn't found out who had been shot. The emergency operator had talked with 'a man' but knew few details about the patient due to rugged mountain intermittent phone service. Actually, Bill had been surprised to find out where the emergency had happened. The coordinates were located on Martin Keiser's claim. What were they doing there? He had no idea.

They arrived at Freedom Mine ten minutes later. The stretcher was quickly unloaded as the three medics prepared for the hike. Bill noticed that

Libby and Captain Holly's patrol SUV was parked but vacant. At least someone was now on the scene. As they paraded down the slope, Bill could now see Officer Libby James rushing up to them. She must have been jogging at a fairly good clip. Libby panted for breath as she spoke, "Down this way everyone. The patient is stable and talking. We're about five minutes away."

"Then it's not Bix?" Bill asked.

"Not Bix but Kevin Donner got nicked by a gunshot. We don't know for sure who the target was but it does look like Donner was it." Bill fell into step with Libby. They moved a distance ahead of the medics to privately talk. "Why him do you suppose?"

"Well, Donner is the most financially powerful player for the Tiptop side. The man has lots of influence down Denver way. He comes from a very prominent family. Apparently, him siding with Tiptop was quite a surprise for the Zoning Committee."

"There has to be more than just the Zoning Committee upset would be my guess," Bill assessed. "You've got to figure that the government has informants here in the county. That Black Hawk Helicopter didn't just fly over by coincidence. Someone had to have ordered it. Plus, this attempted murder happened way too quickly. Maybe the assassin was monitoring the whole meeting then decided just to take out one of the votes."

"Exactly what we were thinking," Libby agreed. "In fact, Captain Jen and I now wonder if all the landowners are in danger. The zoning meeting adjourned with a 4-to-4 tie on the subject of Eminent Domain. Best way to change that vote is through elimination," Libby added then glanced at Bill to let it all sink in.

"I hope you're wrong but it does make a hell of a lot of sense," Bill answered. "Are all the landowners down here?"

"Not all. Emma is with Kevin Donner's lawyer and there's also Howie Page. They're down having lunch in Tiptop," she disclosed. "I'm going to take you all to the site then head into Tiptop and find them. They should be at the local restaurant."

"Who's Howie Page?" Bill asked.

"The one Zoning Committee member voting against Eminent Domain. He's an old geologist who lives near town. Come to think of it, he might also be in danger. So we have four people that need protective custody. Plus, Nathan Abel is still out in the wind."

"I sure hope Nathan is still alive. The plot thickens," Bill speculated. The team would have to find Nathan Abel and soon, he knew.

The group arrived and found Bix, Wally Hall and Kevin Donner talking with Captain Jen. The envoy stopped and listened as Kevin Donner admitted, "Yeah, we all think I'm the target, Captain Holly, but it's not totally a slam dunk. I bent down to pick up a stone about the time the shot came calling. Can't imagine that Bix was the target unless the assassin didn't like her negotiation style. No, it was me… or Wally?" Kevin said as the medics began to check his vital signs and bandage the wound.

"Whoever was the target of this ambush doesn't need for it to happen again," Jen affirmed. "A little protective custody might just be in order; we'll talk later."

"We're ready to transport, Captain Jen," one of the medics said.

"Good," Jen answered, then glanced around the perimeter. She wanted out of this open meadow as soon as possible; there was no cover whatsoever. "Kevin, we'll check on you in Frisco fairly soon. I need to send Libby to Tiptop to inform your lawyer. Detective Smith and I will stay on scene and mark the site. Maybe we can get lucky and find some clues. An empty casing would be nice."

"Then my lawyer will be informed and meet me at the hospital?"

"Definitely," Jen assured Kevin Donner. "I'm not staying here long but the area does deserve a quick search. I can get an investigative team out here later today for a thorough search. Libby, head into Tiptop and inform the group to stay together then escort them to the hospital in Frisco. We can't take any chances at this point. Actually, Bix why don't you ride in and stay close to Emma."

"I can do that," Bix answered.

The parade reversed and was gone in five minutes. Kevin Donner had refused the stretcher and walked out. Libby and Bix lead the way.

"Well, Captain Jen, Libby was telling me about the events. You really think that all the landowners need protection?" Bill asked.

"I think it would be ridiculous not to put an officer on duty for each individual. I'll call the Peak

County police when we get back and see if they agree. If not, then Summit will need to do it."

They began circling the area searching for the shooter's cover. "Sure would be good to find the perp's location before dark," Jen thought out loud.

"Hopefully, the assassin might be a smoker or just careless," Bill mumbled. "This perp could have been watching the whole meeting. What do you think?"

"Looks like it, doesn't it? I suppose the guy could have had a long distance mic trained on the meeting or someone immediately called him right after adjournment? Either way, it was fortunate for us that he missed his target. Maybe he isn't a professional assassin? Personally, I have a feeling Kevin Donner is one very lucky man," Jen concluded.

"Hey, over here," Bill yelled. On the ground behind a large boulder was a couple cigarette butts and then five feet away was the casing. Bill pulled out his evidence bags as Jen marked the area and took pictures. It was their first real material evidence.

***

"Well, here's to a day of surprises," Bix said holding up her wine glass. It was now early evening. Bix had called Bernie from the Emergency Ward and told her to expect four extra for dinner. The couple had, fortunately, bought a roast for sandwiches that would now be used for this occasion. Bernie had thrown in more potatoes after talking with Bix so it hadn't been a big deal.

Kevin was now bandaged with a minor gunshot wound in his arm and instructions to take it easy. There was no hospital stay needed. His lawyer was sent back to Denver; Kevin had decided to stay in Summit tonight. He wanted to get acquainted with the other landowners and explain his plan to them. Having HAPT's Captain invited to dinner was also a bonus to the deal. Bix's invitation had been most welcome.

Now, all were seated around the table ready to enjoy a great meal. "And thanks goes to Bix and Bernie," Wally Hall declared after the toast, "for opening your home on such short notice. I never expected that I'd be wined and dined this evening. It is damn gracious," Wally finished. "Anytime that you all are over in Leadville, a free dinner at The Rusty Bucket will be offered. Of course that goes for all of you," Wally added.

Yes, Kevin Donner felt right at home tonight.

"Here, here," they proclaimed in another toast. Naturally, dinner hit the spot; most of the guests had forgotten about any lunch. Simon managed to make sure that the people noticed him during dinner of course. His tummy was full as he slipped into his comfy bed. Wonderful meal, he mused.

There was then a long pause as the group finished. This gathering wasn't exactly meant to be a festive affair. Reality began to loom over them. Captain Jen set down her wine glass and turned it slowly. She then glanced around the table making eye contact with the landowners. "We need to talk about protective custody for all of you. I know that it will be a total inconvenience but today's events definitely merit protection. I will talk tomorrow with Peak County about surveillance on Howie Page and Emma.

"Emma, maybe you could bed down here until we can get someone to watch your house?" Captain Jen looked at Bix and Bernie for assistance.

"Of course," Bix said without any hesitation. "We'll have a slumber party tonight. Is that okay, Emma?"

"It is beginning to sound like there is no choice in that matter. If you're fine with me being a guest?"

"Of course" said Bernie. "Okay with you, Simon?" On cue the little Schnoodle jumped up into Emma's lap. He was, of course, rewarded with a warm snuggle from Emma.

"Well, that's settled then," Jen nodded. "Wally, I called Chief Carl Hagen on the way to the hospital and he is placing an officer on your door as we speak. Officer Libby James will escort you back over to Leadville this evening, and Kevin, there will be a Frisco officer on your door. Are we good with the arrangements?"

The group nodded together.

"I can arrange for security down in Denver so don't worry, Captain Jen," Kevin said.

"Good," Jen verified. "I had hoped so. Then we're set with security for all?" There was a second round of nods.

Kevin Donner then leaned forward in his chair and began to address the group, "I need to tell you that my coming here with a lawyer today was no accident. We had expected just what might happen at the zoning meeting. There are many people at the State Capitol that will have our backs as this develops. We need to discuss just exactly what that means now. Tomorrow, I go back down to Denver to finalize our case. The State of Colorado will schedule a meeting for the public before the Friday night rally. The Zoning Committee needs to explain their position to Tiptop . Little extra pressure certainly couldn't hurt."

Captain Jen Holly then got up out of her chair and interrupted, "Kevin, it is better that the police manage the security situation and the murder case at this time. I should probably not sit in on this strategy meeting until the state weighs in on police involvement. Maybe a memo later from the state to my office would be best? Something that I can share with the counties appropriately." Jen then eyed Bernie closely. "Bernie, shall we take Simon for a walk? He looks like an airing would be appreciated."

"Great idea," Bernie answered sensing that Jen had something else to tell her. They cleared the table then Bernie attached the leash to Simon and the three left.

The night was filled with stars as they closed the front door and began their walk. It was silent and crisp outside. One of those spectacular nights that takes your breath away. The stellar sky was full of stars encompassed in deep darkness.

"You and Bix do know that I really hope Tiptop can stop this assault on our land,'" Jen said. "We are a small part of a large fight but each movement does make a difference," she added.

"We know, Jen, how you feel and what your job dictates. Have no doubt," Bernie said.

" I need to ask you something before I leave here tonight," Jen said glancing at Bernie. "Did you bring a hand gun with you from North Dakota?" Jen asked.

"Actually I did. That was one of the reasons that I drove rather than flying. The times certainly do dictate new perspectives, don't they? Hope you don't mind?"

"No. Not at all. I'm glad to hear it actually." There was a pause while Simon used this opportunity to relieve himself. Jen glanced at Bernie for a moment then continued, "Bix may also be in danger. She has connections and anyone who is for Eminent Domain knows that. You two need to be cautious and protective of each other."

"You need say no more. I will sleep with one eye open tonight," Bernie said.

"And I will make a note that you have informed me of your carry permit just in case," Jen added.

"Want me to scan my permit tonight and send you a copy?" Bernie asked.

"That would be great. Thanks, Bernie. I do appreciate your openness. Rules have so changed on gun laws that I probably need nothing from you. Actually, the rules hardly exist anymore as you are well aware."

"That's exactly why I carry," Bernie added. "It's crazy.

"Agreed," Jen added.

Simon now decided that it was time to rejoin

the party. They quickly returned to the house. As they opened the door, the group had just finished their discussion. It was about time to leave and try to get some rest after a very arduous day. However, Jen could tell that the group did have something to announce.

Wally Hall was in front; the group stood behind him in support. He began his confession slowly, "I just told these folks something that I now need to tell you, Captain Holly. Yesterday I went over to see Nathan Abel at his cabin to talk with him. He admitted to me that he wanted out of Tiptop and to retire with some money in his pocket. I was totally shocked when I realized that he was going to sell out to the government. Nathan was serious and his son supports that decision he told me. I couldn't believe it. Where was his loyalty? Well, anyway, something needed to be done." Wally shifted his weight and continued, "On the way back to Leadville I figured out a plan to get Nathan out of the picture for awhile. Not to hurt him at all but to get him out of the situation for a little bit so I could see how things would develop. You remember Milt Gray, Captain Holly?"

"Actually I do. The old guy is a trusted friend of Johnny McPherson's. Another case another time," Jen explained. "Johnny stayed with him during the case. I do remember that quite well. He definitely has lots of friends here in the mountains."

Wally nodded, then proceeded, "Well, Milt has been wanting to prospect my property over on the other side of Independence Pass. One of those small gulches before you get to Aspen. So I gave him permission to prospect if he'd take Nathan Abel with him. I told him to stay out there for at least a week and not tell anyone where they were going. That was the deal."

"And you have neglected to tell anyone about this arrangement until now?" Captain Holly said. The group could feel her tension as the situation began to heat up.

"Yes, Captain. That's exactly what I did," Wally Hall confessed. "I know my action was totally unacceptable and slightly illegal."

"Yes, it was. Aiding and abetting would be my guess," she stated.

Kevin Donner came forward at that moment. "Mr. Hall told us, and we advised him to tell you this evening. His actions will be defended by my law team if need be. I believe that Wally is extremely sorry and now realizes how stupid his actions happen to be." Wally enthusiastically nodded after every word of Kevin's statement.

"You do realize that Nathan's son is a lawyer and mad as hell right now?" Captain Jen offered.

"I am aware of that now, and I will instruct my legal team to contact Jackson Abel immediately. We will be working with him and, hopefully, he will not want to file a lawsuit against Mr. Hall. I will be in Frisco so you can contact me tomorrow before I leave on that situation," Kevin added.

He then placed his hand on Wally's shoulder in a show of support . "Let's also realize that it was Nathan Abel's decision to go. No one forced Mr. Abel to do anything. He simply made an adult decision to go prospecting."

"Correct," Captain Jen answered. "Right now then Wally has told the truth; he has told us the entire story. Is that correct, Wally?"

"You betcha," he said with determination. "I was thinking maybe I could buy Nathan's claim, but he wants a hell of a lot of money. My only alternative was to get him out of the picture."

"However, if something should happen to Mr. Abel on his way out of the gulch and back to Tiptop, Wally might be charged as an accessory to murder. I can't speak for the DA's Office," Jen carefully added.

"We are aware of that," Kevin Donner stated. "That situation belongs in the hands of God and the lawyers. Heaven help us," he added wisely.

There was another caveat to this drama that still needed to be discussed. Jen was well aware of the worst case scenario. Right now no one needed any more surprises. She stared at the two gentlemen and then continued, "So, the question becomes, did you tell anyone else about your plan?" Jen was holding her breath at this juncture. A lot of the case details would be determined by Wally's answer.

"Just Bart, my employee, who drove the two over to Sourdough Gulch. He said that he'd keep it a secret. Bart's worked for me for the last two years."

"Bart's last name?" Jen asked quickly.

"Gentry," Wally Hall said.

As the three ladies watched the group head out of Bix's driveway, the quiet settled in. It was sort of an eerie feeling. So much to process and so many new feelings to wear.

"Martin would be so upset if he were alive," Emma said almost in a whisper. She let out a sigh then turned toward Bix and Bernie. "What do you think will happen now?" she asked.

"I think we have a chance," Bix said softly. "I can tell you I'm really happy that Kevin is on our side," she concluded. "He seems to understand how to combat the legal system. And, isn't it odd how we all were brought together? Our lives so different and yet here we are. Did you know Wally before this happened?" Bix asked Emma.

Emma thought for a moment before she replied, " Martin and I knew him because of the property deeds but that was all. Martin said that we should invite him for dinner but it never did happen. Isn't that interesting…what strange circumstances. We are a group of people who value the same territory. Kevin Donner walked the same land that Martin did; they searched for the same gems. Wally Hall kept his claim for tradition for three generations. The land is our common ground isn't it?" Emma looked at both ladies for agreement; they did. "Bix, I'll do everything that I can to help, not only for Martin, but for myself. These are important times, aren't they?" she admitted.

"Maybe the most important times for all of us, a defining moment, I think," Bix commented.

"Yes," Emma said. There was a heartfelt moment of united silence while they absorbed the events. Emma then confessed, "Now, ladies, I could bed down. Suddenly, I feel exhausted." The day had truly drained Emma's energy, Bix and Bernie could tell.

"You have the entire upstairs to yourself, Emma.," Bix said. "Would you like to borrow something to sleep in; I can also offer Simon to snuggle with tonight. Oh, and there's an extra toothbrush up there," Bix added. It took a few minutes to get Emma and Simon organized. Bernie finished cleaning the kitchen while Bix organized the upstairs' guest.

They met downstairs some ten minutes later. Bix fell into Bernie's arms. There they stood together gaining strength from each other. Processing how extraordinary this day had truly been for them.

"How close did that bullet come to hitting you?" Bernie whispered. Her slender body trembled slightly as she acknowledged what could have been.

"I hadn't considered that possibility until Kevin mentioned it. Kevin was the logical target. He had just tipped the scales and given Tiptop new life. I'm somewhat of a bystander in this controversy," Bix tried to convince herself and Bernie.

Bernie wasn't exactly buying Bix's explanation after talking with Jen Holly so she continued, "Jen just talked to me about watching your back and she was glad that I had brought a hand gun with me." Bernie now looked straight into Bix's eyes, "Jen believes that your involvement could be another valuable piece in this puzzle. You are one of the outside instigators that has contacted the press. Honey, Jen believes you're in danger. We have got to be careful."

"So Jen thinks I'm in danger?" Bix asked, rather surprised. Bernie nodded.

"I have to admit that our discussion about me buying an automatic hand gun yesterday did cross my mind today," Bix conceded. "I have to admit that the government changes have scared me. I can't deny what is going on. The nation has gone from peace and prosperity to corruption and greed. Unbelievable how quickly life changes," Bix admitted. She tightened her hold on Bernie. The hug felt so good.

"Did I hear at some point that we are going to visit Melanie Camp at the Coalition in Denver?" Bernie asked while planting a kiss on top of Bix's head. "How about we stop at a gun shop on the way back and take a look," she suggested. Bernie's mind was reeling; so much had happened in the last week. They had gone from 'so glad you came to visit' then 'we need to get you a gun.' Their lives had become so damn dangerous so quickly. Unbelievable.

"It is time," Bix admitted. She suddenly shook her head and moved on with a resolute sigh. Her arms began to explore Bernie's strong back and tapered waist. She then allowed herself permission to stop the anxiety, cease and desist. Bix's mind began to focus on another issue entirely however. They needed each other, she confessed.

"I want to stop thinking about all of this, Bernie; I want to make love." Bix's eyes burned holes into the tall woman holding her. She unbuckled Bernie's belt, pulled off her shirt, released Bernie's bra and plastered herself against warm breasts. The magnetic heat exploded into the arousal of hardened taut nipples . Never relinquishing this sensuous embrace, the two touched and tangled as they maneuvered down the hallway.

All Bernie knew was that she desperately loved Bix with all her heart. They would get through this mess together; they would trust in each other. Bernie then demanded her mind to stop all anxiety and fall into bed. They needed love right now.

It was like Bix had heard her thoughts. She whispered softly into Bernie's ear, "I am so glad that you are here, honey; I was so scared today," she confessed. "You are my rock." Bix reached up and cradled Bernie's face in her hands then pulled her into a kiss. The soft deep kiss grew into collective warm energy. Bernie's arms folded around Bix. They froze time as the delicious kiss shut out the world . It closed the door on evil and opened into warm arousal. Desire took control as the kiss produced sparks. All the clothes came off as they melted together into a heated blend.

Bodies wrapped closely under the covers; intimate touch exploring folds now rocked their cores. Bernie was home as the warmth between her legs came alive. Their bodies communicating; touching, falling then cradled deep into folds of desire. Tongues seeking depths rhythmically devouring. Lights exploded; thoughts gone. Bix felt her body jump as Bernie stroked her intimately until both their bodies spun toward organism. They were safe. Love dissolved all fear as their bodies melted. The future would take a breather tonight.

CHAPTER 14

SEARCHING WITH HELP

"So this is what I know, Carl, one Bart Gentry dropped off good old Milt Gray and Nathan Abel in Sourdough Gulch. Wally Hall instructed them to tell no one where they were going. I guess that request is protocol for prospectors; they would want secrecy. And also, Wally stated that he did not bribe Nathan Abel or force him to go. These two old men just left everything and went prospecting for a silver vein," Jen finished. Her mind was double checking the details as she told Chief Carl Hagen from Leadville on the phone.

"Holy shit! I can't believe it! That son of a bitch, Milton Gray, has gotten himself in crap again. For an old Leadville drunk, he sure as hell can get himself in trouble with the law. I assume you're taking care of one very remorseful Wally Hall?"

"Definitely. He sat down and confessed on the record after his rights were given. The transcript will be sent to the DA and you, of course. Let's keep in mind those two old geezers weren't kidnapped. Pretty damn gullible, but they were invited."

"What's your next step, Jen?" Carl asked.

"Nathan and Milt are, of course, out of cell phone range. I will be dispatching Detective Jerry Neal and Officer Libby James at first light into the gulch for pursuit. The helicopter will drop them off after checking the area carefully. Tyler, our K9, will accompany them. However, I do need to ask a favor of you?"

"Let me guess. I need to pick up Bart Gentry right now?" Carl said turning quickly in his chair and motioning for a Leadville officer to join him.

"Correct. I hope we can find him and keep the raps on this situation until we apprehend those two."

"Me too, Captain Jen. I'll get back with you within the hour." Chief Carl Hagen said then hung up the phone and bellowed, "Get in here, Harry !"

Ten minutes later, Harry Bristol drove the two blocks and pulled into the back alley behind The Rusty Bucket Restaurant. He knocked then opened the door to the kitchen. "Is Bart Gentry here?"

"Hell no!" retorted a gruff voice. It was the cook who turned around and examined the officer. "The little shit didn't show up for work." The cook then thought about the situation. "Why? Is he in some kind of trouble?"

"No. I just need to talk with him asap. Here's my card. Will you tell him to call me if he does show up. Tell him it concerns Milt Gray," Harry said. "By the way, would you know where he lives?"

"Over on 3rd Street. Second house down from the east corner."

"Thanks," Harry said and left. He soon found that Bart Gentry's house was locked up tight. The guy had disappeared. Harry quickly called Chief Hagen.

A BOLO was issued immediately by the Chief. His officers began combing the bars and other late night haunts. If Bart was anywhere in the Leadville area, they would soon know. The Chief then called Captain Jen back with the bad news. Another character was out there in the wind. What else could go wrong?

***

Jackson Abel received his phone call from Captain Jen Holly around ten that evening. He had already talked with Kevin Donner earlier. The whole situation was incredible. His father had gone prospecting? What a dumb move that was. He was, however, relieved to hear that HAPT was beginning a search the following morning. Jackson had investigated HAPT yesterday and learned of their organization and reputation. He felt pretty confident that they'd be able to drag those two old coots back before something happened to them. At least he hoped so.

Jackson Abel couldn't help but feel that his father would have been far safer if he had stayed in Tiptop, but there was nothing that he could do about it now. He even wished that his dad had gone to the zoning meeting so he would have a clear picture of what was happening. Naturally, like most major events in his dad's life, Nathan Abel was there but absent. Shit.

Then there was the entrance of Kevin Donner into the deal. It had been quite a surprise to Jackson. Who would have thought that Donner Realty would become a power player in the Eminent Domain controversy? Plus, coming out on the side of the Tiptop was an incredible surprise. Jackson had no doubt that he would hear back from Donner's Corporation soon. Maybe there was a better offer in the wind than he had anticipated. Siding with Tiptop and Donner could be a win-win situation for him. The plot thickened, Jackson surmised.

***

The Summit Helicopter circled Sourdough Gulch from front to back. They had hoped that the remains of a campfire might give away the prospectors' location this morning. Unfortunately, there were no signs of any cooking fire. The gulch lay quietly below them camouflaging any signs of human inhabitants.

The steep peaks shot up like church towers on the curricular rim then flattened out into an expansive alpine meadow. From the air they could see many old mining tunnels located high above the plateau on both sides. The large meadow was still lush green from the damp summer with numerous waterfalls adorning the cliffs. It was an impressive fall panorama with a multitude of aspen trees radiating orange and yellow colors below the crystal blue sky.

As the copter landed, Officer Libby James and Detective Jerry Neal jumped out. They unloaded the gear and commanded their K-9 dog, Tyler, to stay close. The alpine tundra above tree line was probably their destination. Tyler would have to stay close in this rugged terrain. They assessed their climbing equipment carefully before sending the copter back to Summit.

Libby James had recently finished a climbing course that Captain Jen had suggested. She knew exactly why she had been picked for this assignment. Her computer skills would keep them in communication and her new climbing techniques locked in the deal.

She also knew exactly why Jerry Neal was here. The man was a phenomenal tracker and dog trainer. Actually, he had a reputation that was now utilized all over the state. If a police department needed help tracking, they called him. Neal had also been recruited to teach some courses at the state level. He was becoming famous in Colorado for sure, she thought. Jerry was still stationed in Buena Vista with the Police Department, but his assignments now covered much more territory. Libby felt honored to be working with him. She had no doubt that, eventually, Detective Neal would be promoted and working on the state level. It would be HAPT's loss. His ability would be missed. Bummer, she assessed.

Libby now checked her smartphone to see if Detective Bill Smith had found Bart Gentry yet. Any information that Gentry could give them about where to start this search would be good. Right now it was a massive area, tracking dog or not. There were no messages. At least she knew that they were able to communicate with Captain Jen during this assignment. Good.

The officers finally finished unloading all the supplies. Jerry then motioned the pilot to take off. The sooner the copter left, the better for their team; their arrival had been too obvious. Time for cover. Were they the only team out here looking for the prospectors or not? Good question. The rotors lifted the copter out of Sourdough Gulch.

Now it was totally silent. The cool crisp air surrounded Jerry and Libby as Tyler dog began his surveillance of their area making sure that there were no unwelcome intruders. The K-9 circled their position enlarging his circle each time. Both officers began to concentrate on their provisions and surroundings.

They gathered all the supplies into their packs and headed toward a clump of aspen trees near the back of the meadow. Right now, they felt like sitting ducks out here even though Tyler was giving the all clear sign for their immediate area. Eyes from above could easily be looking down. Even the prospectors would try to avoid them. After all they wouldn't want anyone to find the silver vein first. It was truly a 'Catch 22.'

It did feel like someone was watching to Officer Libby James. If the rising hair on the back of her neck indicated anything, there was someone watching. Jerry now loaded ammunition into Tyler's dog packs; he balanced it evenly. Quickly they made their way toward cover. Conversation was terminated until they moved from this position. Cover, became the priority.

***

Before the Sourdough Team had left Summit, Captain Jen had sent Detective Bill Smith over to Nathan Abel's cabin in Tiptop to get a sample of his scent. Bill had come back with an old shirt. It had been delivered to Detective Jerry Neal for scent detection.

Captain Jen then sent Smith to Leadville to join the police search for Bart Gentry. Chief Carl Hagen had his men doing a second surveillance of Leadville proper just in case Bart was holed up somewhere. He even had his secretary calling Gentry's relatives. The BOLO was out on Bart Gentry loud and clear. If Bart was out partying, he would be found. The town was definitely on alert. Bill Smith teamed up with Harry Bristol of Leadville during this police action. His orders from Captain Jen were to help Chief Carl Hagen and report to Jen now and then. If the investigation brought no results, they would branch out and start searching Highway 24 and 82 over Independence Pass.

Captain Jen Holly was left to monitor the protective custody of the claim owners and manage the media inquiries. She had also decided to visit with Kevin Donner before he left Frisco. The man was a pivotal player in this whole case. Maybe there would be some detail that would help with all the investigations going on.

Jen had also instructed the returning Summit helicopter to do the preliminary search of the highways and Independence Pass for any kind of car accident. Who knew? It might be helpful. Bart drove a blue 2000 Honda sedan. They might just get lucky; she also hoped Bart Gentry was alive and lucky.

***

Officer Frank Mason sat at the communications board in the HAPT Office this morning monitoring all the events. He knew that Bart Gentry hadn't been found yet, Kevin Donner was going to receive a visit from Capt Jen, Officers Neal and James were in Sourdough Gulch, and the Denver media was licking its chops for more information. Chief Marshall Tate from Frisco had become the contact chief at this point for media. Plus, the FBI was sniffing around. Everyone was busy except for him. Yeah, he was balancing all the information but it just didn't seem like enough. He wanted to take action. Frank, dutifully, wrote a summary on email for all the team officers first. Their morning meeting just wasn't going to happen.

Abruptly the private HAPT phone rang. Frank checked where the call was coming from. Bix Bixler was calling in this morning. "Hey lady, what's up?" Frank asked.

"Morning, Frank," she responded. "Just wanted to check in and say that Bernie and I are heading down to Denver. Emma headed home to Tiptop with a police escort early this morning. We, however, have a meeting with Melanie Camp this afternoon. I think the topic will center around another protest march scheduled for this Friday. We'll be at the Coalition Office early this afternoon."

"Sounds like a job," he mumbled. His mood was obvious to Bix; she could tell. Frank understood his job and the importance of team coordination. Nevertheless, it was not like an active role; he was camped on the sidelines today.

Bix softened her tone and added, "We did want to thank you again for your help at the last protest. My heart would have stopped if I hadn't been warned by you about the Black Hawk Helicopter. Thanks again, Frank."

"You're welcome. I just wish that I could be out there in the field this morning. You know what I mean?" he confessed.

Indeed she did. Bix was of Frank's age and understood the questions that seniors face when it came to physical activities. Could they keep up was the main question? On some days you knew the answer was a definite yes, and then, other days there was doubt. Today she had no doubt; yesterday had been the other kind of day. She sympathized, "I understand, Frank. Getting older ain't easy, is it?"

"No," Frank grumbled spreading the gloom.

Bix then offered a suggestion. "Maybe concentrate on finding some type of information that might help one of the police actions? Her mind searched for an example. "Frank, you know Highway 24 like the back of your hand. Maybe advise Detective Smith; I think Bart Gentry is somewhere near the highway. Plus, what can you find out about the silver mine that Nathan and Milt are prospecting? I'm even sure Libby and Jerry could use some help on how to climb Sourdough Gulch. Little hints in their ears never hurt."

"Well…." Frank hedged not quite ready to cave into the concept.

Bix now was full throttle into her pep talk. "Come on, Frank, your team needs you. They just don't know how much at the moment. Make a list then spread the knowledge in an email for all to read. You'll find a way. I have confidence in that. Now, get busy."

As Frank hung up the phone, he couldn't help but smile. He picked up a pencil and tapped it on the desk. Bix was right, damn it. Sometimes you just had to change your approach.

He pulled open a drawer where they were collecting maps of all their areas. Frank began to inspect 24 Highway carefully. His mind began to travel the road. As his finger moved down the fifty miles, he circled one area then moved on. Yes, there were certain switchbacks that were really dangerous. What if an assassin wanted to bushwhack Bart off the road? Frank then circled two more areas. His inspection brought two other circles where the switchbacks could present an opportunity for an accident. That's the way he would do it if he were out there. Well…well, he thought. Of course, his premise was that Bart Gentry had begun to travel back to Leadville. Yeah, this information just might save Bill some time.

Frank, suddenly, bolted upright in his chair as another possibility popped into his head. Actually, Bart's coming and going were, both, possibilities. What if Bart and the boys had been bushwhacked before they got there? Excitement began to stir in Frank's body; his heart was beating faster. Both sides of the road needed a thorough inspection and depending on what side just might indicate if the Sourdough rescue team was wasting its' time or not. Wow. He then wrote the email in detail to Bill. Frank was careful to explain his thoughts.

Having finished that email, Frank then focused on the Hallway Mine that Wally's grandfather had surveyed and mimed years ago. He decided to call some experts on the specific topography of that area. Millie Jean and a couple of old timers in Summit could shed some light on the topic. Mille Jean could provide the plot descriptions plus any specific landmarks in the area that would verify the ascent. Actually, her clerk recording maps might also alert the team about any hidden dangers. Yeah, that could be helpful.

Frank made a list of names to call. If it wasn't helpful, it would still be entertaining to say the least. His attitude began to brighten. He quickly got an email back from Bill thanking him. The GPS coordinates of the potential curves were appreciated. Bart Gentry hadn't been found in Leadville; they were on their way toward Sourdough Gulch, Bill reported.

Frank was surprised as another text came across his phone. This time it was from Captain Jen. She had sent him a 'smiley face.' Apparently, she had seen his email to Bill before she reached Kevin Donner's motel. "Thanks Bix," he mumbled. Frank had to admit that sometimes he just needed a good kick in the ass. His mind now began to concentrate on all the tasks at hand. Now he decided to scan and text his prospector map to the Sourdough team. Libby would get it pretty quick and she would then know more about the terrain. Frank spun into action!

CHAPTER 15

GATHERING FORCE

Captain Jen Holly arrived at Kevin Donner's lodging at 11:30. She hoped that he would be forthcoming with his information. There was no doubt that Kevin was far more involved in this Eminent Domain case than anyone had expected. She knocked at his door. Kevin immediately opened it. He had been waiting.

"Come in, Captain. I have taken the liberty to order us some lunch. Hope you don't mind?" he eyed her carefully then added, "I'm heading back down to Denver today after we meet and some food would be helpful. Parmesan Chicken okay?" he asked.

She nodded. "Thank you. I guess it is almost lunch time."

Kevin then smiled and began, "My lawyer and I will be meeting with Jackson Abel this afternoon." Kevin pulled out her chair at the dining room table. The condo was a nicely decorated suite with a kitchen, Jen noticed. A caterer was busy setting the table. Last but not least, the caterer placed the steaming chicken dish in the center. Their salads and chocolate dessert had already been placed. It all smelled delicious. Jen could see that his gesture was in kindness.

"No wine though. I will have to remain on duty here but your offering is most gracious." She smiled at him.

Kevin waited until the caterer had poured him some wine, inquired if they needed anything else then exited. He settled in the chair across from her and opened his napkin. After a sip of wine he began, "I think Jackson Abel and I can come to terms on Nathan's claim. Of course it would be incredibly advantageous if HAPT could find the old guy in one piece. I'm really hoping," he added.

"You and me both, Mr. Donner."

"That would be Kevin please. I have a feeling we'll know each other pretty well by the end of this adventure. And quite frankly, I plan to stay in touch from now on. Land grabs are going to have a way of becoming more frequent in the future. Ugly to admit but true. Our democracy and land will need our protection. I'm hoping that you and I will be on the same side always." He stared at her with intensity.

The meaning of what he had just said had not been lost on Captain Jen Holly. Who knew what the future could hold? She hoped with every fiber of her being that remaining a police officer would be possible. That her own beliefs could be met as she kept wearing her badge. However, the alternative now loomed its ugly head. It all depended on how long the public would tolerate the present Regime and their goals. Jen Holly, the person, knew that if it came to following fascism, 'this police officer' would have to quit. Lord help me, she admitted to herself. "I will always protect the people of this country," she said out loud and left it at that.

Kevin Donner nodded slightly and then went back into the Tiptop agenda. "Have your officers found Bart Gentry yet?" he asked.

"It now has been established that Gentry is not in Leadville. One of my detectives and a Leadville officer are beginning the search along Highway 24 and 82. I'm hoping that by the end of today, Bart will be found." Captain Jen could have added, 'dead or alive' but she didn't. Somehow not saying those words left more positive thoughts out there.

"Good," Kevin said. "I am sure that Bart will be able to add more information about Nathan Abel's whereabouts."

"So I have a question," Jen ventured. "What is the next action that Tiptop will take? It is beginning to sound like you just might know."

"Actually, the march is scheduled for this Friday. Do you want to know any details?" he asked with curiosity.

"I think that any information that I can acquire would be good for both counties. The state office has now contacted me. I have been ordered to share all the information that you give me to an appropriate source of course."

"Can we talk 'on the record and off the record?" Kevin froze his fork and watched Jen carefully.

"Let's define those terms. If 'on the record' works for the media and Tiptop public, then I am good with that arrangement."

"Then 'off the record' would mean what?"

"For the police departments," Jen stated.

"Then I can do that," Kevin began eating again. "On the record there will be a zoning public meeting and march on Friday. It should be larger than the last one."

"Off the record?" Jen asked taking a sip of her ice tea.

"The State of Colorado will have representatives present along with Capital Regime people. You need to have a good amount of police coverage. Do you want a list of attendance when it is formulated?"

"Please."

"I can get it to you on Wednesday. Is that soon enough?" Kevin asked. His blues eyes twinkled.

"It's going to be huge, isn't it?" Jen asked as she began to understand the implications.

"The Capital Regime will have sent the details of their case to the Zoning Committee by then. The Zoning Committee will be forced by state law to make it available to the public. I figure we'll get a copy tomorrow which means the state can then map out their intentions. So, yes, it will be a big deal. Bix will find out just how large today as she meets with the Personal Property Coalition Chair, Melanie Camp. So 'off-off the record, other details might be had by talking with Bix later," Kevin said with a twinkle in his eye. "You will be privy to information that no other police department will have. I do know that Chief Marshall Tate will also know the intent of the FBI which will be informative. You do know that they still are investigating Capital Regime? Right?"

"Affirmative. Do you have any idea how they'll interact with Tiptop? Can you give more details?"

"Hmmm, from what I can gather, the FBI will stand down, observe and record. The goal is to make sure that the government doesn't go beyond their bounds. Right now the tightrope is holding. The courts are getting the information from ACLU and the FBI. They like to hear that the legal laws are being upheld. The Regime is getting their information from someone close to this situation."

"Specifics?"

"Well, Wally and I think there must be a money trail somewhere. Some Tiptop citizen whose bank account just might have expanded or at least have increased; this person or persons, would then inform the Regime."

"So the case does revolve around water control? Correct?" Jen verified."

"Correct. And, the Regime believes that water does not belong to the people but is under governmental control. If the government can win in Tiptop, then they will enlarge their coup. They do not serve democracy, Captain Holly, but fascism; control over all states' rights. Our state law is the only thing keeping us safe and out of their control."

"Then Tiptop is the first of many small towns to experience their takeover tactics?" Jen asked.

Kevin took a sip of his wine, nodded and then continued, "Tiptop's existing land and water rights are the first case of their assaults. These local zoning folks pushing for growth and money have no idea. The truth is that the Capital Regime will profit and no one else. There will be no business ventures except through the government if they win. So, we have a plan that will be revealed Friday. Not all is lost yet, Captain Holly. We will fight tooth-and-nail. Wally is going to monitor the claim owners and I am going to get us legal action including a plan."

Kevin smiled and placed his napkin on the table. They had finished their lunch. Kevin now changed the topic slightly. "You know, Wally is an honest hard working guy. And ,'off the record,' I fully intend to get him off of all charges. Please tell the DA that if he does not press charges, my openness will flow."

Captain Jen Holly eyed Kevin Donner closely before she replied, "As of this moment, I am not intending to interfere with any decision that the DA might make. However, if I should find out that Wally Hall is more involved in the Sourdough Gulch situation than I have been led to believe, all bets would then be off."

"And well they should be," Kevin confirmed. They stood up at this point. Kevin offered his hand as he said, "Thank you for doing business with me today, Captain. We shall meet again soon, I am sure."

"So we shall," Jen affirmed as she shook his hand.

***

Libby James stared at the homemade map that Officer Frank Mason had texted her. It was far more detailed than the one she had found for their use. In fact, it looked like some old prospector must have drawn it for his own use. She liked the comments. The first climb was titled, 'Traveling Rocks (hell of a climb).'

Jerry Neal was busy fishing around in his pack for Nathan's shirt for scent. Tyler was watching intently knowing that his job would begin shortly.

"You might want to wait before you give Tyler the scent. According to Frank's map, we need to concentrate on the ascent. It does look like these tailings and boulders could be dangerous." Libby handed her smartphone to Jerry.

He eyed the screen. "I see what you mean." Maybe we hold off until we get to the first waterfall. Looks like it might be within 200 feet straight up that way." Jerry pointed at an angle to their right but mostly straight up. They would need to maneuver switchbacks and move slowly to say the least.

"Hang on, Tyler dog, you'll get your chance soon," Libby said, giving him a scratch.

The three began their ascent. Libby and Jerry occasionally used the bush branches for support. As they traversed across the tailings, their footing was anything but solid; each step would produce a six inch mini slide down before stabilizing. It was arduous and tedious to say the least. Tyler's four footed traction was definitely an advantage. He would stand above them with his tongue hanging out and watch their progress.

The sun had just come out full force and the temperature warmed up. Libby found herself sweating like a pig under the strain. She figured that the elevation was 9500 at the base. The waterfall would be 10,000 feet at least. It was feeling like they were going straight up on a rickety old ladder.

Thirty minutes later they had arrived at a cluster of trees with some shade. The break for water and food was welcome. "Not too far until the waterfall," Libby said. "Maybe half a mile according to this map. There should be a mountain goat path over to our right." Libby had decided to only check out the smartphone map sparingly. She needed to keep her battery charged. She had brought a solar recharger but that would have to wait until later if they needed it. She could rig the solar plate to the top of her hat if need be. It would look a bit strange but it would work. The battery storage then would charge her phone.

"I'm thinking that we can definitely wait to put Tyler on Nathan's scent," Jerry calculated. "Frank's map will take us right to the mine. If we find that they're not mining, then Tyler would be able to do a fresh scent. Tyler would also let us know if Nathan has been in the Hallway Mine just in case. I guess we have to consider the possibility that Nathan and Milt never made it. That is possible. " Jerry stared directly at Libby for a few seconds.

She nodded in agreement. Yes, they did have to consider that these two guys had disappeared prior to the climb. What else could have happened, she wondered? Libby then remembered her premonition as they landed about someone watching them. "So Jerry, have you heard any noises that might indicate another intruder or intruders?" she asked.

"Not so far but if that were the case, they could very easily be above us watching. No noise required. I can't tell if Tyler thinks there's more people on this mountain or not. Wish to hell he could talk," Jerry added.

Libby couldn't help but glance up. Her chills had gone away but that didn't mean that nobody was there. It just meant that she had let it be. "Think I'll text the Captain this location," she said. "Make sure that we're still in service range." They waited until a text shot back to them.

Libby read to Jerry the message, 'Gentry not found in L. Bill on highway searching. Stay in touch every 2 hrs. Capt.'

'10-4.' Libby texted then closed off communication.

The shade had revitalized them. Tyler was laying, tummy down, in a small stream of water looking incredibly content. Their position was well hidden. The shade dropped the temperature by ten degrees for them.

"So what's the next climb like?" Jerry asked.

"Well, we climb straight up. No surprise there. Looks like larger boulders with ledges and small grass areas between them. Lots of lodge pole pines of course. Maybe a little easier would be my guess," Libby replied. "It is titled, 'Breather' on the map.

As the Sourdough Team continued, they were

relieved to venture between shade and sun. Their progress was faster and more relaxed. They found the goat trail that was indicated on the map. Naturally, the wildlife had figured out the best approach to the climb. Libby was checking distance when a mountain goat surprised her. He was coming down the path at a fairly decent clip. With absolutely no hesitation, the goat jumped ten feet over to another ledge. He then stood like a magnificent statue eying them. Tyler simply wagged his tail and stared back. Life moved on for both.

Half an hour later the team arrived at the water fall. It was a grotto actually. The deep light green moss cushioned their steps as they approached. It was like walking on sponges, Libby thought. The ledge wrapped around them and provided ample shade. The waterfall fell from a crevice some 30 feet above them. It provided a mist that gently sprayed them. The grotto, itself, was in full shade and tunneled back into the rock some eight feet. The water fell into a small crystal clear pool no more that two feet deep. Libby placed her hand in it to test the temperature. Perfect, she thought. Tyler drank deeply. So far this hike had been dog heaven, Libby realized. Jerry filled Tyler's water pouch for later, then he settled for a rest.

It was now early afternoon. If they had been recreational hikers, this area would have merited a dip. Libby flashed on the thought that she and Marshall could some day take this hike. It was funny how her perspective had changed now that she was part of a relationship. It was so much fun to suddenly fantasize about what they could do together. It still felt novel to her and, in that same breath, so much more explosive. She let herself flash on the idea of making love here. Lying down naked in the moss releasing all inhibitions; releasing their sensual passions with no one to hear. An incredible luxury she allowed herself to realize. Libby then shook her red hair slightly to get her head back on task. She glanced quickly at Jerry to make sure that he hadn't notice her escape into fantasy. He seemed to be in his own world also. Thank heavens.

Libby's eyes then began to scan the next phase of their climb. Oh boy, she thought. Turning on the smartphone to see the map, she saw what she already knew. The pine disappeared becoming small bushes then they would be officially above tree line. This beautiful alpine meadow would be no longer.

More moving rocks and no stability. The one redeeming factor was that she saw burro trails from long ago winding up the steep slope. They had reached the highest ascent. The narrow burro paths traversed above them almost touching the sky. It would be a harder climb than the previous stages. This would be the challenge.

Libby began to think about how the burros persevered. They must have done the climb day after day until they died. These burros would have felt the leather cutting into their sides as they labored. Their hooves taking small steps to survive the challenge while their lungs strained. It was so hard to image, Libby admitted. Poor animals. And now here they were preparing for that same ascent. "This climb was entitled, 'Hell,' on the map," she mumbled.

Jerry had wrapped a damp handkerchief around his neck and tied it; Libby did the same. They divided up some of Tyler's load. The ammo couldn't be left but there were some supplies that they could retrieve on the way down. How they approached this ascent was very important now. The lighter the load, the better. Libby placed her phone and anything else from her pockets into her pack. Better safe than sorry, she thought.

Twenty minutes later they had left the last of the bushes behind. They were clearly in the open from this point on. The rocks clung to the dry sandy ground while sparse little plants of miniature size added the only color to their ascent. Strikingly visible, they plodded up the trail. Tyler had taken the middle position. He was panting; they were sweating.

Abruptly, as if on cue, the team heard one lone boulder break loose from high above them. The sound was distinctive as it eerily echoed from one side of the gulch to the other. The boulder began to dislodge other rocks in its path. Together, the force multiplied in width and speed. Now, 40 feet wide, the rocks became a murderous herd. Ripping and tearing at the ground; throwing weathered wood and bushes like match sticks. Dust clouds began exploding into the sky as the mass screamed in rage dragging their team under with the dust and rubble.

Giant boulders flew off of ledges spiraling high in the air. These monsters thundered down the slope splitting trees and destroying the terrain in their path. It was the total chaos of a violent slide snarling and screaming erratically. Nature's force gashed and scarred the surface of this beautiful gulch during a mere 15 minutes of nightmare.

And then, the slide began to stabilize; the dust began to clear. A few stray boulders continued their roll still seeking their new destinations. The mass erosion ended with one lone boulder falling into place. That sound heralded the end. Sourdough Gulch became quiet once more leaving a whole new terrain devoid of life for now.

CHAPTER 16

PREPARATIONS

"So the state government will be in support of our action on Friday," Melanie Camp proclaimed from behind her desk. "Even the ACLU will have representatives on site. I think all entities realize that the Regime will have a force there also. We need to make sure that our representatives are extremely visible and standing with the public. The Capital Regime won't try to intimidate the public when they see our presence. This land grab will be obvious and the reasons why will be clear by the end of the evening."

Bix and Bernie both were caught off guard by Melanie's all-inclusive announcement. Their jaws dropped and breath had stopped. There was an awkward pause while they processed.

"Then this rally will really escalate Friday? Do I have to inform the media?" Bix asked.

"Nope. I've contacted the liberal media. The

reporters will find out just before they leave for the event so there won't be many leaks. The surprise element will work in our favor." Melanie smiled at Bix and Bernie; this escalation of events was indeed shocking. It would suddenly go from a small town protest to an entire state wide resistance. The legal actions would no longer be in their hands; the fight for state rights would become the focus. This case of Eminent Domain would become a test case for the entire country which was Melanie's goal.

And, yes, Melanie Camp had been on the other end of this stick years ago. She knew how these cases went. There was a point when a small town event could become a sample case headed for the Supreme Court. The town would have to place some faith in the system one step at a time. She hadn't pulled any punches right now with Bix and Bernie. The whole situation needed to be organized and organized now; it was too late to hesitate.

Melanie continued, "Tiptop is holding a legal protest to halt an Eminent Domain lawsuit that has implications for the entire nation. Showing our strength is vital to get the Regime to back down."

Melanie then produced Friday's schedule. "Zoning Committee Public Meeting first then the rally. Kevin is arranging to have a stage set up by the Courthouse for speakers. I'm thinking that the crowd should meet by the city limit signs, north and south, and park along the highway so that anyone who is coming to this event can understand the crowd size by the lines of cars. Plus, the Zoning Committee can't say later that the town was inundated with traffic and hired protesters. The license plates will tell the story. We'll have the media take pictures of the car plates in a way that gets the point across."

"Do you know who the speakers will be?" Bernie asked hesitantly.

"Actually I do not know who will be here from the state, but your MC of the night will be Emma Keiser. I have a speech trainer working with her this week."

"That's a great idea," Bix said. "Tiptop will be delighted, I am sure. One of their own right up there with the bigwigs!"

"I can at least say that the State, ACLU and Personal Property Coalition will be represented. The crowd won't be disappointed at all. The whole country is in distress right now but most state governors who truly care about their land and people are stepping up. And yes, I know the court system is so slow but it does get the job done eventually. Justice is what it is, right?"

"What do you want us to do?" Bernie asked with resolve.

"Sounds insignificant but it isn't. How about organizing ten or twelve people to handle parking on both sides of the city limits. As the lines get longer maybe some ATVs transporting people to town?"

"Maybe some drinking water stands also?" Bix added.

"Good idea. Kevin is also adding porta-potties. You think we could get some of Summit's citizens over there?" Melanie asked.

"We'll work on it. I am sure that we can show

support for our neighbors," Bix said. She began to realize that tomorrow their life would be busy. Bix would make a list of volunteers to call tomorrow. Some ten minutes later, they left Melanie's office.

Bix and Bernie then did one more errand before leaving Denver. They stopped at gun shop. Fortunately, the place was professional with no politics exhibited. Bix worked with the sales people learning more than she had expected. She was happy to report these people seemed pretty damn knowledgeable and, of course, Bernie, was a huge help.

They had decided on a Beretta 92 standard automatic. Bix liked the safety features and the balance of the weapon. They had been able to fire a rental Beretta so Bix could make a proper decision. She had also realized that there was a lot of education to undertake. It wasn't as simple as she had thought. Responsible people would learn how to handle owning a handgun. Actually today illustrated that nothing was simple. She bought ear protection and made arrangements to take some lessons after the rally.

Eventually, they started driving home. Simon had moved from the back seat into Bix's lap for the ride. Some routines would never change, Bix told herself as they turned onto I-70. Nevertheless, Tiptop would change this Friday and fight for their way of life; Bix had decided that protection was her own responsibility today. Yep, sometimes there was a need for change for humans. Dogs needed no change; Simon simply assumed love. She petted him happily and smiled.

***

Detective Bill Smith and Leadville's finest, Officer Harry Bristol, slowly traveled down Highway 24 in search of Bart Gentry. They were fifteen miles into the search with no signs of a car going through any safety rails or tire skid marks either. They had passed Frank's first marked site. Both officers had gotten out of the car and searched both road sides thoroughly. Bill figured that the next sharp curve was another five miles up the road. He was betting on Independence Pass for any kind of accident. The switchbacks were just made for pushing a car off into the 100 feet canyons. The car would then be lost from sight as it tumbled over the edge. They had brought binoculars along for such a situation. Maybe they would get lucky.

As they neared the first location on Independence Pass, they found a roadside pull off. They kept the lights going on their patrol car and walked up toward the switchback. The little hike took their breath away; the elevation was no easy task. Fortunately, they had also brought some orange traffic cones along. That way, traffic might slow down.

Low and behold, there was the evidence; the skid marks and one section of curve guard rail bent all to hell. The metal rail had been thrown onto the outer side of the road. It looked like two cars had produced the skid marks. The story was there, Bill thought. Gentry had been forced off the road; it was no accident. The officers peered over the ledge. The

Honda was 50 feet straight down in a rocky ravine. The car's rear end was teetering on a massive boulder below them.

The two officers determined that ropes would be needed to descend down the steep slope. Bill got out his carabiners and ropes. Harry called for the ambulance and then set up a pulley system to lower Bill down. The steep slope was piled precariously with rocks. Bill descended slowly toward the Honda.

He tested the stability of the rocks carefully as Harry lowered him. This rescue would be difficult. Bill surmised that the ambulance crew would have a hell of a time pulling anyone up and out of that car. He began to hope. Hope that Bart was in the car and breathing. "Just one little miracle, dear Lord," Bill whispered. From the direction of the tire tracks and skid marks, the officers assumed that Bart Gentry was coming back over to Leadville. Bill was now less than 10 feet above the wreckage.

"Bart? Bart Gentry?" Detective Smith yelled. He waited a few seconds for any kind of response. Nothing. Damn. The next ten feet were made more treacherous by a small stream escaping from under the rocks. The terrain had become slick and mossy. Bill rubbed the moss from the rock faces as he tried to stabilize his footing. Naturally, a few rocks dribbled down the slope toward the Honda. One hit the rear glass and sent a crack across the entire window. At least the glass was keeping stones from falling directly into the interior of the car at this time.

Bill finally found himself parallel with the

wreck. He leaned down and let his eyes search the darkened interior. Nothing was moving. As his eyes adjusted to the darkness inside, Bill could finally make out the shape of a body slumped over the steering wheel. "Bart?" he whispered. Bill signaled Harry to pull him up so that he could move to the other side without causing the Honda to slide down the slope. He carefully opened the driver side door and felt for a pulse. There was none. Bart Gentry had left this world.

***

Officer Frank Mason had been texting Officer Libby James for the last hour with no results. He had finally decided to simply call her. Never mind the noise that it would make. He had to know if everything was all right. Nothing. He let it ring 10 times then hung up. Frank then called Captain Holly. It had become an emergency as far as he was concerned.

"Capt, I can't make contact with Libby and Jerry. I have been trying for half a hour thinking that maybe their direction had changed and messed up our service. But now, it's been too long."

"Call Chief Tate for me and tell him to meet me at the office," Captain Jen said. "Also, get in contact with Bill and have him head to Sourdough Gulch. Marshall and I will meet him there at the entrance in 45 minutes. I am also calling to request a copter. And, you did the right thing, Frank. Thanks."

***

Detective Bill Smith sped down Highway 82 toward Sourdough Gulch. He had his siren and lights going in pursuit. Before Bill had left, the medics had been able to pull Bart Gentry's body out of the car. Bill had helped move the stretcher up the slope along with the two medics. Gentry had probably not felt much after the first contact with the boulders. 50 feet had done its damage. The medics had called the ME from Leadville to transport the body. According to the medics, the patient was pretty broken up. The poor guy just hadn't been lucky.

Harry had stayed on scene to wait for the police investigators and to direct traffic. Bill had no doubt that Harry wouldn't be home tonight until late. Actually, Detective Bill Smith realized that he might not be home at all tonight either. Frank had offered to notify his wife. That was a relief. Bill was glad that she knew at least where he would be.

What he would find was totally another issue. The uncertainty began to pulsate through his body. It wasn't like Libby to drop communications at all. Bill began to imagine that something terrible had happened. You just couldn't help it. As he pulled up into the trailhead, he saw Captain Jen and Chief Marshall Tate waiting for him.

"Grab your pack, Bill. Ranger Bend from the Forest Service called me about 15 minutes ago. There's been a rock slide recorded up there. Frank printed me off a map which indicates the route that Libby and Jerry took," Captain Jen said. "We'll assume we can follow their route."

"I grabbed a whole supply of medical stuff from Frisco before I left. Here," Chief Tate said while he handed out supplies to be stashed in their packs. They hurriedly compiled.

"The Forest Service will have a volunteer team here tomorrow if we need them," Jen added. "I have ordered, asap, a medical ambulance to stay down here until we contact them. They will establish a Medivac Camp with lights and tents within the next two hours. Frank is staying in the office tonight and coordinating the medical teams and Forest Service with our team. We are to report in each hour so that he can stay on top of the events. Can you think of anything else for now?"

Both men thought then shook their heads.

"Good. Let's go," and with that, Captain Jen began jogging up the climb. It was late afternoon and the light was short in the gulch. She knew that the faster they moved through the first phases of the climb the better. At this point there were no signs of the rock slide. It had to be much higher, she calculated. Frank had marked the last communication location for her on the map. That's where Jen was heading.

Chief Marshall Tate was beside himself. Libby just had to be all right. He wouldn't let himself think otherwise at this time. He and Libby had been doing some high altitude training for the last couple of months. With the pace that Captain Holly was setting, he had to thank his stars that Libby had made him train. There was no doubt that he was in top physical shape but elevation changed the game plan in many ways. They quickly found themselves in the second phase where the tailing piles slowed their progress. Slip-and-slide became the norm.

***

Frank had just gotten the Medivac Unit organized and it was about ready to head down the road. He had just finished informing Breckenridge and Leadville about what was happening. Chief Josh Anderson from Breckenridge had become the point man on informing the media. Lucky him, Frank smiled. Chief Carl Hagen from Leadville had let him know that Gentry was deceased. Harry Bristol was directing traffic at the Honda scene. "Whew!" Frank mumbled as he took his first break in hours.

No sooner had he exhaled once when the office door opened and Howie Page from Tiptop came sauntering in. The man was in no rush from what Frank could tell. "Howdy Frank. Thought I'd stop by and chat if ya got a minute," he said and plopped down on the couch. "Man, you look frazzled," he proclaimed.

"Well, kind of," Frank growled, then thought better of it. Howie didn't know. Besides Frank had been left in charge at this point. Take a deep breath, he told himself. "We got officers out doing all sorts of pursuits today. If I get a call, don't be surprised. What's up, Howie. How's Tiptop?"

"Oh, it's doing fine. The Zoning Committee is in one tail spin and the public is beginning to hate their guts. Same old, same old," Howie chuckled.

"You don't say," Frank said, stretching and relaxing his shoulders.

"So I've got some information for ya that I recently found out about our all important leader, Betsy Jonquin. Figured it might be something you all need to investigate," he said then leaned back.

Frank played Howie's game. The man would sooner or later get around to the point. It was a waiting game. He inhaled and counted to five. "So what ya got?"

"Well…did you know that her husband has been talking up the Eminent Domain thing? He's been telling people that it would be economically good for Tiptop. These Zoning types sure don't get it, do they?"

Okay he had Frank's interest now. "So what are you thinking?"

"I'm thinking that he's a little too enthusiastic. Maybe he's thinking of all the money he's going to make or thinking about the money he has already made. You know what I mean?" Howie's eyes began to twinkle. He had picked up some clues from these greedy people during the Zoning Committee meetings. The Jonquins were just too quick on the Eminent Domain offer, he thought. He'd been watching them.

Frank sighed, then asked, "What do you figure is going on,? Who is the husband? Buck Jonquin?" Frank tried to quicken the pace.

"Well, he's an ex-military officer and quite a hunter. If I had to bet on how the Regime knows what's going on, I'd start looking there if you know what I mean."

"So how did he and Martin Keiser get along?" Frank asked.

"Funny that you'd ask. I heard they got into it awhile back about the future of Tiptop. Started yelling at each other. Buck Jonquin wanted expansion and Martin Keiser wanted peace."

"Anyone witness this disagreement?" Frank asked.

"Just everyone in the bar. Happened a couple of months ago before there was any Eminent Domain conversations. It was like Buck knew something in advance. Ask Emma. She'll remember one night when Martin came home pretty steamed," Howie finished with satisfaction.

"I'll chat with Emma and pretty quick. Thanks, Howie," Frank stated with enthusiasm.

"Anytime. You coming over Friday for the protest? Word has it that it's going to really be something. There's now a Public Zoning Meeting before the rally. Guess all sides will be present. That ought to be something."

"So I hear," Frank answered as the phone rang. The noise brought Frank back to the craziness that was going on in the office. "Excuse me, Howie. Duty calls." He put on the headset and said, "Yes, Captain." He paused and listened then replied, "Medics should be there within the hour. Have you seen any signs?" Frank took some notes then hung up. "So, Howie, I've got to get busy. Can we finish this conversation later? Oh, and yes, I'll be at the protest Friday."

Howie got up ready to leave. He turned back and said, "Martin Keiser was a damn good man.

You ain't going to lose sight of his murder with all this Eminent Domain business going on?"

"Absolutely not, Howie. We're on it. I promise you that," Frank said.

"Well good. Buy you a beer soon?"

"Thanks and I'll collect." Frank waited until Howie had shut the door before he sprang into action. Captain Holly wanted him to contact Pitkin County. HAPT needed to inform them of the events since Sourdough Gulch was out of Lake County and in Pitkin County.

CHAPTER 17

SLIDE

Libby, Jerry and Tyler dog had heard the rocks begin to tumble. The force gathered steam; it screamed with a roar hurling the massive rock slide right at them! They ran straight down the slope throwing their packs off to enhance their speed of escape.

Tyler took the lead barking out his message; Libby and Jerry followed him. Tyler's survival instincts kicked in as he dodged and leaped over the moving ground. Somehow, he knew where he was going; the humans simply followed. Thought was impossible in this mounting chaos!

Boulders began to roll and rumble passed them. Libby could feel the vibrations and power of the rocks rolling around her. The immense growl of force screamed in her ears. She had never been so scared in her life! Every bone in her body wanted to look back but there was no time. No time, no anticipation ; she prayed and ran while her body dodged the descending boulders. Her focus was on Tyler; he pushed them faster and faster downwards.

Abruptly, Tyler ran parallel to the oncoming slide and disappeared right before Libby's eyes! She followed him blindly not knowing why until she saw the dark entrance of the grotto. Libby dived in not caring what she hit or who.

Well she hit Jerry who had been right beside her. They crawled into the deep darkness and held each other. Tyler sat on his haunches in protection mode guarding them. They watched the boulders plunging over the entrance with horrific noise then rocketing on down the slope.

Tons of rock passed the entrance. Finally, the terrain was able to stop the slide's forward momentum. Now the debris reversed its direction and began to fill the grotto entrance like a jar filling with liquid. The grotto opening began to shrink in size! The slide was now piling the debris into their enclosure!

Jerry grabbed a skinny pine tree pole and lodged it out the grotto entrance as the slide debris began to close in around them. Dust now filled the grotto with a brown thick cloud; their vision was gone, the air was polluted. All three began to sneeze and cough almost to the point of choking. They covered their faces with their damp bananas.

Jerry moved the pole gently packing the gravel around it. Libby figured out what he was doing, air hole! She sprang into action. They constantly moved the pole back-and-forth so they could dislodge it later. He had aimed it directly up toward the sky.

Five minutes later they were trapped in darkness. The grotto cavity had now shrunk to half its size. An occasional rock could be heard traveling past outside, but the slide was finally over.

"Unbelievable," Jerry whispered as he removed his bandana from around his nose. He took a moment to pet Tyler. "You did good, boy. Thanks." Jerry then began to slowly pull the pine pole back into the cavity. Libby guided it gently into their area; their attempt worked! The stones remained solid; their fissure was open! As Jerry pulled the last three inches carefully, he breathed a sign of relief. "Thank you, Lord."

The air coming in through the small fissure smelled amazing. This exchange of oxygen began to temper the dust. Fresh air spread throughout the grotto. Sunlight filled the small fissure; it was beautiful. It was a single ray of hope, Libby mused. She quickly glanced around the cavity and found that they did have water. Again, a small miracle. Yes, they were trapped and could die in here, but there was light and water. Now all they needed was the most incredible miracle of all; someone to find them!

***

As dusk began to settle, Jen realized that they had to turn around and head back to the Medivac Camp for the night. It was just too dangerous to continue in the dark. The distance had been much farther than they had thought. In fact, the team hadn't reached the slide area yet. They did find some of the Sourdough team's supplies stashed neatly behind a bush. The team had a least made it this far. That was a good sign, Jen thought in relief.

Chief Marshall Tate aimed his search light ahead. He scanned the ascent for any signs. "There's the slide 400 feet above us," he said.

Jen glanced below and could see the lights of their camp. She yelled, "Libby? Jerry? Tyler?" They all listened while staring into the wall of darkness. No sound. It was eerily quiet and serene. At this point, Jen had to make a very unpopular decision. "We need to head down and wait for first light; we then can be back up here in half an hour. It's just too dangerous; the slide isn't stable yet. It's still shifting."

Marshall yelled again before they left the area, "Libby, answer me! Are you there?" Nothing. Only silence answered.

"So sorry, guys, but we need to go down and get food and some sleep then hit it right away tomorrow. We couldn't be doing them any good if we fell in the darkness or miss them." Jen placed her hand on Marshall's shoulder, then turned and began descending. Bill followed.

Marshall was the last to leave. He listened intently for any sounds of Libby. Finally, he pulled himself away and followed Bill and Captain Jen. He knew it was the right decision but he felt so damn helpless. So lost. His body began to climb down but his heart stayed on the mountain watching and listening. They approached the camp some twenty minutes later. There was a big pot of stew simmering on the campfire. Marshall was handed a huge bowl first thing. He felt like he was eating rocks at first then pure hunger kicked in.

Captain Jen Holly immediately got on her phone and ordered two copters out at first light to search the mountain side. Frank had already sent out the order of course. She and Frank began talking about how people survived during rock slides. "Usually, miners would look for an air hole then start tunneling," Frank assured Jen. "When you get up to the slide, watch for old claim digs where they could jump in for protection," Frank suggested. "How's Chief Tate taking it?" he asked.

"Not well, of course. He was last off the mountain tonight. Rational reasoning did finally kick in and he followed us down," she said.

"Good. You'll find them tomorrow. I just know it." Frank then began to inform her of the latest developments. "Captain, I just had an interesting conversation with Howie Page about the Jonquins. Seems like he thinks that Buck Jonquin might be a person of interest. I'd like to head over to Tiptop tomorrow and have a chat with Buck sort of an unexpected visit. Would that be okay? Of course after you find our team," he added.

"Certainly. As soon as we can bring them off the mountain, head on over. Call Frisco Police and get them to monitor our phones," Captain Jen said. "And, Frank, if you sense that Jonquin might be armed and dangerous, call for backup. Jerome Walker could get there pretty quick."

"Will do and thanks, Captain. I sure hope you find them safe and sound tomorrow. My thoughts are with you," he added. "May the stars be shinning on them tonight."

Jen felt exactly the same way as she cut off communication. Before sleep the rescue teams mapped out what looked like potential locations to search. Each team picked a location. There were now other police officers and forest service present. They would be able to comb the mountain for sure. As the stars came out, all hearts were focused on the mountain. Their minds were determined; preparations were set. They hoped for the best.

During the night Marshall would get up and occasionally flash his light up on the mountain side scanning the areas. He tried to be as quiet as he could. Sleep hadn't been an option for him. He scanned for any light or movement. Captain Jen came up behind him and placed her hand, once more, on his shoulder. "We'll find them, Marshall. Have faith."

"It's just so unbelievable to me. I guess I've never been on a rescue where someone I love is missing. It feels so surreal, Jen. HAPT certainly has one hell of a purpose, doesn't it?" His intense blue eyes focused on her face. He was searching for answers to so many questions.

"When the opportunity to start HAPT occurred, I jumped for that very reason. Police are placed in so many situations where lives are taken. The public forgets how many people they do save. HAPT is our pay-it-forward team in so many ways."

Both officers then stared into the brilliant sky. A shooting star suddenly abandoned the atmosphere and headed toward earth. Jen pointed then made her wish knowing that Marshall had already hoped.

Morning dawned with mountain sounds echoing. Marmots chirped, birds searched and a gentle breeze brought cool temperatures just above freezing into camp. The first light hit like an alarm clock for the teams. Coffee was on and being poured. Breakfast was served quickly. Within thirty minutes the people were ready to move out. Captain Jen communicated with Frank then she gave the order. Four separate teams headed up the mountain. Their trained eyes began to search the ground for any signs immediately.

Jen lead her team through the bushes traveling in the same direction as last night. She held the map tightly in her hand referring to it when need be. As they moved upward, they could see the other teams. Communication was kept between the search teams with radios; the four county police department offices were listening. All officers out on patrol were monitoring. There was a strange quiet permeating over the mountain communities. If thoughts could move mountains, then that force was there.

The surreal morning was spectacular. The sun radiated and sparkled off the trees that sent dew raining down on them. It was like nothing had ever happened in this biome. The slide's secret was being held tightly. Of course, they were not up as high as the alpine meadow yet. This area hadn't felt the destruction and chaos. The serene morning and wildlife went about their own business as usual. Animals had to feed. A female deer and two fawns grazed ahead of them. The team had interrupted their breakfast. Mother and fawns moved off into another area. The teams kept going higher.

They reached the tailing area some thirty minutes later. The slip-and slide tailings slowed their progress. All four teams could see each other at this time. They waved back and forth. Radio communication stated that nothing had been found as of yet then came the reassuring comments about it being too early for discovery. Their progress moved cautiously.

Marshall felt impatient. His mind knew that the teams were well trained and approaching the area correctly, but his heart was racing all over the tailings screaming for Libby. He had flashes of their last hike together pulsating through his mind and heart. He flashed upon her beautiful red hair bouncing in the sunlight in front of him. How the warmth of her eyes and endearing freckles melted his heart.

All at once Marshall realized all the things that he hadn't told her. He felt remorse, regret and oh yes, love. It all engulfed his heart. God, he did feel love; it took his breath away. How could he have been so stupidly silent these last months? Yes, he had been under stress because of his new position as Chief in Frisco. Yes, he had lost focus; Libby wasn't secondary to his job! No, she was the primary reason that he was here; that he existed. Damn, he loved her and wanted to be with her for the rest of his life. My God, he wanted to marry Libby.! The reality was crystal clear to him now; his future loomed before him. 'Dear Lord, make it so,' Marshall prayed.

"Libby? Jerry? Come, Tyler," Captain Jen

abruptly yelled. It was almost like she had sensed some of what Marshall was feeling. His throat went dry with emotion as he stayed in control . Then came a similar yell from another team. Each team echoed the chant. About five minutes later Jen's team yelled again; the process continued as they all climbed. All four groups were brought together as one team as their ascension continued. The power of their voices became strong and unified.

***

"Did you hear something?" Libby said from the back of the cavity. Her sleep had been interrupted by something she sensed. Not to mention that Marshall's face had appeared in her chaotic dreams. His warm presence had suddenly halted the slide in her recurrent nightmare. When darkness had entered their air hole, she and Jerry had decided to get some rest then when the morning light would come, they could start digging.

Tyler then answered with a conciliatory bark; he sensed or heard something also.

"Maybe. I'm not sure, Libby. Our minds could be playing tricks on us. I hope not," Jerry said then moved closer to the fissure air hole. "Come here, boy. Listen, Tyler."

Libby could hardly breathe. If there had been a sound, she didn't want to miss it again. Then she let herself listen. The sound was far away but she felt fairly sure that someone was there somewhere.

"Help! Help!" Jerry yelled in the air hole. Tyler barked. Libby spun into action and let out a whistle.

They stopped shouting and listened again. Hoping for an answer. Nothing. No one. It was the longest few moments of Libby's life; her hope so fragile.

"Hello? Whistle again. We hear ya," came a voice from the distance.

Libby didn't recognize the voice but it didn't matter. She let out a couple more whistles and waited. Jerry petted Tyler enthusiastically. They focused on the air hole. Staring and listening. Abruptly the sun beam was replaced by shade.

"Are ya in there?" A face appeared.

Jerry was sure. "Yes! We're here and needing help. Can you get us out?"

"We can try," said the voice. Let us dig over to the right and stay away from your air supply. "Okay?"

"Okay," Jerry answered. He moved over as far from the fissure as possible and slowly started to lift the rocks away. He handed them to Libby who placed them in the back of the cavity. They removed the stones carefully and piled them with precision. If it all caved in again, they wanted to leave an area for them to occupy.

The old prospectors outside, however, weren't nearly as organized. They threw the rocks back over their shoulders not even caring to look. Their goal was to remove as much rock as they could in the shortest amount of time. Milt Gray and Nathan Abel grunted and groaned with the weight of excavation. Sweat began to appear on their old brows from the strain; they diligently worked on in the early morning dawn. The sun had just come up.

Nathan could now hear that whoever was inside was also making rock progress. It began to look like they could get the job done. Obviously, the trapped people were about four feet back in this closure, he surmised. From his calculation, they were maybe a foot apart at this point. He began to anticipate seeing hands soon. The tunnel was almost cleared. He was glad to know that the ceiling of their tunnel seemed safe and wouldn't collapse. Miners always looked up. Ceilings could be hell if you weren't careful. Luck was with them for now.

***

Captain Jen suddenly got an idea. She stopped and stared at Marshall. "Call Libby's phone again. I know that you did last night but try it now. Maybe we can hear the ring."

Marshall pushed his blond hair back with his hand and braced himself for a 'no answer.' "It's ringing," he said.

The team on their right suddenly stopped then yelled, "Something is ringing. Hold on!" They quickly scattered and began removing rocks. All teams had now stopped the ascent. "We found Libby's pack with her phone in it. There are no signs of a tunnel, however." The team then waited for Captain Jen's response.

"Please have one of your team transport the pack back to me. I'll ask Chief Tate to relay the pack over here . He may be able to find something significant in it. Everyone, stand down for a break. Make sure that you have water before we start up again. Ranger Bend, please mark where the pack was found and take pictures for the investigation."

"Will do, Captain. The pack is on the way," Ranger Bend responded.

Marshall moved quickly across the tailings. The two men met some five minutes later and the pack was exchanged. He carried it back to his team. It felt good to at least have something of Libby's in his arms. It would have to do for now, he mused. As he approached Jen and Bill, he gave the pack to Jen. She opened it and pulled out all Libby's belongings. Jen arranged the articles carefully. It was now apparent that Jerry and Libby probably had no food or water on them. Not a good sign, Jen thought; she dismissed the implications. Stay positive she demanded of herself as she shook the pack upside down.

Detective Bill Smith now assumed that Jerry and Libby had been caught in the slide. Could have been a good thing or a bad thing, he calculated. His eyes began to inspect the items as Jen carefully arranged them. He picked up a picture that Libby had placed in a safe zipped compartment. It was a selfie photo of Marshall and Libby embracing on a mountain top. Bill handed the picture to Marshall in hopes that it would help. He knew how the guy must be feeling right now. Bill promised that when he got home, there would be a huge hug for his wife of 15 years. Bill couldn't imagine losing his Bonnie like this. Even the silence wasn't painting a good picture right now, he mused. Had Libby thrown the pack off or had it been torn from her body? They were getting closer to the answers, he knew.

The mountain search had become more subdued, Bill noticed as they continued on up. Marshall attached Libby's pack to his; she might just need some of these things when they would find her. And, they would find her, he told himself with new resolve.

Some twenty minutes later, Jen saw the smoke! It was spiraling from a campfire she thought. "Look guys, over there. I see smoke. Got to be a signal! Let's get the hell up there!" Jen ordered the other teams to their destination. Men and women began scaling the mountain side with new enthusiasm. Someone had started that fire. Thank God!

As Jen's team rushed up the side of the mountain, a familiar bark was heard. Tyler jumped down off a ledge and licked Jen's face happily. He was ready to escort them to the gathering.

There, seated around a morning fire drinking coffee was Jerry, Libby, Milt Gray and Nathan Abel. Libby dropped her cup and ran full charge into Marshall's arms. Milt, added more water and grounds to the coffee pot. Looked like they were going to have some very welcome visitors if Libby's reaction was any indication!

CHAPTER 18

VORTEX

Officer Frank Mason let out a sigh as he leaned back in his chair at HAPT Headquarters. Bless her heart, Libby was okay; in fact, the whole damn team was okay. What a relief. He had sent out the rescue message over all the airwaves. The county now knew that their own people were safe and sound. One for the little guys, Frank thought.

He pulled his gray mustache playfully and thought about how he could now make a difference. Officer Mason wanted to begin his part of the investigation. Captain Jen had given him the okay to transfer calls to the Frisco Police Department and head over to Tiptop. Seemed like HAPT had only been able to put out the fires instead of investigating lately. They had gone from one crime scene to the next. Frank really needed to add his two cents worth now. He had a lead on the Keiser murder, thanks to Howie's visit.

Howie Page had really gotten Frank

investigating Buck Jonquin's finances. Frank could
now actually see that there was lots of questionable
money . Jonquin hadn't sold any property lately on
the market, but he had stockpiled large checks from
Capital Regime. Why not? The Regime had plenty
of money. They had been syphoning off various
government departments for quite awhile. No more
public services so the money just piled up for their
convenience. Buck had gotten quite a shitload of
dollars for his efforts. Was he the one who killed
Martin Keiser, shot Kevin Donner and maybe
started that damn slide after killing Bart Gentry?

Hell, Buck could have run over to Sourdough
Gulch yesterday morning and simply let a rock roll
just for spite. All it would have done was delayed
HAPT from finding Milt Gray and Nathan Abel but
maybe that was his intent. Frank's hand, suddenly,
froze on his patrol car door handle . Buck would not
only get money for murder but he would also stand
to profit from the construction of more reservoirs
and dams. The man thought he would be set up for
life. His dirty deeds would bring power and wealth
or it could bring him his own death. The fascists
just might consider getting rid of Buck to keep the
scheme under cover eventually.

Frank's mind began to explore the possibilities
as he headed toward Tiptop. The two questions that
were nagging him were, 'why keep Nathan Abel in
Sourdough Gulch? Why not let the HAPT team get
him back to Tiptop quickly?'

If Betsy Jonquin had been right about Nathan
wanting to sell, then why not let HAPT do its job?
Or, had Buck heard something else from other

sources? Maybe Nathan had talked with his son, Jackson. Could Jackson Abel have changed his mind and would now tell his dad to vote with the Tiptop locals? Nathan was definitely a wild card thanks to Kevin Donner.

Frank then began to think about the entrance of Kevin Donner and his fortune into this quagmire. Yep, Donner's decision had been quite a shock to the Zoning Committee. It was one thing to go after a poor mountain town, and another thing to go after an influential man with state and financial connections. Kevin Donner's talks with Nathan Abel's son just might have gotten back to Buck. Gossip did travel fast in small towns, Frank assessed as he ascended Hoosier Pass. Maybe Buck needed to keep Nathan in the gulch as long as he could. The old prospector did have the deciding vote at this point. Hell, Buck might have been told to stop the old guy from casting a vote. All the circumstances just might have changed.

Jackson Abel might have seen the advantages of being on Kevin Donner's team since they were both from the Denver area. Kevin might help Jackson Abel's law firm by sending some business his way for that vote. Frank's blue eyes sparkled as he conjectured what might be.

His patrol car began the descent into Peak County now. Frank had checked on Buck Jonquin's military career before he'd left the office. The man had been a general and did have ample training as a sniper. Martin Keiser's murder would have been a piece of cake. Buck's expertise in recognizance missions would have been extremely beneficial to the Regime. Retired General Jonquin knew the terrain and had military contacts that could facilitate the planning of Keiser's murder. All the government had to do was send him the laser weapon and there you have it.

Yup, collecting and creating the weaponry for that mission would have been an easy challenge for him. His military friends could have even assisted him with the creation of the laser weapon and, of course, there was always the internet. Either way, Buck could become a lethal threat. The other missions might have been more difficult because they weren't planned. Their execution would have had to be quick and effective.

Kevin Donner's failed assassination attempt could be attributed to spur-of-the -moment reaction, plus, Buck might be out of practice. The man was a lot older now, but he still had the training, Frank surmised. How easy for the fascists to convince Buck, tempting him with money and power. It was indeed a small world, Officer Frank Mason confessed as he entered Tiptop. It was time to rattle Buck Jonquin's cage and open this case up.

***

The coffee was dark and strong but it tasted great, Captain Jen Holly thought while sitting on her rock around the small campfire. She was now so relieved to just sit and listen. The other teams had met them and decided to head back down. Striking camp and returning to their jobs had to be considered priority. The story of what happened on the mountain would be explained later. In essence, their volunteer duty was over.

Captain Jen began to listen with care. Was it an accidental slide or something else was the question that had to be answered for her. Telling the story from the beginning was important at this juncture. Captain Jen then tuned into what Libby was saying.

"So we just blindly followed Tyler," Libby began. "I threw off my pack so I could stay up with him. That dog really moves when he wants to. The grotto was our savior. Tyler knew exactly where it was. Then it was lights out," Libby finished glancing at Jerry to continue.

"I did the old post out the door for an air vent routine as we waited. We could breathe and had water so the night was somewhat comfortable. Thank heavens for Milt and Nathan at daybreak." Detective Jerry Neal then looked at the prospectors to continue.

"Well, we was taking a break up at the mine," Nathan said. "Ya see, we're looking for the silver vein. We've been working hard for the last 48 hours. We was having a smoke when we spotted some guy down the slope wedging out boulders. Didn't see him though until it was too late to stop him. He was bent on starting a slide."

"Bout the time he let the damn boulders go, I spotted these three," contributed Milt Gray as he pointed at the Sourdough team.

"Did you get a good look at the guy?" Chief Marshall Tate asked.

"Nope. He was too far away. After he got the boulders going, he split like a flash," Nathan said while pouring another cup of coffee. "Sitting up there gave us quite a perspective. Last night we saw your camp and figured it was a medivac. We decided to wait until after the slide settled over night. So this morning at first light we headed down to the last place that we'd seen these three. We figured if they had a brain, they'd have jumped into the grotto."

"Then it was an individual, not two or three perps starting the slide?" Captain Jen asked just to make sure.

"Yup," both prospectors said. Their shaggy old beards blew in the breeze as they sat enjoying their morning coffee and campfire. It was a beautiful morning to have company.

These old gentlemen were quite a sight, Jen assessed. It was like stepping back into history: rugged heavy boots, hand rolled cigarettes, dirt crusted hats. These two old gentlemen presented quite an image that she would never forget. Too bad that the case demanded action, she conceded. It would have been nice to simply stay and find out about their mining but it wasn't meant to be.

"Well, gentlemen, thank you for the coffee. I think it's best that we all decide to head down, Jen said tossing her coffee remains into the fire embers. We'll take you back to Leadville then?"

"We ain't going," Nathan Abel stated. "Knowing how this would probably happen, I wrote out a quit claim deed here that says Jackson, my son, owns Smoky Quartz Claim from this day forward. Jackson can do the voting on Eminent Domain that way. Whatever he decides. I just need you all to sign as witnesses, then I'll sign this here deed." He handed the quit claim deed to Captain Jen Holly to sign.

"But you do realize that these people are dangerous and are shooting at the claim owners? Ben Gentry is no longer with us; these people are playing for real. If you stay up here, I can't guarantee your safety," Jen said. "What prevents them from coming back?"

"Nothing I guess except we'd be ready for them now. Both of us have a rifle plus if you let it get out about the quit claim deed then I'm not a target anymore," Nathan said. I figure Jackson can handle it; I raised him right. How about you tell Chief Hagen in Leadville to send Harry Bristol over to get us Friday morning? That way I can watch the rally festivities," Nathan suggested.

"Are you sure?" Libby asked hardly believing her ears as she signed the deed. The two crusty old geezers were at least offering something of a compromise, she reconnoitered. But still....

"Damn straight. There's silver up here and we aim to follow the vein. Neither one of us has much more time for this kind of prospecting. Way I figure it, it's now or never," Nathan Abel proclaimed. Both old guys nodded in agreement. They had obviously discussed this issue in detail.

"Besides, I don't know if I could climb up here again. Hell, it's a lung sucker. Damn near had a heart attack the first time," confessed Milt Gray. "Been spending too much time in the Leadville bars, I guess," he confessed.

"So your minds are made up?" Captain Jen

clarified. "And you will promise me that Officer Harry Bristol will find you ready to transport at 10 on Friday?

"Yup," they said and crossed their hearts.

Captain Jen really couldn't make them come down. They were adults. At least there was a dash of compromise here. She had to hope that Jackson Abel would understand. She really had no choice. Captain Jen Holly stood up, all 5' 7" of her, and placed her hands on her hips. It was her best stern mother impersonation. Using her pointing finger at them, she declared, "I swear if you're not down there on Friday at 10, I will come back here and throw you down!"

"Yes, ma'am, we swear!" they said in unison like school boys crossing their hearts twice as they stood up. Jen was amused and satisfied.

Bill and Marshall couldn't help but chuckle slightly. The scene was too funny. After recovering somewhat, Bill inquired, "Before we head down without you, is there anything that you could tell us about the guy who started the slide. Anything? Something that just comes to mind now?" Detective Bill Smith asked as he waited to sign the deed. He looked at them with hope in his eyes.

"Well, now that you mention it again, I do recall thinking he had on cowboy boots," Nathan Abel added as he signed the quit claim deed and handed it back to Captain Jen to give to Jackson his son.

***

Bix Bixler took careful aim at the target. She and Bernie had spent all day yesterday arranging transportation and water booths for the rally. It was now two days away and things were looking up. Melanie Camp from Property Coalition had hinted that Kevin Donner and Jackson Abel were becoming great friends. It sounded like maybe the vote was now leaning toward not allowing a governmental purchase. At least the town might be winning that battle; obviously, the courts then would make the final decision. That ruling could take years and higher courts. Maybe by that time, the US could have a legal election without Russian interference. One could hope.

This morning they had gone to the outdoor gun range for distraction. She and Bernie had decided to try out her new Beretta automatic handgun. She definitely needed a timeout from all the rally details. Phone calls made and lists finished, Bix was done for now.

Bix concentrated on the target. She hadn't shot a gun since she had been in her twenties when she worked late nights. This adventure was going to be a new challenge. The gun grip didn't seem too bad, she assessed. Bernie had said to pull the trigger slowly with a soft squeeze. Bix brought the site into focus before she even touched the trigger. Front site aimed to the middle of the two back sites had been the instructions. Breathe; bam! It was over.

Her attempt had landed a little to the left of the center. Not bad she thought. Society always made such a big deal about the recoil on guns. It made you think that women would always fly off their feet and land on the ground because of the recoil. Not so. More hype than fact, Bix assessed. She wasn't shooting with some kind of elephant rifle for heaven sakes. The discharge had been more noisy than threatening, she concluded. Bix now took aim again and this time hit above the bullseye. Maybe years of cutting wood and lifting weights did strengthen your grip.

"Relax your grip," Bernie said.

The most distracting part of the gun range, Bix decided, was simply getting comfortable with racking her gun and being careful. The vocabulary was new. 'Rack' instead of loading the bullet into the chamber of the gun; 'brass' instead of bullets. 'Cartridges' plus the rest of the lingo. Then, of course, there was so much to know about safety. The gun range seemed like a friendly place and her practice was being monitored by everyone there including Bernie.

To be fair, Bernie had been patient and rehearsed with her at home before they came. It reminded her of play rehearsals. Finding your comfort zone was an individual thing that instilled confidence. You had to be in your own quiet zone of concentration and routine each time you acted. Preparation was key to success.

Okay then, she aimed again and this time was way off center. Well, maybe there was more to this than she had expected. After an hour of practice, Bix felt exhausted. It was intense. However, the routine had given her an escape from her other stresses.

As they headed home from the gun range

Bernie asked, "So what do you think? Are you feeling more comfortable about having a gun?"

"I need practice is one thing I know for sure," Bix said. She crossed her arms and then continued talking, "It certainly changes the victim game, doesn't it? I believe that I could place my Beretta in the glove compartment of the car after more time at the range. Guess you need to feel comfortable." Bix glanced over at Bernie before saying more.

Bernie listened then added only a nod; she knew that this was just the beginning of their many philosophical conversations on this subject. Bix would need to justify how she really felt. Bernie wanted her to carry a gun for protection; it was that simple. Maybe her love for Bix motivated how she felt, but Bix did get into many police situations because of her friends and knowledge. If she kept putting herself out there, then precautions were needed. Bernie wisely stayed silent.

"Protection is such a huge concept," Bix concluded out loud. "I know that if someone did threaten my life, I'd want to be able to defend myself. Damn," she murmured. "Bigotry has added such a horrible dimension to our lives since the last election. You know, I read that one out of five women now own a gun for defense. All the negative conversations about women have really changed society viewpoints. How this Regime could treat women with so little respect is beyond me; we will persist. It's a whole new can of worms out there, isn't it?

Bix was, of course, conflicted. Her thoughts were filled with concerns of how to reach a balance.

To own a gun peacefully was the bottom line, she considered. Would she ever be comfortable with seeing people carrying guns openly in public? Not hardly; she didn't want to be at the risk of strangers making stupid decisions. That concept was too precarious for her but in the glove compartment for personal safety could be a compromise, she decided. And she had to admit that she had enjoyed the shooting range as long as the target resembled a dartboard and not a person. "So maybe once a week at the range might be a good idea?" Bix said.

"Sounds like a plan to me; we could do that. You should also get on the internet or read books about technique. Hell, I learned from my father when I was eight," Bernie remembered. "We hunted; it was ranch life. Now that I've taken the courses on carrying and hunting, the training is more complete." Bernie continued carefully, "The range here provides concealed weapon and safety classes. Maybe you could sign up after I take off for North Dakota again?" She glanced at Bix.

"Think I just might do that. For me that makes sense. Besides, victim is such an ugly word."

"Yup," Bernie said as she turned off Highway 9 and headed down to the house.

"Glad I called Melanie this morning before we left," Bix intentionally changed the subject now that they had returned home. "Hard to believe that the rally is just two days away. Maybe we could go for a hike this afternoon? Take Simon with us. I sure could use some more outdoor therapy."

"A hike sounds like just what the doctor ordered. Sure beats pills, doesn't it?" Bernie smirked.

"Yes it does," Bix answered smiling.

Simon met them at the door hoping to be included in the next activity.

CHAPTER 19

ENCOUNTERS

Officer Frank Mason put his Ford Interceptor in park. He could sense tension in the eerie silence. There was a car in the garage but Buck Jonquin wasn't in sight. The front door was wide open; a privacy screen door kept out the insects and small critters. "Hello?" he yelled out the car window and waited for an answer. He had a funny feeling though. Frank called retired sheriff Jerome Walker's home phone and waited through ten rings. No answer. "If you get this message, call me. Might use some backup." He disconnected figuring that his phone number was listed on the machine.

Frank now decided to get on with it so he opened the car door, unsnapped his holster clasp and approached the house cautiously. His eyes darted quickly around the yard. What the hell, Frank thought as he walked closer. "Buck? Are you home?" he asked.

"Don't even think about pulling your gun. I got

a Colt 45 aimed at your chest. It's your heart or your balls if I aim lower. Now take your gun out with two fingers and drop on the ground now. Now!" the demanding voice yelled. Buck was behind the darkened screen; Frank calculated that he had no choice. Buck Jonquin must have planned for this occasion. Frank slowly complied and dropped his gun on the ground.

"Now raise your pant legs slowly. Now, with the same two fingers, take out your backup weapon and toss it."

Frank complied. How had Buck known that Frank was coming to question him? News sure traveled fast for this suspect. Almost too fast. The hair on the back of Frank's neck was standing straight up; he had chills. Buck had a partner was the logical conclusion. Frank's heart was pounding loud and clear in his ears.

After all these years as a cop, he had made a damn foolish mistake. He should have waited for backup. He could have even called Breckenridge. His simple announcement of his destination over the police channels should have had more detail. Or, was someone listening to the police radio? He should have considered that scenario. Frank admonished himself; he had been an arrogant son of a bitch.

"Step away from your weapons and put your hands on top of your head. Come on in, Officer Mason." The Colt 45 pistol barrel slowly opened the screen door. Buck stayed in the shadows of the front room. "Well, come on in the fucking door, fool."

The handle was cold to Frank's touch. Right now he had to hope that sometime later, Buck would let down his guard. Right now he focused on the Colt Commander gun barrel. The man wasn't taking any changes. Frank would either meet his maker or get lucky.

At least Captain Jen would be trying to contact him eventually. The team members always reported in every couple hours. No response on his part tonight would alert the team at least by tomorrow. Time was on his side, kinda. If he made it until tomorrow.

"Now take hold of that radio piece and rip it off your shirt. Now!" Buck racked his automatic gun quickly; he could have at least 16 cartridges in that magazine. So he hadn't racked the gun earlier but played safe. Something to remember, Frank thought. He took hold of his radio microphone and disconnected it.

"Turn around." Buck did a body search then pulled off the rest of Frank's radio receiver. Frank was now without, period. Buck was thorough no doubt about it. He heard the chair creak as Jonquin sat back down. "Turn around, you fuck. So what do you want?" he asked.

Frank turned around slowly and looked at Buck Jonquin now comfortably seated in his desk chair. The Colt 45 Commander was sitting on top of a pile of desk papers but still aimed directly at Frank. Buck waited for the answer. "Talk, you shit," he hissed.

Frank began talking while trying to keep his voice as casual as possible. "Just came by to find out what you think about this here protest. As one of the top realty fellas in the county, you must have an opinion about any gossip that you might have picked up."

Buck eyed him closely. "Why don't you sit down in that chair and we'll talk a spell. So you came to find out what I thought about this fucking mess?' Buck's eyes gleamed with intensity. There wasn't anything casual in his tone. He knew more about the visit than Frank had figured.

"That would be correct," Frank answered looking as sincere as he could under the circumstances. Play the game, he thought.

"Well, I think the government is gonna win this encounter. Ain't no doubt in my mind. They got the power. The Blackhawk copter was just a hint tossed at these poor local saps. The town ain't got no idea on how to play politics. The deck is stacked against them for sure."

"If that's so, then how does Kevin Donner fit into their Eminent Domain case?" Frank asked. "I hear tell the State of Colorado is on his side."

"He's gonna do a lot of talking but when it comes to push, the Regime is gonna win.
This state ain't got the power to make a damn bit of difference when it comes to who owns the water rights. Fascism is here to stay, Officer Mason. And the cops are going to find that out pretty quickly. You gonna have to beg or fuckin dry up pretty soon."

"You sure about that, Buck? You got some kind of crystal ball that's telling you about the future or are you in contact with someone… or something?" Frank asked, then held his breath and waited. Buck was beginning to piss him off.

"It don't take a lot of brains to check out what the government could order the military to do. Deer hunting rifles don't stand a change when armed troops parachute in, do they?" he blustered.

"And you have reliable sources? Who's supplying you with this information? Or, are you just guessing, Buck?"

"Retired military doesn't mean down and out," Buck retorted. "I keep my hand in the action. The Regime is watching the events very closely and this could be all it takes for them to establish military control."

"With Russian money right?" Frank shot back. "You getting some of that money, Buck?"

Buck leaned back in his chair and eyed Frank closely. How much did this cop know, he wondered? Was Frank fishing or had he more information? It also was important to know if this old fart had decided that he had killed Martin Keiser or not. Buck hadn't thought that HAPT could be that far along in the investigation to tie him to the murder. They might be able to tie him to firing on Donner, but Keiser? He thought all the activity was keeping them on defense; maybe he needed a little more information. Buck ventured forward cautiously, "How would I be able to receive any money? Hell, who has put that gossip out there?"

"Doesn't take much computer research to find out your involvement, Buck. Everyone in the county knows that you were a general in the military. You brag about it enough. Your bank account has had quite a few transfusions lately. Where'd the extra money come from? You haven't sold any property for the last month."

"Hell, this ain't my only property interests," Buck shot back. "Besides, yeah, some of my old friends have taken an interest in Peak County politics. Nothing wrong with financing someone to keep an eye on their projects. Certainly isn't against the law."

"To the tune of two million dollars?" Frank asked casually. Yes, he had found all or some of Buck's off shore accounts. Frank had his contacts also. Officer Mason was venturing onto a pretty slippery slope here, he knew. Buck's eyes twitched; Frank watched the tension begin to mount. Buck glanced at the Colt 45.

"Maybe that's none of your business, old man."

"Maybe it just might be," Frank retorted. " I hear from sources that you and Martin Keiser got into a brawl at the bar about a mouth ago." Frank decided to go for the jugular vein; a confession would do just fine. Go for broke. He had nothing to lose.

"Hell, that was just cabin fever talking. I haven't made any secret of how I feel. My opinion is that we sell the land and then make a profit off of the water just like the government. There's a deal to be made and property to be sold. Not to mention the workers that would come into town and help our economy. This place needs more population. Martin didn't buy that argument so we exchanged verbal words and a few punches. No death threats exchanged, so what's your point?" Buck waited a few moments to let that soak in, then he continued, "Yeah, I'll take money for monitoring the situation. That's all that I do."

"Well that's interesting. So what if you did more than just monitoring? I keep wondering about Keiser's murder and all the military equipment used. Then there's Donner where the sniper sure arrived quickly. I mean, Donner had barely opened his mouth and voiced his opinion when a shot hit him. How was the government involved and so quickly? Or maybe, it was someone closer to the situation acting for the Regime? Well, the cigarette butt and cartridges ought to tell a story soon."

Frank was now in it big time; the accusations just kept rolling. "You see, Buck, even the slide in Sourdough Gulch was done by a single perp. There weren't any Blackhawk Helicopters swooping down and firing at our team. The Capital Regine hasn't played fascist war on the community yet because of the publicity. If they were to give any orders now, it would be to tone down the assault in my opinion. The last two attempts have been all hints and innuendoes. One individual in Sourdough Gulch sliding boulders. One car taking out Gentry. Before that, a sniper shot at Kevin Donner. Only one direct hit, Martin Keiser. It's got to make an old man wonder," Frank finished, knowing that he had probably gone too far.

"You got any proof for those wild accusations, Frank, or are you just shooting the breeze here?"

"Oh, a little of both." Frank leaned back in his chair and waited.

***

Chief Marshall Tate could hardly take his eyes off Libby. They had just arrived home so she could clean up. Her clothes were scattered on the floor as she made a trail toward the shower. Marshall's heart leaped as he picked up her clothes. Her scent filled his nostrils; he closed his eyes as the sensation took away his breath. Marshall quickly placed her clothes in the hamper.

His body was now drawn to the shower like a magnet. He threw off his uniform and slipped in beside her. His arms then surrounded her naked warm body. Libby moaned; she clung to him feeling the warmth and safety of his caress. She was home. His body fit so perfectly around her. The hardness of his erection was tucked in between them.

"Would you marry me?" he whispered. "Last night I was so afraid that I wouldn't see you again, be with you again. I love you so much." Marshall was surprised how quickly the words had popped out of his mouth. So much for being romantic, he thought. Yet, he couldn't help it. He wanted Libby in his life forever. No minutes wasted but forever.

"Marshall? So much has happened. We both experienced chaos. You were gone; I was gone. Just like that." Libby snapped her fingers; her radiant green eyes grabbed his heart and pulled. "I never expected to be in a rock slide; you never expected to be in a rescue party. It was all so unexpected. So immense."

Libby kissed him softly, paused, then

confessed, "Did you know that I could almost feel you last night, smell you? Your eyes, your touch; I wanted you so much." Libby's hand then pulled his penis down until he was nestled against her center. She gently rocked him, back and forth, across her mound; Libby closed her eyes as her fingers nuzzled him sensuously.

Intense arousal exploded through Marshall; air rushed into his lungs. He felt her cradle him in her folds. With every bit of strength that he could muster, he let Libby take the lead. Waiting for her to open up and take him into her core. Libby's hand then freely guided him into her body. His penetration dived deep. He pushed in and up slowly; she pushed down until both bodies melted and blended; they were there, home together tightly holding each other inside secured by body warmth. Their bodies heated in the moment, sensuously aware of holding tight what they wanted and needed.

Marshall then began to sense a wild sexual force begin to rock his body. He plunged deeper and deeper, in and out; the frantic sensation starting to bring Marshall home. Libby rode him gloriously, abandoning all inhibitions, her legs tightly twined around his waist, her breasts smashed against his lips. He sucked her hungrily. Faster and faster, mounting and coming until Marshall exploded with one last giant thrust. He barely had time to breathe before Libby's orgasm began sending them both into another fit of arousal. He could feel her body pulsating then vibrating beyond known passion as she rocked and moaned. Love surrounded them and embraced them stripping away all the anxiety of the last two days; they were speechless, finally motionless. Marshall then began to scrub Libby's body in the warm water as he explored each vital inch. His lips gently kissed her freckles and nose. So content. Right now it didn't matter what time of day or what had happened; they were together in this moment.

Libby then captured his hands and stared into his eyes. She traced his mouth thoughtfully with her finger. She then pulled him into a kiss that was deep and open. Her tongue slipped into his mouth seeking comfort. Quite suddenly, Libby pulled back for a second and stared at him. She cocked her head to one side, searched his eyes, then simply whispered, "Yes."

***

Captain Jen Holly headed back to the HAPT Office in Frisco. It had been an incredible day. The best part was that everyone was safe; she couldn't have been happier. Still, the question of why had someone decided to delay or kill the team played in her mind. Why start a slide? Was the perp trying to destroy or simply delay Nate Abel's return to Tiptop? Somehow, delaying Nate's vote seemed most logical. Keep Nate in the mine until after the meeting and Friday's rally. His vote would have changed the balance in favor of the town was Jen's guess. Then one had to think about who ordered the perp to stop Nate? Was he or she under orders from Capital Regime or from someone closer? Jen couldn't exactly wrap her head around the whole situation. The good news was that the plan had been averted.

She would need to call Jackson Abel tonight and inform him what had happened in Sourdough Gulch. Jen knew that he would be relieved to hear about his father and absolutely surprised about the Quit Claim Deed. Probably not happy about Nathan staying in the gulch but somehow she knew he wouldn't be surprised. Of course Jen hoped that he and Kevin Donner had reached some type of agreement. An agreement that would make Tiptop's position in the courts much stronger was her hope. Captain Jen Holly, however, would need to be silent about the conflict. Her job demanded neutrality.

Martin Keiser's murder seemed like their piece of the puzzle for now. Her team didn't need to be neutral when it came to that investigation. The law was clear about murder jurisdiction; the body had been found in Summit County. They were ordered to investigate period. It was time to solve this murder before anything else happened.

Detective Bill Smith could now begin to work with Frank on Buck Jonquin's involvement as a prime suspect. Jonquin's military ties and political opinions did bring him to the forefront . Frank was already working on Buck's financial picture. He and Bill could dig deeper starting tomorrow morning. She was looking forward to Frank's report on his first meeting with Jonquin. Jen had heard Frank's announcement come over the radio. She concluded that what Frank had learned this afternoon would be first on the morning agenda. Good. HAPT needed to focus on the Keiser murder investigation. They could now concentrate.

In her mind, Jen began to wonder how many conspirators there just might be in Tiptop. Those folks would be Keiser suspects for sure. Buck couldn't have committed all these crimes by himself. There had to be more locals helping the government, and as far as Jen knew, no legal suit had been filed yet. It sounded like it would come out in the Zoning Committee Public Meeting. At that time the state would also become involved. How would Kevin Donner's plan change that venue? Maybe Eminent Domain was just one part of this puzzle. The bottom line was, who had the control, state or Regime? Jen figured that the courts would ultimately make that decision.

If the plan was for the government to control American waterways, then all the states would have to comply or be cut off, and their authority destroyed. Tiptop's controversy was one of the first national actions of this Regime. It could be a test case. So far Capital Regime hadn't been successful. Eliminating Martin Keiser should have scared the town into compliance, but it hadn't. Donner, being shot, should have scared him away, but it didn't. He was more resolved than ever. Now Nate Abel's vote would be placed in a Denver lawyer's hand that just might sway the vote and the media.

The fascists seemed to be using a wait-and-see tactic to play it safe. They hadn't come out with guns blazing. Other than the helicopter, they had kept a low profile. The whole country was in such turmoil these days that it was hard to know who was giving the orders and what agencies would oppose.

So it looked to Jen like maybe a few radicals were trying to push the Regime agenda before the government was ready. These radicals had exposed their hand before the coup had any success.

That left HAPT to uncover these radicals. Who knew? If the small town militants could be brought to justice and publicized by the media, then Capital Regime might just back down. Expose the criminals; expose the Eminent Domain plan. It could delay any legal litigation until after the midterm elections. That was a great concept.

As Jen parked, she noticed that Frank's car was gone. She quickly headed up the stairs to the office to see if he had left a message for her. Regardless, Jen would get out a text tonight. The team needed to meet tomorrow morning bright and early. It felt like the quiet before the storm right now. It would be all hands on deck tomorrow. The Tiptop Rally was two days away and HAPT needed to be close to solving these crimes. Two days....

CHAPTER 20

BUT, NO FRANK

Buck's eyes stared hot coals through Frank at this point. This cop needed to at least disappear, he thought. Buck really didn't want to kill him, however, things were just spinning too fast. The carnage was adding up. He had been ordered to stand down by the Regime. Nevertheless, they weren't here and didn't know what this loud mouth cop might cost them. Some type of compromise had to be made. If he could delay Frank Mason until after the takeover, then all would be well. Some type of containment might work. Later, the leaders would be able to dismiss any charges filed against Buck. Their control of the area would change things for sure.

Obviously, Frank wasn't the only cop that would point the finger at him for Keiser's murder. However, if HAPT went into a frenzy searching for Frank, there would be a delay. More time for Capital Regime's intervention in Tiptop would change everything, and the sooner the better. Buck was hoping that Friday's rally would bring the town under Regime control. Their representatives would be here. It was past time for the change of control, he calculated. Buck now made his decision. There just might be a way to simply delay Officer Frank Mason. If he lived would be up to him and not on Buck's shoulders. "Time to get up, Frank, and take a ride. I think you'll drive." The Colt 45 pointed in the direction of Frank's patrol car.

Frank just couldn't help it as he got up. He just had to ask, "So you killed Marten Keiser, didn't you?"

"Doesn't really matter, does it?" Buck said coyly. "He was a goner any way that you look at it. The government needed that job done. I take orders from people in control." Buck's angry eyes beamed with self righteousness. Frank watched him become carried away with politics and power. "When the water rights and land are in the Regime's hands, I will become a hero. This movement ain't playing around, old man. They will own the fucking country soon and nothing or nobody is going to stop them. I am on the side of that power, and you are just a bump in the road."

Unbelievable, Frank thought as they moved toward his car. Buck Jonquin was delusional. He really did think that Capital Regime would cover for him. His traitor friends had filled him with dreams of corruption and military control. Fake news and fake goals controlled retired General Buck Jonquin's mind.

Frank opened the car door and slipped in

watching Buck closely. He was at a loss for words right now. Jonquin was literally crazy with cult propaganda. The man was dangerous as hell, Frank assessed. Was Frank riding to his grave? His only hope was that Buck would get carried away in his enthusiasm and let Frank grab hold of Mr. Colt.

Buck directed them toward the Freedom Mine. Was there some secret entrance that no one knew about? Was Buck going to simply shoot him and dispense with his body in the mine? Holy shit!

"Yup, you just got too close to the answers, old man. If you had waited until after the papers were signed then we wouldn't need to be taking this ride." Buck let the Colt 45 indicate that they were passing the mine entrance.

Now Frank was confused. "Where are we going, Buck? You at least can tell me that."

"Oh, I think it's going to be a surprise. Keep moving down this road and no funny business."

"Did you start the slide?" Frank asked.

"Nope. I left that one to my partner who fucked that attempt all to hell. Sometimes, you just need to do the work yourself but what's done is done."

"How about Donner? Is that your work or your partner's?"

"Oh I went for Donner to at least slow him down. If he had held still, Kevin boy would have missed the whole damn rally like I had planned."

"So your partner only did the slide? Who is your partner by the way?" Frank asked as he held his breath. If he ever got out of this situation, he would at least have the answers. One could hope.

"Good try, you son of a bitch. I think I've said enough at this point. You can stop the car now."

Frank put the car in park and looked around. They were on Martin Keiser's property. What in the hell was Buck going to do? Simply shoot him out here so the coyotes could munch on his remains?

"Shut the motor off and get out with your hands on top of your head again," Buck commanded. He kept Mr. Colt aimed directly at Frank's heart. Buck didn't take his eyes off Frank as he rounded the car. "Now we're going for a hike. Walk."

"So what are the plans for Tiptop when the government takes control?"

"Well, the way I hear it, the old town will get bulldozed down just like what happened in Dillon in the sixties. We'll have a reservoir constructed right where the buildings are now. The government will then add small living quarters for the workers. Eventually, deluxe condos with costly price tags will line the reservoir. I'd say a couple million dollars to buy into the gated community."

"So Tiptop completely goes away just like the old mining town of Silver City," Frank assessed. Silver City had been a little community of 5000 population in the silver mining days. Then it had become a ghost town when the silver vein was gone. Some rich man came along and bought all the buildings in the fifties. It had eventually been rebuilt on private land for the man's guests. Regular folks of the mountains had lost one piece of their past without even realizing what had happened. Their history was just plucked out of the ground and forgotten. No buildings left in that community. How fitting that the same incident could happen again. Frank shook his head as that nightmare played.

"Hell, it won't be so bad. Landowners will be compensated and provided with opportunities somewhere else," Buck added.

"What? Like on a reservation? Flatland with no future? You really don't care about your neighbors do you? Or maybe destroying the environment in this fragile mountain terrain doesn't matter. None of that bothers you, huh?"

"Not in the least. Times got to change," Buck added with pride. "We'll be governed by a stronger alliance. Controlled for the betterment of America without democracy. It ain't worked for years. Water rights will be controlled by the new fascist military; states begging for water if they don't comply. Sounds good to me."

"You really are a son of bitch, Buck. What's your wife think about this whole plan? Betsy has lived in Tiptop all her life. How could she possibly agree with you?"

"She doesn't know," Buck admitted as he brought the butt of Mr. Colt 45 down on the back of Officer Mason's skull. The thud was loud and clear. He dropped like a stone. "Good night, Frank," Buck said with satisfaction.

He pulled Frank by his feet toward the old cistern. Hell, people had used this hole for trash for years. He tossed Frank in with the rest of the debris head first. Actually as Buck Jonquin stood above the cistern hole, he realized that he hadn't checked to see if Frank was still alive. He'd hit him pretty hard. Well, it didn't really matter, did it? Dead or alive, Frank was going to miss the rally. Frank's question about Betsy had really pissed Buck off. Betsy was one piece of this scheme that he hadn't figured out yet. What would be her reaction when she found out? He had no idea. Buck still had to deal with her. Shit!

***

It was 6:30 in the morning when Captain Jen Holly arrived at the HAPT Office. She had stopped by the pastry shop for goodies this morning. She selected a treat with enthusiasm. It just felt like a small celebration needed to happen. They had survived all the shit that the anti-Tiptop constituents had handed out. Now, another page would turn and they'd figure out who were these perps.

Jen opened her computer and checked her email. As she scanned down the rows and rows of incoming, her eyes suddenly spotted an email from Frank. It had been dated yesterday around 3:00 in the afternoon. By then Frank would have known that all the officers were safe, she knew.

Jen opened it and her cream buff froze in midair. Frank had gone to Tiptop to interrogate Buck Jonquin late yesterday. He had left her an attachment to explain. The information was all she needed to realize that he had made quite a dent in Buck Jonquin's credibility. Money, army general and ties to the precarious new government were all great motives. Jen would have Frank explain in detail when he got here today. It was all a great start. In her mind, she kind of wished that Frank had waited until he had someone to go with him but she understood his enthusiasm. Buck did look like a strong suspect. It certainly wouldn't hurt to casually find out Buck's perspective. Not get too involved but do the preliminary investigation with Buck was Frank's explanation. Just to let the perp know they were out there watching.

It sounded like Frank felt there must be someone else helping Jonquin. One mole just didn't balance with all the incidents that they had experienced. Gossip may travel fast but there just seemed to be more ears involved than Buck by himself. Maybe Betsy was also a prime suspect? She certainly was in a position to find out what was happening. However, physically, her interaction was hard to fathom.

The door opened and the team burst into the office at 6:45. No lack of energy, Jen noticed. The volume of talk was high and excited. They made a beeline for the pastries. All except for Frank who wasn't there.

Anyone seen Frank yet?" Jen asked.

"Nope," Bill Smith answered before inhaling his croissant. Didn't see his car at his house when I passed so I figured he was already here."

"Well, let's wait a few minutes for him. He has been extremely busy while we have been dodging rocks," Jen said feeling slightly uneasy. He was usually the first one through the door on normal meeting days. Granted, they were early but still.

"Funny," Libby mumbled as she made her selection from the pastry box. Libby also knew Frank should have been first. Hunger, however, won her attention as a vanilla cream puff was selected. She smiled, selected a napkin, then proceeded to sit and eat.

Detective Jerry Neal and Tyler dog had stayed with them today. Jerry knew that Captain Holly was in full pursuit on this case. He had called Chief James Marten last night and begged for Summit duty. It hadn't been too hard although Marten had hinted that he would miss Tyler more than Jerry. Naturally, Buena Vista wanted to be in on the gossip when it happened so Marten had acquiesced. The high country had all eyes on Tiptop these days. What happened over there could easily mirror future events for all of them. A frightening concept but unfortunately a sign of the times, Jerry calculated.

After being seated for about ten minutes, Officer Libby James pulled out her cell phone and dialed Frank. "Maybe he overslept," she said. The team's eyes focused on her and waited. It rang the usual four times then went to answering machine. When she disconnected, they became quiet.

Their eyes then turned to Captain Jen for guidance. She decided to read Frank's email while they waited. Why not? It would give them a head start this morning. "I got an email from Frank around 3:00 pm yesterday. Of course, I didn't check my mail until this morning. I'll start filling you in before Frank gets here. Hopefully, he will arrive in time to tell us about his interview with Buck Jonquin. Who knows, maybe we can detain a person of interest before the day is over,'" she added.

They listened as Captain Jen read the email.

The team was torn between listening and watching the door. Frank hadn't shown up yet. A tension began to permeate. No Frank, why not?

"Well, team, we need to ask Buck Jonquin about where Frank is," Jen decided. Her stomach began to churn. Frank needed to be found now! "And, I think we need a search warrant immediately," she declared. "Let's not take any chances. Buck is now more than a person of interest when you add the disappearance of Frank to the list," Captain Jen added.

Bill got up from the couch and headed for his desk. "I'll call the Courthouse and get one of the judges to sign on the dotted line then head over to Jonquin's.

"Sounds like a plan," Captain Jen said. "Libby partner with Bill; while he deals with the warrant, you inform all the police stations. Why don't you two go by Frank's house and make sure that he isn't there before getting the search warrant. I guess something could have happened at home. Notify Jerry and I, asap, after you have searched his house. If he's not there, we'll head over to Jonquin's immediately. I see no reason to delay. We have a missing officer, ladies and gentlemen, if he's not found at home. Bill and Libby, keep in touch. Stop by the hospital just in case on your way out of town." The team left the office; the pastries were abandoned.

Detective Jerry Neal and Tyler drove Captain Jen Holly toward Tiptop. They had their lights on as they headed through the outskirts of Frisco toward Breckenridge. Libby called in that Frank was not at his house. The search had to begin.

Jen decided to call Bix and have her spread the word about a possible search with the locals. They just might need as much help as they could get. "Bix wanted to let you know that Frank is missing. It would seem that he didn't come home last night after going over to Tiptop. Will you put out the alert to the locals for me?"

"Oh my, of course. What was he going to do over there?" Bix asked.

"Interrogate Buck Jonquin." Captain Jen could sense the worry and silence on the other end of the phone. She finally asked just to make sure that they hadn't been disconnected, "Are you still there?"

"Yes. You be careful. That man is known as a political sympathizer and a hot wire. I don't like him. Betsy made a poor choice when she married that loud mouth. Have you called the hospital?"

"Libby and Bill will stop there before they come to Tiptop. Bix, don't tell the locals about Buck but just say Frank was going to Tiptop. Jerry and I are on our way over to Jonquin's house now. Libby and Bill are following with a warrant. See what you can find out about Frank's whereabouts and call if you have any information. I'll let you know what happens as soon as I know."

"Promise?"

"Promise," Captain Jen disconnected. Her mind was spinning. Please, God, don't let us find a body, Jen thought. She had assumed that the team would be over in Tiptop but not this quickly and under these circumstances. Jen looked up Jonquin's address on her cell phone, then settled back for the ride.

Their radio interrupted her thoughts. It was Libby. "Bill and I will be on the way to the hospital and then the courts in the next fifteen minutes. I have finished calling all the police stations. Marshall wanted to know if you want more back up and so does Chief Anderson over in Breckenridge."

"Not at this time. Let's not disturb Tiptop until we've searched Buck Jonquin's residence. Tell them both to be on alert though in case the whole thing goes to hell," Jen said. "If we don't get any answers from Buck, then an all out search will need to happen so stand down until further notice."

"10-4." Libby disconnected and ran across the HAPT parking lot to jump in Bill's waiting patrol car. With lights on they headed toward the hospital then Breckenridge Courts.

***

Bix quickly called Emma Keiser first while Bernie and Simon Schnoodle paced. "Emma, we have a problem this morning. Officer Frank Mason has disappeared somewhere over Tiptop way. Can you put out the word?"

"You bet. How long has he been missing?"

"From what Captain Jen said, I'd say since yesterday afternoon and, yes, they are checking the hospital. He could have run off a switchback or something so we're probably looking for a car accident."

"Oh, Lord. The folks will start looking on this side of Hoosier Pass right away. Most people are out-and-about today anyway. Doing stuff like getting in supplies just in case the rally takes a turn for the worst. Well hell, things couldn't get much more crazy, could they? You know I'm going to call all the claim owners," Emma sputtered. "Who knows what the Regime could be up to? I mean maybe they're picking up all of us? Wouldn't hurt to inform everybody about Frank."

"Maybe a call to Kevin Donner and Jackson Abel might be a good idea also," Bix said.

"And you might think about calling the Coalition and telling Melanie Camp. A missing police officer just might be of interest to them. After all, they are constructing a case against Capital Regime.

"I'll do it next before I contact the Summit locals. Bernie and I will comb this side of Hoosier Pass for any signs of an accident fairly soon. We need to make sure that he didn't drive off a switchback on the Summit side."

Half an hour later the couple , accompanied by Simon, were diving up the first switchback of the pass. Three other groups were up ahead searching. They would cover the area from the summit to the bottom in the next hour. Simon's nose was out the window checking for clues. He wasn't sure what he was looking for, but it did seem to need attention.

The Breckenridge Police were patrolling from Frisco to their town limits and beyond. Chief Josh Anderson hadn't put out a missing person's report on Frank yet, but the county was buzzing with activity. Chief Anderson was waiting impatiently for Captain Jen Holly's call. He had pretty well decided that if Frank hadn't been found within the next hour then it was time to get a full force out there.

Chief Josh Anderson then picked up his phone and called retired Sheriff Jerome Walker over in Tiptop. That old man could become their best resource pretty quickly. He'd lived near Tiptop all his life and knew the area like nobody else. Walker also knew Buck Jonquin's property lines if they needed to search on foot. If it came down to a search of all of Peak County, Jerome Walker could be a valuable asset if he would help. Of course, that was the question. Walker was an ornery old cop that lived by his own rules. Hadn't followed the rules ever. Josh Anderson had never figured out how the guy hadn't been fired years ago. He wouldn't have lasted a month in Summit that was for sure.

Josh listened as he tried to contact the old coot. It rang at least eight times before Jerome answered, "What the hell do you want at 7:30 in the morning? This ain't another damn call about Frank Mason is it? Don't you people ever talk to each other before you fly off the fucking handle? I got the whole damn town calling me. I'm getting my fucking pants on!"

"Well do you know anything?" Josh said.

"I just checked my damn answering machine and Frank told me he was heading out investigating. He said that if he needed backup, he'd call me. Ain't heard shit."

"Have you told anyone about this conversation?" Chief Anderson asked becoming impatient.

"Well hell, no. The Tiptop snoops have kept me busy. I haven't heard from any police as of yet."

"And you didn't call Frank back yesterday?" Josh said flabbergasted by how little concern Walker was showing.

"Frank is an adult. If he had needed help yesterday, he would have let me know. Now let me get my pants on!"

"How could any officer disregard the need for back up like that?" Josh assessed.

"Look I told you, I didn't check my messages until this morning," Jerome grumbled.

"You know, that's just not good enough. If you aren't going to monitor your damn phone, then don't call it police business! You can't have it both ways!" Josh yelled.

His abrupt comment was met with the slamming down of the receiver. Josh then proceeded to call Captain Jen Holly and report the conversation. He held his temper in control until he had given her the information.

"We, also, just heard back from Bill and Libby. Frank is not at the hospital either. My officers will arrive, warrant in hand, at Buck Jonquin's for backup within an hour. I believe it's time for immediate assistance," Captain Holly declared.

After the communication was done, Chief Anderson began to boil. He thought about calling Jerome Walker back, then decided the hell with that! How could that man be such a hard ass when dealing with his own brothers in uniform? Chief Josh Anderson of the Breckenridge Police Force was hot and, come hell or high water, his force was going to help! Walker be damned! "Call a meeting of our department in 20 minutes! Order both off- and on-duty officers to get the hell over here!" Josh screamed at his poor dispatcher who jumped out of her chair in shock. Captain Josh Anderson spun out of his chair and attached his weapon belt. He was moving now!

CHAPTER 21

ON THE SCENT

Captain Jen Holly and Detective Jerry Neal turned off their lights and slowly approached Buck Jonquin's house. Jerry had thrown in one of Frank's jackets that they had found at the office. He now had Jen offer it to Tyler. The dog inhaled and immediately recognized Frank's scent. He whined slightly and looked at Jerry. If Frank had made it to Jonquin's house, Tyler would let them know for sure.

They carefully checked out the surrounding area near the house as they approached. It looked all quiet at this time. They pulled up, unsnapped their hand guns, leashed Tyler and opened the patrol car doors slowly. If Buck Jonquin had them in his sights, it was important not to make any quick moves.

"Take it slow and easy," Jen whispered. Then she yelled politely, "Hello, Mr. Jonquin, can we approach?" Captain Jen had plastered a fake smile on her face. Jen then handed Tyler's leash to Jerry as they both stood in front of the car. The screen door opened slowly. Jonquin came out and leaned his Winchester 30-30 rifle up against the house. Jen noticed that it was still in reach but he had put it down.

"What the hell do you want?" Buck asked placing his hands to his side in a non threatening stance.

Jen thought that could be a good sign for now. The man wasn't relaxed but he wasn't ready to shoot them either. Jerry reached down to release Tyler.

"Don't let that dog off leash in my yard!" Buck demanded then scratched his unshaven face reconsidering his tone somewhat. " I don't want no dog activity upsetting my livestock." His eyes were intense and definitely not matching the tone.

Detective Neal patted Tyler indicating that he should stand down. Buck relaxed then and asked, "Why are you here?"

"We're looking for Officer Frank Mason. Have you seen him lately?"

"I ain't seen him. Why?" he responded.

"He was suppose to visit you yesterday afternoon," Jen said casually.

"Well he never made it. No, I ain't seen him. Been mighty quiet around here. Why? Is he missing?" Buck asked with fake innocence, Jen observed.

"His report yesterday would indicate that he came over here in the afternoon. Officers are required to report their destinations," Jen added.

"Did he call in to say anything about meeting me?" Buck asked. "You think I'm lying or something? Well, I ain't. No, Frank Mason did not come here."

"The last we heard from him was his report. It just seems odd to me," she offered.

"I don't give a shit if he didn't follow orders. None of my business," Buck said obstinately.

"You mind if we look around, Mr. Jonquin?" Jen asked trying to sound casual with her request.

"Hell yes, I mind. You got no right. And, no, you can't look around." The tension began mounting. Buck's blue eyes glared at both officers then he took a step back toward his Winchester rifle. He crossed his arms slowly, then asked, "Are you implying something, Officers? Cause, Mason did not come by here. You hear?" Buck turned to go back into his house then said, "Time to leave, Officers, I'm through talkin."

"Mr. Jonquin, you will need to stay on the deck here," Captain Jen Holly ordered. "We have a search warrant coming. It should arrive within 20 minutes or so. Why don't you sit down in one of those deck chairs? We are planning to search your house and property. You might just as well relax."

"Bull shit about relaxing. You have no right," he yelled taking steps toward them off the deck.

"Stop!" Jen yelled. Both Officers drew their guns while Tyler growled. Jonquin ran his hand through his salt and pepper crew cut hair while holding his ground. He wisely stopped his forward aggression and stared at them. He should have never left the deck without his rifle. Buck now realized how foolish his anger had been. The standoff lasted a few seconds while Buck Jonquin reconnoitered what the next action would be.

"You two will need to get in your damn car and wait there unless you plan on arresting me right now for not having seen your officer. I'm through talking."

"And you'll need to sit a spell in your deck chair in plain sight, Mr. Jonquin. Actually, on the west side of the deck away from the rifle or the door until the warrant arrives. That would be an order, sir." It was the only compromise that Jen was willing to make, Buck realized. This bitch was deadly serious.

The silent intensity held for a moment before Jonquin finally said, "Suit yourselves." He slowly wandered over to a chair and sat. His eyes never left Jen's face. He leaned back and crossed his arms. He didn't stop staring until they got in their patrol car. The silent truce was on.

***

Bix reached over and touched Bernie's arm. "Turn in over there," she said pointing. "I'm thinking that we just might want to search a couple of these more obscure roads just in case Frank was forced off Highway 9. Someone could have set up an ambush."

"Good thought," Bernie answered, slowing down and taking the right turn. The road turnoff was almost a 180. She then gunned her automatic up the steep slope. When they reached the top of the ascent, the view was spectacular. Bernie realized that she was looking down on the whole Summit Valley. The mountains loomed on both sides. In the distance she could actually see Dillon Reservoir some 20 miles away. Unbelievable .

"Drive on down this road please. There's a Colorado Springs water gate two miles down here; it just might be one possibility."

Bernie slowly maneuvered the ruts as they approached the green colored gate. As they got out, Bix opened the glove compartment and handed Bernie her 357 Blackhawk Revolver. "Just in case," Bix said.

"Just in case," Bernie answered and attached the holster on her belt. Bix secured Simon on his leash. The little guy just might smell or hear something that they couldn't, she reconnoitered.

They walked around the gate and followed the road. Simon was happy to be out at this point; it was an unexpected pleasure for him. He hiked along, enthusiastically, with his nose to the ground. Bernie and Bix inspected each side of the road for any signs of activity; Simon did likewise.

The early morning rain had cleaned the tree pollen off the ground plants and awakened the smell of pine. Chipmunks scurried out of Simon's path as they walked. It was a beautiful day with no signs to interrupt the peaceful environment.

Bix knew there was a cabin about half a mile ahead of them. Simon was quiet except for his overly active nose; Bix watched him closely. She knew that he would smell an unwelcome stranger before they would. Frank could be tied up with a guard in some place like this. Who knew what had happened to him, she concluded. There were many options and so little time.

She pointed to the left side of the road. Bernie saw the old weathered wood cabin peeking out of the forest. They walked carefully toward the cabin clearing. Fortunately, there were plenty of trees and bushes to cover their approach. They moved around to the back of the old relic. Bernie had pulled out her revolver and Bix had tightened Simon's leash. They quietly moved toward the one window on the back. Their approach, silent and intense.

Simon's eyes stared up at Bix, expectantly, waiting for his orders. His little body was ready to react.

Bernie, slowly peeked in the widow and scanned the interior from side-to-side. Her eyes focused on each shadow closely then moved on. She wasn't going to miss any movement or have any surprises.

Bix felt the tension in her body mount as she looked into the interior for the first time. Deserted. The dusty wooden table had one chair and the bed had only springs. Bix then relaxed and decided to breathe. No inhabitants and, unfortunately, no Frank. 'Bittersweet' was the word that Bix felt. She had been scared that he'd be there and then, she became saddened by his absence.

"Shit," she mumbled. "Time to move on," she told Simon. The little black dog wagged his stubby tail at her and waited to see what they would do next. They retraced their steps back to the car.

Bix had already decided that McAdam's Gold Mining Refinery would be their next stop. There were all types of darkened rooms in that historic site. Her resolve strengthened. Frank needed to be found soon, and they just might be the ones to do it.

***

The smell came first; wet dirt, rancid food and dried blood attacked Frank's nostrils. His body became repulsed and forced him to throw up. The stars that showered his consciousness exploded like the Fourth of July as he lifted his head up from the stagnant ground.

He forced his eyes open. There in front of him were plastic water bottles, old Styrofoam food containers and his blood mixed in for color contrast. Frank pulled himself up and sat holding his throbbing head. Had to be a concussion, he calculated as awareness slowly crept into his world.

Sound suddenly entered the cistern. Some 30 feet above the opening were two crows flying across a crystal blue sky. They squawked at his visual intrusion then Frank became aware of the sound of their wings moving gracefully through the air. The motion itself was such a singular awareness. Life was moving and living beyond him. He then began to look around trying not to move his head too quickly. If he kept his head level and quiet, the stars didn't come back to torture him. Staying awake would now become his challenge.

Frank was in a hole some 25 feet below the surface. People must have used it as a trash container on hikes. He knew that he was in the back country. Buck Jonquin had hauled his sorry ass out into the wilderness then dumped him like garbage. From the feel of his head, Frank figured that he had been thrown head first. There seemed to be two throbbing injuries. One on the back of his head and one on top.

His mind now remembered that Buck had hit him probably with the Colt gun butt. He had gone out like a light. The top head injury had to have been from landing, head first, in this fucking hole. As reality began to take hold of his senses, Frank realized that he was lucky to be alive. "Thank you, Lord," he whispered. Hearing his voice shocked him as it echoed off the dirt walls. The depth of his environment brought half sun and half shadows into his world. He would be able to tell the time of day by the sun's movement. Frank spied an old rusty nail and marked one line on the wall next to him. Day one, he calculated.

***

The Police Patrol car roared down Buck Jonquin's driveway some 20 minutes later. Buck opened one of his eyes and watched the cloud of dust rising from the gravel road some half mile away. He knew that they were bringing the warrant and turning his page. That damn dog would find evidence of Frank Mason's visit. Jonquin was in a shitload of trouble.

His arrest was happening entirely too early. Why couldn't it have waited until after the rally and the Regime invasion? The control would have shifted nicely; the Regime then controlling the mountain lands and water rights through Eminent Domain. Buck would be free of any charges after the coup. The power in the mountains was shifting and the cops would be either fired or working for the government. His case, at that time, dismissed.

Unfortunately, things weren't working out as he had hoped. The charges of murder and abduction of Frank Mason could go to court before the invasion happened. He had abducted a cop and the worse part was that Buck hadn't checked to see if Frank was alive. What a fucking stupid mistake. If he told the cops where that old fart was and Frank was dead, then Buck was up for two murders. Holy shit!

Jail! That was another nightmare that he would now have to face. The population was a sicko mix. White Supremacists didn't rule at the present. Black gangs did. Buck would have to wait until the White Cult Movement released all the white men from prison and put them in the army.

The present reality was that some inmates in the next couple of weeks could attack him for his beliefs. You had to figure that some of those guys had families out there who were going to lose their health care or had race issues. There was a shiv with his name on it out there for sure- either a white guy or black would try to take him out.

The government movement had to bring the population down to compliance somehow soon, Buck reconnoitered. Taking away health care, then democracy, would turn the tables. Fascism was here to stay, he speculated. The money would shift to the government and control would become reality. The stupid Congress was playing right into the fascist's hands. The takeover was imminent!

Nevertheless, Buck's problem now was that he should have followed orders and only killed Martin Keiser. He just simply got too involved and had put all his faith in the Regime. Now, there was a price to be paid. Why hadn't he just stood down and waited? Well, it was too late now. His chances of becoming rich over the land speculations were pretty well over. And his marriage to Betsy would probably be over also. She didn't sign up for a husband who was a jailbird.

Suddenly, doubt flooded Buck's mind. He hadn't played the 'what if game' for a long time. His loyalties and ego might just have gone too far. What if the Fascist White Cult didn't win? Had he been right to side with this government coup? Would they actually be able to take control? Create a third world country with deteriorated infrastructure and healthcare was the goal. Well shit, at this point it didn't matter to him. Nothing really mattered. He was a goner! Buck sprang for his Winchester and dived off the east end of the deck.

Jen and Jerry had been watching him closely. His movement was quick and slightly unexpected. Tyler barked and scratched the patrol car window in his enthusiasm to pursue. Jerry unleashed him quickly and got out. Captain Jen with gun drawn approached the deck first. She moved quickly making sure that Buck hadn't doubled back and into the house. Jen peered through the windows carefully as she moved to the east. Jerry and Tyler

were now right beside her running on the deck.
Tyler gave the signal that Frank Mason's scent was
present.

So Frank had been here, Captain Jen realized.
They moved around to the corner of the house and
inspected the side yard. It had been cleared of trees
and was pasture mostly. No Buck Jonquin in sight.
Jen was surprised that he could disappear that
quickly. However, he was trained and this pursuit
wasn't going to be a piece of cake for them. How
could he have run 100 yards that quickly she
questioned? Then her eyes spotted on the side of
the house a vegetable cellar. People rarely built
these storage places anymore, but Buck had created
one. The double doors were shut.

Tyler pulled Jerry directly to the ominous
doors. The dog focused on the closure turning his
head from side to side as he listened. Jen glanced at
Jerry and nodded. They could hear Libby and Bill
now opening the front door upstairs and calling to
Jonquin about the warrant. Their footsteps rushed
around through the rooms. Finally, Bill yelled, "All
clear."

Buck had used the cellar! No doubt about it.
"Let's go," Jen said.

She placed a hand on the right door but before
she pulled it open, Tyler barked an alarm. "He
thinks it might be booby trapped," Jerry said.
"Careful, Captain."

Jen grabbed her flashlight then inched the door
open and looked in. There was a wire attached to
the door by a eyebolt. "We need wire clippers," she
said.

Jerry's eyes glanced over at the barn. "I'll find some. Stay put," he whispered. He motioned Tyler to stay and then rushed toward the open barn.

Libby and Bill then came around the corner of the house. "What happened?" Libby asked.

"We think he's in here," Jen whispered. Jerry came back with some cutters. Jen opened the door one inch again, Libby aimed the flashlight and Jerry slipped the wire cutters over the wire and cut. Bill was watching the perimeter of the area just in case. The cellar was open within a minute.

The officers moved to the side of the opening and pulled their guns. Captain Jen counted to three with her fingers held high before they rushed the entrance. "Hands up, Police!" was met with pure silence. Their flashlights scanned the cellar as they entered. Libby then flashed upon a tunnel dug in the far wall. "Over here, Captain," she indicated.

The tunnel was just large enough for escape. As Jen peered in, she couldn't see any light at the end. Buck Jonquin had made quite an elaborate tunnel.

"Unbelievable," Bill mumbled as he looked. "Where do you suppose this ends?"

"Good question. We have backup coming from Breckenridge. We're not going to lose this White Rabbit today," Captain Jen Holly said. "So far Buck's on foot and Tyler's got the scent. Bill, call a search helicopter in case Buck's got a vehicle hidden somewhere. Actually, tell everyone to watch for Frank's patrol car also. Got a hunch," Jen said.

CHAPTER 22

ESCAPE

Officer Frank Mason could hear a helicopter somewhere in the distance. It hadn't traveled across his telescopic view yet. Unfortunately, this deep cistern was now his home with the dirt walls becoming all too familiar to him. The dampness was so penetrating that he had now piled debris up making a seat. His concussion symptoms were dissipating; that was a relief. Frank could now prop himself up and move with minimal pain.

He had also organized the trash debris into a pile of potential tools. If you could call a rusted gallon gasoline container, one yard of old canvas, a half pound of 16 common nails, a medium sized plastic bucket, some 30 feet of rotten old rope and a rusty beer can opener, tools. From his pocket he had added his lucky flint stone to the inventory.

The copter motor now quietly moved off into the far distance; it wasn't coming for him this time, he calculated. Frank sighed as reality settled. It was time to see if he could move enough to figure out how to get out of this damn cistern.

Frank examined the dirt walls closely. He took inventory of the various shapes of rocks sticking out and tried to map his climb. Some stones were large enough to help create steps, he thought. Others, would simply fall onto his head. Near the top rim he spied a Smoky Quartz Crystal sticking out. It teased him; the prize that he would have to reach to get out of here. Slow and easy Frank thought; one step at a time.

His attention then began to focus on the movement of clouds above him. They were beginning to cover the sun switching sunlight off and on; blinking at him then taunting him. Thunder clouds were finally forming; it wasn't the monsoon season so there were only occasional rainstorms. He had been ignoring the formation, not trying to get his hopes up. A little rain would produce water for him. Concussions made people thirsty, he seemed to remember and, yeah, he was thirsty. Real thirsty.

Moving slowly he placed the plastic bucket in the center of the cistern pit. Frank dug a shallow hole with the can opener, then placed the bucket in it. He opened the canvas and spread it out. Using the tall gas container for height, he attached the canvas to the handle with nails. He was able, finally, to shape the canvas into a convoluted funnel. Hopefully, this arrangement would produce more potential water in his bucket. It was all a wait and see game of course. What was it, 'watched pots never boil,' Frank remembered. Ignore it, he demanded of himself.

Frank pulled himself over to the wall of the cistern and, with the beer can opener began to dig his first step. As he hollowed out the first step, the clouds opened. It was a hard rain that pounded down on his environment. His body welcomed the feeling. He hadn't realized how dirty he had become. His tongue caught the first drops and then more. Frank glanced over to see if his invention was working. Yes! The water was collecting in the bucket. The only problem was that his newly constructed step was washing away. "Oh well," he mumbled. The water, he calculated, would keep him alive. Good.

***

"Libby and I will crawl through the tunnel since we're the smallest on this team," Captain Jen Holly said. "Bill, you and Jerry take Tyler out and see if he can figure out where Buck's exit might be. Maybe we can trap Jonquin in the tunnel. We could get lucky." With those commands the ladies, flashlights and weapons drawn, disappeared into the tunnel.

The guys watched until they could only see darkness. Would Buck Jonquin be caught in his own escape route? Jerry and Bill wondered as Tyler stuck his nose deep into the tunnel following Libby and Jen's scent.

The tunnel was pitch dark. It was just large enough that Libby and Jen could walk with a bend at their waists. It wasn't the most comfortable posture but it sure beat crawling. Buck had to be crawling.

The earth reeked of dank smells. Roots occasionally reached out like spiders from above to stop them. Jen was trying to ignore her claustrophobic tendencies as this tunnel rapped them in darkness; a darkness so complete that her mind began to play tricks on her. How to sense moving forward even became a challenge. Libby was behind her and that was the only indication of direction. Both ladies would occasionally pause and listen. Their environment was positively quiet, yet, they kept up their guard just in case.

"I'm starting to feel like a mole," Libby whispered. "Or what I think a mole just might feel like. My shoes are becoming icicles. This place is cold and damn musty!"

"Yes it is. How far do you think we've gone?" Jen whispered.

"Far enough that I've lost direction and if gravity wasn't a certainty, I wouldn't even know up and down," Libby answered. "50 feet?"

"Probably. We should be in the middle of that meadow east of Buck's house. Haven't seen any light in front of us yet," Jen stated. "This tunnel really was a project. Wonder what his wife thought he was doing? Hard to believe she's not in on this quite frankly," Jen said.

"You got that right. She must have seen piles of dirt somewhere. Really hard to hide mounds and mounds."

Jen began to flash her light on the ceiling of the tunnel in case an opening of some sort appeared before the ending. Buck had been thorough, she reconnoitered.

"Hope he didn't tunnel under all his property," Libby mumbled.

"That's for sure. I've been watching the ceiling pretty closely for an escape hatch," Jen said. From somewhere Jen began to sense air movement hitting her face. "Whoa, what's that?" She abruptly stopped as Libby collided into her backside. It was fresh air coming from somewhere. Both officers flashed their lights onto the ceiling ahead. Some ten feet in the distance they could see a square outlined by small rays of sunlight . Sure enough, it had to be Buck's escape hatch!

They aimed their flashlight beams on the outlined perimeter of the hatch. Their faces were now illuminated as they talked. It reminded Libby of Girl Scout Camp gossip meetings, the ones that took place after lights out. However, this situation could mean real danger with weapons drawn. What would happen when they opened the hatch? Would Buck Jonquin be there ready to blow their heads off?

"Careful, Libby," Captain Jen Holly whispered. They listened and waited for any sounds. Nothing. Before opening the hatch, Jen decided to flash her light forward into the tunnel ahead. There, occupying the end of Buck's tunnel, some ten feet ahead, was a large water proof ammunition storage cabinet with plenty of room for rifles and handguns. Jonquin had obviously moved his arsenal out of the house and into his tunnel. Unfortunately for them, they could see that he had taken four or five weapons with him. Armed and dangerous was definitely an understatement at this juncture.

"Ready?" Captain Jen whispered.

"Ready," Libby answered as cold chills gushed down her back.

***

"Let's go," Jerry said. He and Bill retraced their steps back out of the vegetable cellar and into a slow rain that had just started. They stopped by the car for rain ponchos and to radio a message about the escape. The reply was quick; help was twenty minutes out.

The officers then went back into Buck Jonquin's house for an item that would give Tyler Buck's scent. There was an old military shirt tossed over a kitchen chair. Tyler inhaled then raced out the door. They followed as quickly as they could. Tyler made a beeline straight from the cellar toward the meadow. His head was down sniffing deeply as if he could sense the tunnel.

"I'd say he's got it. Let's go!" Jerry yelled as he followed his dog.

They moved due east quickly scanning the area for any signs that might give clues to Jonquin's whereabouts. Some five minutes later, Tyler stopped moving and barked at a bush. It moved! A whole patch of ground and bush flew open like a submarine hatch!

Both officers assumed the stance with weapons drawn until Captain Jen's head popped out! "Wow!" Jerry yelled. "It's you! Straight out of the military books! How long did that tunnel take him, I wonder?"

"Doesn't matter since it worked," Jen said, then crawled out and helped Libby climb out. "He obviously has planned for his escape for a long time. "Okay, the way I see it, one of us needs to go back to the house and direct the teams coming in. Who would like to hunt Mr. Jonquin?" Three hands flew up into the air without hesitation. Jen sighed and grumbled, "Leadership, damn. Okay, get going and find that son of a bitch before dark! Radio in every thirty minutes. I want to know when and where he appears. Assume that at any moment the command to launch a helicopter with re-enforcements will be priority. Now, get the hell out of here and stay safe! Jonquin had his arsenal stored down there. He's now extremely dangerous. Radio back when you make contact."

They didn't have to be told twice. The team raced down into a gulley up ahead.
Captain Jen Holly walked back to the house. She had wanted to go, but it wasn't the right call for her to make. As she got close to Buck's house, she could hear sirens coming down his driveway. The Crime Scene Team were ahead in the race and second came Chief Marshall Tate from Frisco. Coming in last was Chief Josh Anderson with the Breckenridge Troops. Buck Jonquin's house would now become their control center.

First words out of Captain Jen's mouth, "Let's get a helicopter up looking for any hidden cars, especially Frank's, at this time! My team is out there and Jonquin is fully armed! We're tracking him."

***

Detective Jerry Neal held Tyler's leash tightly. Buck Jonquin could be behind any bush or hell he could be the bush, Jerry thought. Fortunately, Tyler would alert them either way. The tracking would be extremely dangerous when the technique could end in an ambush. "Let's spread out maybe 20 feet apart. We don't want to miss him as we travel forward. Tyler will be able to get the scent, but the exact location maybe more difficult. I've never tracked a professional army sniper before like this. We need to also watch for any booby-traps. Remember the cellar. His plan might be to get rid of us, one cop at a time."

Libby and Bill nodded. They were perfectly content to follow Jerry's command. He had been trained and had the experience. It mattered if they could pick up on Jonquin's clues; Jerry and Tyler took the lead. This situation would definitely be a challenge.

Tyler led some ten feet in front of Jerry. The rest followed watching the ground then surveilling the distance as best they could. The K-9 moved quickly back and forth zigzagging. It became obvious that Jonquin was covering his tracks as he traveled. Tyler would, once and awhile, move backwards to retract the scent again.

Jonquin could have buried himself anywhere, Jerry figured. The terrain was flat and arid in nature. Sage, yucca, and wild rose bushes spotted the landscape. A few shrub trees added some height.

The ground was a mixture of sand and clay. There was an occasional gulley that could hide a sniper easily.

Buck could spring up at anytime and fire at them. Jerry motioned to Libby and Bill to get down as they approached the next gulley. He pointed along the horizon so the officers would scan the area closely. Jerry held Tyler for a moment then rushed the gulley leaping into a summersault then he went flat down into the gulley. His rifle scanned the bottom closely. Nothing. He waved to Libby and Bill who moved into position. They checked the terrain thoroughly before moving forward. Their heads popped up as they scanned the ground ahead.

Tyler was anxious to go ahead; he pulled on his leash. Jerry gave him some distance and watched. He was 16 feet out and moving back and forth quickly. The scent was obviously strong. Jerry motioned for the officers to approach his position.

They were finally together and moving out when Tyler suddenly began to make a circle as he smelled the ground. A frustrated whine escaped from Tyler's mouth as he moved back and forth in a flurry. Jerry hadn't understood what was happening until the AR-15 rifle let loose an avalanche of bullets from in back of them! The spray was intense.

"Back in the gulley," Jerry yelled! The officers quickly scrambled. It turned out to be the best surprise move that they could make. Buck hadn't expected them to retreat. He was plummeted with bullets as they turned in full run! The few seconds that Buck had to duck their barrage got them back to the gulley safely.

Now Jerry realized what Jonquin had done. He had doubled back and simply dug a hole for himself. Buck had let the officers pass him. Turning the tables had been definitely a good surprise technique. From his position Jonquin would have taken them out if they had run forward. Their retreat had worked. Jerry also considered that Buck just might be a little out of practice. Thank heavens. They were pinned down but so was Buck Jonquin.

Buck's cold eyes peered out from under the shrub bush hat. He was dead set on killing them one way or the other. Staying alive was not their option, Buck promised himself as he pulled out another 60 shot magazine and loaded his AR-15.

Jerry then made radio contact with the Command Center to bring up more troops. If it was a standoff that Buck wanted, he'd damn well get it!

***

"So what in the hell did you think he was doing with all that dirt?" Captain Jen Holly questioned the dark haired lady with quivering lips next to her. They were once again in the cellar now showing Betsy Jonquin the tunnel entrance. She had arrived home from work a few moments ago expecting to find her husband waiting for dinner. Instead, her house was being trampled by the Crime Scene Team. The living room had been arranged so that their communication radios and monitors could function. Some ten officers were busy keeping track of the actions taking place. Jerry's report was producing a scurry of activity in the living room upstairs.

The shock on Betsy's face seemed genuine, Jen noticed. Chief Josh Anderson had remained for the interrogation also. He watched Betsy closely for her reactions and answer now that they were downstairs inspecting the tunnel. Betsy's mouth opened and closed like a goldfish in a tank. Her eyes watered up and she whimpered, "Buck didn't like me to come downstairs into his man space. He kept his guns and personal papers down here. I didn't know. I respected his space; he called it his privacy cave."

"It was more than a man cave, Mrs. Jonquin. Did you ever notice all the dynamite and weaponry Buck was collecting?" Chief Josh Anderson asked as his arms encompassed all the shelves piled with ammunition. "It's a frigging arsenal down here!"

"Like I said I never came down here. Buck could get awfully mad; I had my rooms upstairs. That's the way we lived. Gardening was our one hobby together. Buck was making me hotbeds for my plants with the dirt. I never asked him where he got it. We have plenty of land here; why should I care? Buck just kept filling the new hotbeds with dirt from his truck every weekend. I was pleased with our progress. I swear I didn't know; I just kept planting."

"And you expect us to believe that?" Chief Josh Anderson shouted while staring intensely at her.

"Weekends, I'd be either doing town business or selling real estate. Buck pretty much took care of the house. He worked more during the week. We'd take some week days off to be together. Those were the days that I'd garden and catch up on the laundry." She leaned down and stared into the tunnel again. "Where does it go?"

"Some fifty feet out into the pasture," Captain Jen said.

"Oh my," Betsy exclaimed "He must have worked on it during the weekdays or at night when he cleaned his guns down here. I had no idea."

"Did you know that Buck was working for the Regime? That he was for Eminent Domain and had connections?"

Again, shock registered on Betsy's face. "We both thought that selling the land and water rights to the government was the best option. The town needed to be able to grow, and it was our civic duty to comply. I have never said anything else to the committee. The town Zoning Committee, except for Howie Page, had always been for development," she offered. "It was a done deal until we got involved with the landowners and Kevin Donner. Now the whole thing has changed. Everything's changed after Martin Keiser's death," she mumbled. "Buck did have government contacts from his military days but actually working for them now? I don't think so."

Betsy's eyes twitched slightly, Jen noticed. Actually it looked like his wife might have a few doubts surfacing. In fact, she was downright hesitant so Jen pushed. "Not death, Betsy, but murdered," Captain Jen added. "Did you know that Buck and Martin got into quite an argument about a month ago in the bar? The topic was Eminent

Domain, Betsy." There was a pause as they listened to the surveillance helicopter going over the Jonquin's ranch house.

Betsy finally answered the question, "I heard about it from Buck. He told me that Martin was really hot on the issue. Wait a minute, you don't think Buck had anything to do with Martin's death?" Her eyes suddenly enlarged with shock. Betsy shook her head in quick denial. "Oh, no. He'd never kill Martin Keiser. They weren't friends but they were neighbors!"

"The murder had all the characteristics of a military operation. Someone who knew how to rig up that drone with a laser. Someone who could obtain the supplies without anyone knowing. Your husband had the training and connections, Betsy," Chief Anderson stated matter-of-factly.

"Noooooooo," screamed Betsy as she fainted dead away.

***

Chief Marshall Tate had decided to lift off in the helicopter joining the surveillance team. Buck Jonquin could have stashed away Frank's vehicle in Tiptop or outside of town. He was too smart not to have hidden the patrol car somewhere. It also made sense that Jonquin would want it close to the highway for a fast getaway.

They were starting their search in Tiptop thinking that the car could be hidden on any of the back streets. Marshall had the description of Frank's car plus the plate information. He and the pilot inspected the town streets first before heading out into the fields. So far they hadn't seen any signs of it. Marshall also remembered that Buck's truck was in his garage. The two men had to have escaped in Frank's patrol car.

"Let's head out onto the claims. We're wasting our time here. No cop cars."

The pilot nodded and circled back out to start covering the mountain terrain. They headed up near the Freedom Mine to start their surveillance. It looked pretty isolated at this time, no vehicles, no people. Marshall recorded on his map what area they were covering.

"Let's search the mining claims. The Saddle Tree Claim is first, Kevin Donner's. The helicopter took six passes over the top of the property. Wally Hall's North Star Claim was next. The same results, nothing. Marshall's eyes then spotted the signs of a an old lumber road running across the top of the claims. "Let's set down on that road and see if we get any signs of fresh tracks."

A few minutes later both men stared at the car ruts. They reached the same conclusions; Frank's patrol SUV had gone west across the claims.

"Let's go," Marshall yelled over the copter noise. They followed closely making sure that the tire tracks were still in view.

"Copter 4 come in," came the voice of Captain Jen Holly over the radio.

"Chief Tate here. 10-4."

"The team has made contact with Buck Jonquin out on the Saddle Tree Creek Claim. Sending Copter 2 over that area with reinforcements. 10-4."

"We've just found Frank's SUV tracks on an old lumber road above North Star Claim heading west now. We're in pursuit! 10-4."

"Stay with Frank's vehicle if you find it. I repeat, stay with the patrol car in case Jonquin makes a run for it," Captain Jen ordered.

"10-4," Marshall said.

The pilot upped their speed, still following the road. The dust became a cloud above them as they moved along with the nose of the copter facing down. It was like a small tornado out in the middle of nowhere.

"Hey, check out over there behind those scrub bushes," Marshall yelled. They landed and there was Frank's car. The keys were in the ignition.

Marshall inspected it quickly. He found some blood stains on the steering wheel. "I want you to head back to Control Center in case more troops are needed or any other action," he ordered. "I'll stay here and wait. Someone needs to keep an eye on this vehicle. Inform Control Center of my location,"

The pilot nodded, ran back to the copter and lifted off.

CHAPTER 23

BATTLES

Without any warning, Buck Jonquin heaved a stick of dynamite toward Jerry's position. The sandy soil mushroomed high into the air hurling threatening debris. After the explosion settled, Bill and Libby watched to see if Jerry was okay. He nodded to them and motioned for the firing to continue. Jonquin fired back this time not using any more dynamite. The exchange of fire became intense.

Bill and Libby both crawled forward. Each going wider so that Jonquin was slowly being surrounded. Buck then managed to retreat back away from them. From scrub to bush to boulder, the officers dodged his bullets. Constantly moving faster to keep the focus off Jerry who was now moving in a slow crawl straight toward Jonquin. The wider Libby and Bill zigzagged, the more effort it took to keep track of them; Buck was busy.

Jerry and Tyler began to move more aggressively

toward a large boulder in front of Jonquin's position. Libby and Bill sent a barrage of bullets at Jonquin simultaneously. Buck ducked under cover while Jerry and Tyler rushed to the boulder.

Then like an army of one, Jonquin took control of the situation. He heaved more dynamite as Bill and Libby then retreated with a diagonal move that separated them from Jerry's position. Jonquin, like a ghost, suddenly jumped into another gulley and disappeared.

The advantage was Jonquin's. The man knew this country like the back of his hand. He was moving with a purpose that neither of the officers understood. His direction was unclear to them. Buck's firing had slowed considerably as he retreated, then changed direction.

From above, a helicopter had spotted the battle. It moved lower to the ground and deposited a dozen Breckenridge Police near HAPT's position. They spread out like spiders circling the area. The commotion was loud and impressive. Libby and Bill took advantage of this action and rushed forward together as one unit. They rushed toward Jerry's last location.

Libby quickly flew around a boulder. She fell spread eagled on the ground as her eyes suddenly spotted a shadow advancing. Libby brought her rifle sight up and took aim. Her heart was in her throat!

* * *

Frank marked another day gone by on his prison wall as late afternoon began to settle. He could hear a bunch of rifle fire going on somewhere in the distance this afternoon. Obviously, Buck Jonquin was out and running. There had to be at least two helicopters out there searching and circling but none of them came across Frank's limited vision.

There was quite a conflict going on. The burst of bullets fluctuated like waves; the characteristics of pursuit, he calculated. The question was who was pursuing whom. The copters told a story of more reinforcements after Jonquin. That, at least, was his best guess. However, if they didn't get him soon, nighttime would become an advantage for Buck. Jonquin knew every inch of ground around here. He could probably slither out and make some strategic escape during the night.

"Damn," Frank mumbled. The sound of his raspy old voice actually scared him. He hadn't heard a human voice for awhile, he figured. Things were not looking up on the home front here. Even this pursuit was happening in the far distance. No one was coming his way; it wasn't a search and rescue effort anymore. "Shit," Frank grumbled as he began to feel sorry for himself.

Even the coyotes were beginning to smell his impending doom. It would be dusk soon, and they would stare down at him imagining a juicy meal. Dusk was the hardest time for Frank. Always had been; it seemed to play chords of despair. It was hard. Hope would vanish with the fading light; that, was Frank's reality. His drinking water was almost gone. He was past being hungry, just weak. He even had to admit that the mouse in the cistern was beginning to look a little tasty. Frank quickly ignored the little critter. Tomorrow, he might have to reconsider.

From his calculations the rally would start tonight. He had to wonder if Tiptop was going to be saved. Donner was a pretty smart cookie and so was Nathan Abel's son, Jackson. Frank did have hope for them at least. He smiled slightly and let out a huge sigh. Tiptop would be crowded; who knew what would happen. The landowners' attempt to keep their claims just had to work.

Frank then stared at his failed attempt to dig steps on the side of the cistern. Even though he had pounded in sticks as handrails, the height of the cistern was just too much. Most likely because he couldn't pull himself up, secure himself then work on both a new step plus handrail at once. He had even tried to use the old rope to stay on the fourth step but it was too old and rotten. Actually, Frank had to admit that his age, plus the need for food and clean water played a huge role in his failed attempt. Frank allowed himself to let out another long sigh.

He would allow himself anything that he wanted at this juncture. Self pity was included. Why hadn't he waited until Captain Jen had gotten back before he had left for Buck Jonquin's place? That question was burning a hole through his stomach right now. He had been so stupid. Just an old man who didn't seem to accept the age factor. He had needed backup. Someone to sense what Buck had been thinking. Someone to get the drop on Jonquin first while Frank tried to talk him down. Captain Jen could have done that for sure. She seemed to always sense the future before it happened. Her mind jumped quickly and correctly. Frank had needed that action; he had needed her. "Damn," he repeated.

Well hell, life goes on he decided when the coyotes yipped and yowled as they began their nighttime hunting with enthusiasm. Stocking up before winter was their priority. At least he was safe from them right now. Later, he couldn't say. He couldn't think about that.

There was one bright spot going for Frank. He had made a sky lantern out of the canvas and sticks. The wick was braided out of the rotten rope. He had saved some of the better rope to tether the lantern above the cistern location. If he finally got lucky and the night noises became human, he could launch the lantern into the sky. He had his lucky flint in his pocket that he always carried for fire. He could hope that someone would see his beacon. Preferably not Buck, however. Buck Jonquin would kill him. Frank would be a trapped goner. Let the team catch that son of bitch. He'd take his chances later.

Frank listened to the assault progress. He figured that possibly he just might be able to interpret what the rifle fire meant. Apprehension would definitely have a different sound to it. Right now it was obvious that the suspect was running somewhere in the distance. Was the action coming closer? He wasn't sure. Patience, he told himself. Frank so desperately needed the action to end at the cistern location. This story had to end with him being found alive. Frank felt a chill crawling up his back. The goose bumps were carrying doubt. He pushed that thought away with force. Maybe death was his ending but, by damn, he'd fight it every inch of the way.

Frank let himself think about a human voice searching for him. Acknowledging him. One human voice. Now even the conflict with Buck sounded better than just sitting here dying. Any human contact would be better than none. He would send that old lantern up no matter what! He fell asleep listening. A little catnap was all that he needed, he told himself. If the assault routine changed, Frank would wake up, he calculated.

Miss Mouse listened to Frank's breathing calm down. She cautiously crept out of her hole to hunt. The mouse began searching for any insects that had fortunately fallen into their common home. Dinner was waiting , she reckoned. The cistern was alive with crawly insects and water condensation. All ripe for the pickings. She gently sniffed at Frank's relaxed hand in greeting. It was definitely nice to have another live being caught in the cistern she thought. Life was looking up for this mouse.

***

It was now late afternoon. Bix Bixler and Bernie Holden had decided to wait before checking out anymore backcountry cabins. They went home to take a break and eat. Frank's rescue would just have to wait; the Tiptop Rally would now become priority. Bix knew that she and Bernie weren't going to be in on the Buck Jonquin capture. If they had any luck during the evening, someone would tell them that the police had got Buck. Or killed Buck, she then thought. This capture had really taken a dark turn. Buck Jonquin was part of the evil no doubt.

The reality was that Jonquin represented a part of the government that wasn't working for the people but for foreign entities and the Regime corruption was from within. The United States was under siege and the mountains were, unfortunately, playing a dangerous role. Bix was sure that there had to be little battles taking place all over the United States. Each aggression meticulously planned by this incredibly powerful opposition. Their forces were also trying to control the media while dividing the country. The public was left both confused and amazed. It was like juggling balls in the air, Bix thought. The massive amount of balls to balance became more prevalent, leaving the public in a position to try and control these attacks.

Be that as it may, tonight was just one of those little ball juggles where a small town had to deal with the corrupt Regime. Tiptop was center stage with the state of Colorado watching closely. The question of control, state or anti-American force, would be decided soon for these mountain people. Water rights and Eminent Domain would be topics in everyone's mind at this rally. Their survival as a small town was indeed in danger. 'Tip the Top for Justice' echoed in Bix's mind. It was the correct slogan, clear and loud, and, unfortunately, up for grabs.

Nevertheless, Bix and Bernie's job tonight

would be much more mundane in nature. Life went on even during a revolution, Bix realized. You had to still take care of the little things like parking. No matter what happened, the public needed to be smoothly transported from the large parking lots on both sides of Tiptop to the protest. Residents of the little town had volunteered their pasture lands on the north and south outskirts of the town to accommodate the cars. People would park and walk or be transported by ATVs plus some volunteer cars. Summit's volunteer parking attendants had come through big time. The transport process would start around 5:30 even though the protest wouldn't start until 7:00.

Bix's mind flashed suddenly on the other small population of Tiptop who denied any problems in the world. The enablers. They had no idea how close this country was to revolution. They simply denied the existence of a foreign power and corruption by ignoring the facts. Denying the media and their neighbors. Just like the stubborn population of Germany during the Nazi Regime. *Mad Magazine* said it best, 'What me worry?' For them, democracy was intact; no big deal. If you didn't recognize a problem then it didn't exist, Bix decided for them.

She shook her head and looked at Bernie. They both were having fairly deep thoughts, Bix realized. How many times had they sat down and talked about the state of affairs? Didn't do any good to rehash the situation now. Bix fell into Bernie's arms and gathered strength silently. They needed a moment too for each other.

Bix had to admit that out of all this current despair, their love became incredibly wonderful. Bix was so proud of Bernie. No denial of the political unrest but the strength to confront it. They were together and that was everything. Confronting the situation was actually therapy in some deluded way. You had to deal and not deny, Bix calculated.

Speaking of dealing, there was the community meeting at 6:00 that Bix wasn't going to miss. Bernie would just have to direct traffic for both of them during that time. It had been decided that the Zoning Committee would meet one hour before the protest. Bix wanted to be there. She and Bernie would probably miss the public speakers beginning at 7 because of their traffic management. People would still be arriving by 7:30 was her bet but the Zoning Committee meeting was crucial to what would be the actual outcome of the evening's events.

Kevin Donner and Jackson Abel, both from the Denver area, had helped arrange the meeting; they had a proposal for the Zoning Committee. Bix had no doubt that these two could very easily determine the Eminent Domain case with some type of proposal. Too many lawyers involved not to have some type of deal offered at the last minute. How intriguing was that, Bix thought. Apparently, Melanie Camp and Ranger John Bend had also been sequestered to talk at this meeting.

Bernie stared at Bix for a moment as they finished their hastily made ham sandwiches. "So what do you think Donner and Abel will tell the committee?" Bernie asked.

Bix tossed a piece of ham to Simon before answering. "I have no idea, but I would think that these landowners have created some type of proposal to halt the Eminent Domain proceedings. You don't invite the Personal Property Coalition and Forest Service CEO's to sit in just for giggles. They must have organized some type of alternative," Bix said then popped her last potato chip into her mouth. "Not being a lawyer, I have no idea. Hopefully, the people of Tiptop will be the winners in this situation."

"Seems like everyone but Frank Mason might be a winner tonight. Damn, I wish we had found him this afternoon. I hope you have some more ideas about where Buck Jonquin might have stashed Frank, and I sure hope he's alive," Bernie added. Her green eyes softening as she spoke. The silence in the room was filled with concern. They were two people trying to strengthen their resolve.

After a long sigh, Bix tried to answer Bernie's question, "I do have a few more places in mind for us to search. Somehow as we drove away from Tiptop today, I became more convinced that he's over there somewhere. Buck didn't have a lot of time to spare. He had to make a quick decision on what to do with Frank. Even with some help, Buck would still have Frank's car in Peak County. I know that the police have set up highway barriers to search cars; the mountain police have been trying to stop Buck Jonquin's escape. It has changed the focus. I would image that even old Jerome Walker has been ordered to search for Frank."

"Somehow that old guy just doesn't seem to be

all that motivated," Bernie added. "Enthusiasm about anything doesn't seem to play well in his mind. I could be wrong but he's down right negative."

"Well, even so, the old geezer does still feel that Tiptop is his responsibility. He was forced to retire from Peak County but he still believes he's the sheriff of Tiptop."

"Hmmm," Bernie mumbled not totally convinced. "Where are we going to look after the protest?" Bernie asked. Her eyes explored Bix's face again. She wasn't quite done with this topic. "Honey, I think Frank is alive. That's what I think," she added.

Bix went deep into her heart at this point. She searched for that answer. As hard as she tried, Bix couldn't imagine that Frank was dead; she just couldn't entertain that thought. The man was a fighter and knew survival skills for the mountains. If anyone could stay alive, it was Frank.

However, looming in the depths of her mind, Bix was beginning to feel a need to hurry. The nights were getting colder. They were close to the first hard freeze, she knew. To think that Frank was tied up and not able to find his way out was definitely concerning. Buck would have made sure that Frank couldn't get away. Damn it.

Frank might be hurt also played through Bix's thoughts. What if Buck had seriously hurt Frank? She couldn't let her mind wrap around that one; the thought was horrible. Lord, keep him safe and lead us to him. "Amen," Bix whispered to herself as they departed for Tiptop. "We will keep looking," she promised Bernie out loud. "God helps those who help themselves," she concluded closing the door of Bernie's car.

Simon was in the back seat delighted to go again. It had been decided that he could wait in the car until after the Eminent Domain meeting. Bix would then bring him along to ride with them as they transported folks to the rally. Maybe they'd have some time to search for Frank later. Who knew; Simon could help he knew.

CHAPTER 24

SCRIMMAGES

It was Tyler looking at her and wagging his big brown shepherd tail. Libby lowered her rifle and inhaled deeply. "Hi boy, you scared me big time. Where's Jerry? Find him, Tyler," she commanded.

The K-9 turned around and headed back through a turn in the arroyo in back of the boulder. Libby crawled after him; she could hear Jerry's rifle fire ahead. Tyler licked Jerry's face to announce their approach. He motioned Libby over to join him.

"We got him on the run. I think we need to push him toward the cliff over to the west. We'll trap him as the other teams begin to move in. Those reinforcements are going to join us soon. "Head out, Libby, and keep moving Jonquin toward the cliffs. If you can signal Bill to join you, let him know the plan." Jerry then aimed his rifle in Buck's direction and crawled ahead another four feet. The slow charge was on!

Libby circled back around and slithered out of

the arroyo then headed west. She could see Bill on her right. With hand motions, Libby made two fingers walking toward the cliffs. As she pointed at them, Bill nodded and moved ahead. Their advancement began.

Detective Bill Smith let off a barrage of fire angled so that any eastern movement by Buck wouldn't happen. He then crawled forward. Suddenly from overhead, the whirling rotor noise of an approaching helicopter startled him. His concentration had been so focused that he had missed the distant sounds of the machine. The dust began to spin around him. Bill covered his face for a few seconds until they landed some hundred feet away from him.

From the bowels of the copter came at least ten more policemen clothed in military garb. They advanced toward Bill's position. He waved and made eye contact with the troops. They covered the distance quickly to Bill's position. "We're herding the suspect toward the cliffs so he will be trapped and surrounded," Bill shouted over the copter lift off noise. "Cover the area to the east and west so he will not try to escape from our perimeter. He has been occasionally throwing dynamite in our direction by the way. Make sure that you keep an eye on how close you are to him. His rifle scope is accurate up to 300 feet." The team nodded and took off without a word. Bill fired several rounds for cover as the team moved into the formation.

From the air, the copter pilot surveyed the situation before he radioed into command. "The teams have perp surrounded and moving toward the

Ute Buttes. Ten officers covering west, HAPT is in the center and another team is to the east. Perp will be surrounded and trapped within ten minutes. 10-4."

Captain Jen and Chief Josh Anderson from Breckenridge were both listening. It was a chess game, Jen thought quickly. She grabbed a piece of paper and drew the battle dimensions using x's to signify their men and a circle for Buck Jonquin.

Josh began to scurry through the pile of maps to locate the Ute Buttes. "The terrain is extremely rugged and steep. Looks like you'd need climbing gear to go over the top. Plus, Jonquin would be a sitting target if he started to climb," Chief Anderson said.

"That leaves either surrender or charging the teams in a suicide attempt," Captain Jen calculated. "Unless he has enough dynamite to light up the area. I have a feeling that he would rather die trying to escape before surrender. What has he got to lose at this point?" Jen asked. Her mind began to spin. What would she do became the question. "Where's Frank's car in relation to this battle?"

Chief Josh Anderson scanned the computer screen and found the GPS location of Frank's abandoned car. It is due east some two miles in the distance! "He'll be moving east immediately then if that's his plan!" Josh yelped.

Captain Jen then communicated her commands into the radio for all teams to hear. "Jonquin will begin an assault on the eastern side of the Buttes. He is armed with dynamite and will begin using it any moment. His goal is to reach the vehicle on

Smoky Quartz Claim two miles east of your position. Do you read? 10-4."

"We hear you loud and clear," was the unanimous answers.

Detective Jerry Neal is now in charge of this operation, be so advised," Jen commanded leaving no doubt in any of their minds.

Immediately, Jerry came on the air not missing a beat. "Breckenridge East Team retreat as the dynamite begins. Line East Team and West Team along his route but do not charge the suspect. Do you read? Do not charge him. 10-4."

"We read. Moving out now. 10-4."

"West Team, pull in your ranks tight so that the suspect will not advance in your direction. Stand down with your firing at this time. Create a line that contains but do not advance."

"10-4," West Team answered.

"HAPT, move out and head directly for GPS coordinates of Frank's car. Chief Marshall Tate is there and standing guard. He will need HAPT as reinforcements. Now move!. Tyler and I are moving out now. Catch up with us! 10-4."

"Moving out. 10-4," was the comment from HAPT.

Captain Jen then commanded both copters to send observations back to the command post. Copter Two was commanded to watch Chief Tate's stakeout closely. Jen then radioed Marshall who had been listening. "Chief Tate, do you read?"

"I do and am positioned near the car but not in it. Jonquin will probably have kept at least one stick of dynamite just in case he thinks there is a stakeout."

"Good plan," Josh broke in. He then stared directly at Jen. She knew exactly what the order given now had to be.

"Apprehend suspect if possible, Chief Tate. Frank's location is priority. Do not, however, let Buck Jonquin escape at any cost. Do you read? 10-4."

"I read, loud and clear. 10-4."

Chief Josh Anderson nodded at Captain Jen. She had made the right call. Now Tate's training would play a huge role in the capture of Buck Jonquin. They just had to wait and see what would happen next.

***

Marshall Tate began to sweat. He realized that his location was going to get mighty busy. He examined his surroundings carefully. It was now time to decide where Jonquin was most likely to enter the perimeter. The road was not an option; the copters could spot him too easily. There were cliffs to the east and arid terrain to the west with very little cover available. Marshall examined the center approach. "Yeah. Right down this terrain using shrubs and gullies for cover," he mumbled. It was the best option, Tate decided.

Marshall then focused on Buck Jonquin's transportation. He opened the car door and calculated Jonquin's actions. Buck would go there first and try the ignition key. Why not have him get into the SUV then and try to turn over the motor? Buck would then be focused on the car instead of him. Time to disconnect the starter, Marshall decided.

He left the key in the ignition and proceeded to pop the hood. He quickly disconnected spark plug covers. For good measure he then pulled off the wires and threw them into the bushes. This car needed to be totally disarmed; he couldn't take any chances on that one.

Now it was time to figure out where his position would be for the arrest. He closed the hood quietly and began to inspect his surroundings. He couldn't be seen from the rearview mirror and/or side mirrors. Okay then. Marshall Tate focused on the closest areas. His intense blue eyes narrowed. There was a sinkhole in the ground some three feet deep and fifteen feet from the car. It was shaped like a small basin. Could be natural or an old grave; either way, it was perfect.

There was a convenient pile of weathered wood next to the hole. Bingo! An old miner must have dug it, he calculated . Some landowner could have had a test well going here; the well had come up dry or the guy had never come back. Actually, he thought, it didn't really matter how it got there; the point was that it was close to the SUV and perfect for his cover location.

Marshall carefully moved the longest old boards over the sinkhole balancing them like a roof. He went back to where he had displaced the weathered wood and left enough there to cover his disturbance. Buck was trained to look for such clues; Marshall couldn't take any chances. His cover would be on the passenger side of the vehicle and hopefully out of sight for awhile. He crawled into the cavity and made sure that he could observe Buck Jonquin's approach. He carefully pulled a gray stocking cap over his blond hair just in case. Now it was time to wait.

At 6:00 p.m. promptly and some 400 feet away, Marshall thought he had caught a glimpse of movement. Were his eyes fooling him or had that actually happened? He shook his head to pull the observation into total focus. Marshall raised his binoculars up to spot the location. He held his breath. Yes, that damn bush was moving!

It was not an apparition but a well trained military man in a perfectly camouflaged ghillie suit. There were even branches sticking up to illustrate new growth. The detailed suit blended into the terrain colors precisely. The retired military sniper had decorated the ghillie suit with sage and bush remains from the area! Marshall marveled at the detail. However, the giveaway was that it moved some ten feet at a time. Watching patiently, Marshall could finally detect Jonquin's boots out the back of the suit. The man's disguise was almost perfect except for the boots! This was one professional military sniper ready for combat. Marshall began to sweat again.

***

The High Altitude Pursuit Team rushed ahead. Tyler had moved out in front of Libby, Bill and Jerry. The Shepherd would occasionally glance back to make sure that they were all present and running. Detective Jerry Neal had decided to let the

K-9 lead them on Buck Jonquin's trail; time was of the essence. He couldn't stop to find footprints. Their orders were to keep moving. The capture was priority.

Up ahead, Jerry could see a small open meadow. Tyler had slowed down and began sniffing around the area frantically. Somewhat frustrated by the delay, Jerry halted the team. Something just wasn't right. The three took cover and watched. No one seemed to be there so they, again, began to slowly move forward. Their eyes scanned the area intensely.

Near the back of the meadow, Jerry spotted a black metal bipod with a mounted AR-15 attached; it was aimed in their direction. It peeked out of the long wildflower stems. The 30mm scope mounted on the rifle was an accurate and lethal accessory to say the least. Detective Neal dropped quickly to the ground; Libby and Bill followed suit. Their eyes questioned him; he pointed at his discovery.

The team focused and listened. The atmosphere was quiet. Only Tyler's activity made any sounds. Their eyes watched the K-9's intensity as he circled and sniffed. The AR-15 aimed toward them was like an evil ghost. It peered out of the dried wildflower stems with barrel pointed directly at them. The sheer evil and potential of this weapon now had their full attention.

They crawled closer. Jerry couldn't help but stare at the barrel. It was mesmerizing. The black rifle was on guard even though it stood abandoned. Why was it here? Where was Jonquin, Jerry wondered?

The team was now 20 feet from this weapon. The rifle's history was so lethal, he thought. It had been used in Iraq and Afghanistan. The scope accuracy was within 1.1 inch at 300 feet. Had Buck run out of ammunition, Jerry wondered? What was the reason?

The German Shepherd began to growl at them as they got within 10 feet of the rifle. Tyler began barking and wagging his tail at the same time. At first Jerry didn't understand then suddenly he knew! The rifle's magazine wasn't empty! Tyler knew; he had combat training!

"Stop!" Jerry yelled. "Watch your footsteps! Tyler is indicating an IED somewhere in our vicinity. Backtrack! Follow your own footsteps backwards and be careful for heaven's sake!" Jerry exclaimed.

CHAPTER 25

STRATEGIES

Promptly at 5:45 pm Bix Bixler walked toward the courthouse. She quickly moved through the overflow crowd at the entrance and wrestled her way into the rotunda. Now, Bix could hear the spectator noise from the courtroom upstairs. She climbed the old wooden stairs quickly.

Obviously, the Zoning Committee had thoughtfully scheduled the largest room in the building, the courtroom. Still, this room was brimming with the noisy audience. Unbelievable, Bix thought. You prepare for an event like this, but you never quite understand the ramifications until you're there. Jerome Walker, the old retired Peak County Sheriff, was actually managing the courtroom doors. He nodded to her and opened the door for her. Bix was relieved to know that she was on the proper attendance list.

The meeting was packed! The importance for Tiptop, Colorado, was so obvious . After these people voiced their defiance, the legal team's battle would begin, Bix mused. This case would, eventually, end up in the court system. Who would have thought it? It would be interesting to see Betsy Jonquin's handling of this boisterous crowd, Bix speculated as she looked around the room.

Emma Keiser, from the gallery seating, waved her hand in Bix's direction; she had saved her a seat. Bix voiced the customary 'excuse me' comments down the row until she landed next to Emma. They both rolled their eyes at each other signaling their shock at the immensity of the audience. "Incredible," Bix Bixler whispered to Emma.

"I know. I got here at 5:00 and it looked like this then. Who are all of these people?" Emma asked as she looked around.

"State and national representatives? There must be a ton of lawyers in this room," Bix surmised. Her eyes then spotted the state contingency perched four rows back from the front. They sat silently staring straight ahead. The not-so-silent media occupied the last two rows on both sides of the aisle in the gallery. Their reserved seating was busy and noisy. "The news media is eating this up," Bix mumbled as she leaned toward her friend. "I guess that's a good thing," she added trying to convince herself more than Emma Keiser.

Dispersed throughout the rest of the courtroom gallery were the concerned people of Tiptop all packed in like sardines in a tin can. The frustration and amazement epitomized their expressions; their town had been invaded!

If Emma hadn't been nervous before, she was now. In her left hand she held her speech for the rally and with her right hand she grabbed Bix. They sat holding hands for support. "Haven't ever seen this many people come to a county meeting in all my life," Emma whispered. "I don't know half of these people in this room," she added. Her eyes registered total 'deer-in-the-headlights.'

Overwhelmed best described Emma and the local residents, Bix decided. "Me neither if it makes you feel better," Bix said as she scanned the multitude. Bix then began to look closely at the composition of the crowd. Actually, it did make sense, she observed. The opposing parties had taken opposite sides of the room. Strangely enough, Kevin Donner and Jackson Abel had organized their group in the defense area, while Capital Regime occupied the prosecution side of the courtroom. All the Capital Regime lawyers were adorned in expensive suits that were inappropriate for Tiptop. The cost of their shoes alone would have financed the town's budget for a year. Clicking briefcases and whispers occupied their focus. The Regime Representatives were two rows deep. The heap of paperwork on the front desk was being arranged by a group of four lawyers who were, obviously, leading this delegation.

To combat this legal government army, were three very determined men, Jackson Abel, Kevin Donner and one meager lawyer. They sat stolidly silent waiting for the proceedings to begin. It was obvious that what they were going to present had already been organized and prepared.

Their advocates sat behind them. Bix was surprised to see Millie Jean Marvel from the Clerk and Recording Office there. She was dressed appropriately for court and held a folder of information tightly to her chest. Also in the same row was Nathan Abel, Jackson's father, back from Sourdough Gulch as expected. His expression was one of reluctant attendance and discomfort. He looked absolutely trapped. Forest Service Ranger John Bend and Melanie Camp from the Personal Property Coalition finished out the row. Jackson Abel and Kevin Donner's team was ready. Melanie Camp talked quietly with a gentleman on her right. Bix figured that Melanie had brought a lawyer for advice and support from the Coalition.

"Martin would be shocked by all these goings on," Emma whispered to Bix.

"I'd think that he is probably having a good giggle up in heaven over all this commotion. Martin always did like a good murder mystery," Bix added. "Don't you think that he sensed how important the property had become?" she asked Emma.

Emma Keiser sighed and thought that question over for a few moments. "I suppose you're right. Martin did know what Eminent Domain was going to do to our little community. Water rights were never lost on Martin; he knew how important they were. Ever since the Dillon Reservoir was constructed by Denver, Martin had been wise to that trick. Back in the fifties and sixties," Emma continued, "people were living in their own 'Sleepy Hollow' thinking that water was a right and not a commodity. The lawyers knew, didn't they? Now, here we are facing a fascist government trying to take control of our water and land. My dear husband just didn't realize that he would be the first rock to fall in this drama," Emma added while shaking her head.

Bix tightened her grip on Emma's hand. "I know." The circumstances should have been different, Bix thought. Buck Jonquin didn't have to murder Martin, she calculated. "Your husband was a good man, Emma. In fact, I think this whole case of Eminent Domain could have been handled with less publicity if Martin hadn't been murdered. You have good neighbors, Emma. They do understand the worth of land and water. Please remember that Martin didn't die in vain. Fate had a purpose for him and it just might have been to save the whole town of Tiptop."

"Thank you, Bix. Sometimes, a person loses sight of the big picture when grief settles in," Emma confessed. "My speech will be for Martin; may God rest his soul," she declared.

Finally, the judge's door opened and the Zoning Committee members began to enter. Bix and Emma then realized that Betsy Jonquin was absent from the group. In her place stood a gentleman who was not from Tiptop. His presence brought recognition from the media and left the Tiptop spectators curious.

This impressive stranger had to be from the Colorado Capitol, Bix concluded. He remained standing after the committee members sat down. His imposing presence spoke volumes. The tall blond stranger simply waited until the entire room became silent before he spoke. "Ladies and Gentlemen, I am Attorney General Warren Hopper. I was requested by the Tiptop Zoning Committee to represent the State of Colorado in this preliminary meeting. I have agreed to facilitate this meeting in the absence of Mrs. Betsy Jonquin. Mrs. Jonquin has recused herself from the proceedings. Her husband, Buck Jonquin, is now being sought by the police as a person of interest in the murder of Martin Keiser, and, therefore, her request for recusal has been granted."

The audience let out an audible gasp! The community now realized how their little world would change forever. These proceedings had just elevated into the history books. State rights versus national rights were in the balance. Whatever happened here today would create a precedence for any and all states who sought the freedom to govern their own people and property. Not to mention, the fact that one of Tiptop's own was now deeply involved in the murder and abduction of a police officer, Bix deduced. How much more real could it get, she thought? Tiptop, was now listening in shocked silence.

Suddenly, a jolt of a very different kind hit Bix. She hadn't expected this premonition at all! Like an explosive force, Frank Mason's psyche overwhelmed her thoughts. His spirit hit her like a hammer sending her heart pounding. Frank was calling for help; she knew it! The importance of the proceedings became irrelevant. She and Bernie needed to find Frank now! "Emma, I have to go. You'll be fine and the town will be fine but Frank needs help. I just know it!"

Bix didn't wait for Emma to answer. She got up and immediately began to exit. As she left, her eyes frantically searched the room for any signs of the HAPT Police Officers. Bix wanted desperately to talk with Captain Jen Holly, but it was not to be; none of the team was there. Who else could help? Bix froze for a second before she departed the room. She searched the gallery faces for help one last time. She then left, shutting the old wooden doors quietly.

Bix was surprised to find that the rotunda was now empty. The overflow crowd had abandoned the courthouse for the rally. Her thoughts shifted gears. She needed to find Bernie, and they needed to get some help. An idea popped into her mind as she ran down the steps and out into the dusk. Maybe, she did know someone who could help.

***

Frank pulled himself up into a sitting position once again. He had awakened this time with a jolt. His body had twitched sending an electrical shock wave throughout his being; this uncontrollable force attacked with pain. His suffering was now immense. Frank would have peed his pants with the jolt if he had not been so dehydrated.

He hadn't wanted to wake up. It was night now. His constant dreams were far better than this ugly reality. Relentless chills dominated his consciousness. They ripped through his nerves; it was like being buried in the cold moist ground with zero control over your body. Frank had been thrown in this grave alive. His life was ebbing away. The chills constantly reminded him how weak he was becoming.

Frank had to admit that he was weaker. Who was he kidding, he was becoming a lot weaker. There was no comfort in being awake anymore. The semi-conscious state beckoned him back. It was a blessing to abandon the cistern; to be swept away into deep vivid dreams.

Frank plunged into visions of his youth. He was a young man again, climbing the mountains with contentment. The young man smiled as he hiked through his alpine surroundings. The smells of summer beckoned him and filled the breeze caressing his body. Green pine filled his nostrils and the sun beat down on his face. A much younger Frank climbed easily with the renewed energy of youth.

Frank was so thirsty. A small stream appeared in the alpine meadow that he had entered. The water had dug a deep trench in the moist earth. Soft green grass and watercress clung to the shore of the deep narrow stream. He cupped his hands and tasted the cold mountain water. The water origin so near to him. This water so clear and pure; he was the first recipient. It was, oh, so inviting and good.

The old man smacked his lips loudly as he tasted the imaginary water. His tortured body then produced another spasm that shook Frank awake. The stark damp cistern encompassed him. How uninviting the old man realized again…and again. Frank's fight was exhausting. His energy was spent, so depleted. Why bother, Frank admitted to himself. He allowed himself to snuggle back into his semi coma.

Miss Mouse was closely watching Frank from the entrance of her domicile. She was beginning to feel less intimidated by her human companion each day. As Frank began to slip more often into sleep, Miss Mouse began to be more curious about his condition. Somehow, this little creature was beginning to sense that her human companion might not be around much longer.

Actually, in a cold hearted way, a decaying body would bring more insects into her life. There would be months of a carcass feeding frenzy. That circumstance would be a good thing for her survival. However, the smell of decay could bring predators into her existence. If a coyote got down here, she'd be in extreme danger. Oh, my!

Miss Mouse had no control over the situation. Life was that way. She had to admit that there was enjoyment in their strange companionship. The human even talked to her now and then. He hadn't ever threatened her. Co-existence wasn't so bad; she'd leave it at that for now. A moth had just landed on Frank's pant leg. Miss Mouse rustled over for the kill. It would be a tasty treat.

***

Chief Marshall Tate quietly put his binoculars down in his sinkhole cover. He could now watch Jonquin's approach without them. The sniper was making his way to Frank Mason's car with extreme caution. Buck Jonquin finally tossed half of his ghillie suit to the side and proceeded in a crouched position for the last 20 feet. Marshall could hardly breathe as he watched a hand come up out of the remaining costume and open the driver's side door. Buck slithered in and turned the key. Quiet. Nothing. Marshall could actually hear Buck exhale as he whispered, "Fuck."

Jonquin froze for a second as he absorbed the unexpected reality. He then made his decision. Buck Jonquin, bolted with lightning speed across the seat then throwing the passenger door wide open! His compact AR-15 began to spray bullets in all directions. His fire exploded while his darkened eyes searched the area. The choice of Jonquin's escape door was what Marshall had expected. However, he had not expected Jonquin's instant attack. The bullets enveloped the entire area until Buck Jonquin saw the weathered wood pile. His eyes narrowed; Buck had his target. He took aim.

"Stop. Hold it. You're under arrest!" Marshall yelled one second before Buck sought cover behind a boulder then launched a massive amount of ammo toward him. The bullets hit all around Marshall sending dirt and metallic smells into his nostrils. The constant fire tore splinters from the wood and hurled them into Marshall's skin. The noise was deafening; he covered his face and flattened against the ground. Jonquin wasn't going to throw his guns down and surrender. There was no room for a peaceful capture, Marshall realized.

Chief Marshall Tate pulled himself out of his cover and rushed toward the car. He would have to be able to fire back from another position for any advantage. He quickly shot four rounds in Buck's vicinity, hoping to get him out from behind the boulder.

Jonquin must have stopped to reload another magazine into his AR-15. The man then came out just like Marshall had hoped. Marshall fired ten rounds directly at him as fast as he could. The havoc of continuous fire brought results. Marshall had aimed low trying to keep Jonquin alive. At least one of the ten rounds must have hit. There was a pause.

It became quiet, deafeningly quiet. Almost uncanny, Marshall mused. Finally, he could feel his body breathing again. His ears were still ringing as he slowly advanced toward Jonquin's body. The man's darkened face registered no response; his eyes glazed over and were lifeless. Marshall leaned down and felt for a pulse. None. The man was dead. Marshall inspected Jonquin's legs for any direct hits but couldn't find any evidence.

Then, he saw that one bullet hole in Jonquin's upper chest. It was located specifically above his protective vest. How could that be, Marshall wondered? He knew that he had deliberately aimed low. Maybe a ricochet or something? Marshal sat back on his haunches and thought.

Well, all sorts of strange things did happen in combat, he speculated. You just had to wait for ballistics to have the final say, Marshall decided. Still…it was strange and too simple.

A major frustration now hit Marshall. He realized that there would be no information about

Frank Mason's whereabouts from this corpse. Yep, that was the bottom line, Marshall thought. He just hated the outcome. Hated the fact that he couldn't do anything about it.

A couple minutes later, Marshall heard the HAPT Officers approaching. Tyler came bounding out of the gulley some 30 feet from Chief Tate. Marshall hadn't reported in the kill yet; he had been lost in the surreal outcome. The K-9's appearance brought him back to reality. He reached out and petted Tyler who had now sat down with him next to the body. The warmth of the dog brought Marshall's focus back. The drain of combat had sucked away all his energy. He really did feel exhausted.

"Marshall!" yelled Libby who came bounding out of the gulley. She approached quickly and suddenly realized that her, 'knight in shining armor,' hadn't quite recovered from the conflict. She could feel that something was wrong. "What happened?" she whispered sitting down beside him. Her hand found his as she stared into his eyes. There weren't any signs of a wound, she noticed. "You okay?"

"Kind of," he mumbled. "I wanted to find the answers about Frank and bring this creep in alive. None of that was possible and it doesn't exactly make sense."

Jerry and Bill joined the two. They sat down to listen. Marshall recounted the confrontation as best he could. "It was like I didn't shoot him. I fired ten rounds all at the ground up and yet he was hit in the chest. I don't get it," Marshall finished.

After a few moments, Jerry went over to the body and inspected the entrance wound. He took several pictures and then rolled the body over and inspected the exit wound. The others watched him silently. It was intriguing.

Finally, Jerry announced, "That's because you didn't kill him."

"What?" they all said in unison.

"You didn't kill him, unless you were standing behind him. The entrance wound is in his back. Check it out," Jerry added and pointed. The officers moved closer and examined the wound.

"How do you know?" Libby asked Jerry.

"The skin tells the direction of the bullet by which way it folds. I'll bet that he was hit with a 45mm. not your 9mm. Check out the size of the opening," Jerry added.

"If Marshall hadn't killed Jonquin, who did?" Libby asked in shock. "And, more importantly, where did the killer go?"

The team began to inspect their surroundings; their guns were raised and Tyler was out circling the area trying to catch the scent.

Marshall quickly reported to the Command Center. His message then sent the Command into another tailspin.

A high alert was issued by Captain Jen Holly to all the area police. BOLO was sent out statewide. "Be on the lookout for a fleeing suspect headed out of Peak County. Approach with extreme caution!"

CHAPTER 26

TESTIMONY

"Therefore, it is the opinion of the Forest Service that to allow these landowners to donate their claims to the State of Colorado is in the public's best interest," stated Ranger John Bend. "Open land is a vital part of preserving our Colorado wildlife. The Forest Service whole heartedly agree, with their proposal." John Bend let his breath out. He was being questioned by both sides. It was indeed a 'hot seat.' He kept his focus as best he could.

"We completely disagree with Ranger Bend. The National Mandate must be honored," retorted the Regime Lawyer as he stood up. "This case of Eminent Domain is for our national security," Lawyer-Suit-Number-One emphasized. "Therefore, it is far more important to our nation than the existence of some state wildlife preservation. The nation, as a whole, would receive benefits from this claim that far outweigh the meager pleasure of a newly established reserve. In fact, our administration has made it perfectly clear that national security exceeds any state preservation of wildlife. Capital Regime has continuously removed all environmental laws for that reason; the national economy and security must be the priority goal."

"Please sit down and let Ranger Bend finish his statement, sir," AG Hopper applied the wooden gavel as he took control again. "This meeting has already given you ample time to present your case. It is in the best interest of this committee and the state to hear the Forest Service Representative's testimony," AG Hopper declared. He then waited for order.

The crowd now understood why the governor had sent AG Hopper to Tiptop. His attendance brought a much needed balance to the proceedings. Lawyer-Suit-Number-One finally sat down. The 'suit' released a dramatic sigh of frustration as he reluctantly became silent.

Hopper turned his focus on Ranger Bend, "Do you have any more comments before we move on?"

"Actually I do. Specifically, the river is very important to various fish populations and other forest wildlife. Wildlife recreation is a major resource in Colorado. Our state thrives when tourists, from all over the world, can recreate and spend money in Colorado. Not to mention that this water commodity belongs to all ranchers, miners and other citizens of many states. State covenants say that the property owners can't change the river flow or accessibility for good reason. The river flow allows survival for everyone from here to California. This origin of water has an enormous effect on our nation. When dams interfere with the flow, the repercussions are immense and damaging. Water evaporates when man interferes with the quality and quantity of this natural resource. The process of purification is extremely important to our environment."

Ranger Bend then took a breath before finishing his presentation. He allowed himself some opinions as he continued, "Why should the Regime Government be allowed to intervene when their intent is not for the good of the people but for government control of that population? Water is the right of the people. Water is a moving commodity that brings life to any existing landscape and population through crops and public consumption. To confiscate this commodity from the public, is outrageously wrong."

The crowd came unglued at this point. The Regime Delegation looked cautiously around the room. It was becoming a little uncomfortable for them.

"Order!" Attorney General Hopper yelled and banged the gavel once again. He stared down the noise and then proceeded. "Any more questions for Ranger Ben."

There was silence. "Thank you, Ranger Bend, for coming today. Did you say that an urgent call will necessitate that you leave this meeting? Is that what I heard?"

"Yes, sir."

"In that case, thank you and enjoy your day," AG Hopper said with a smile. "We appreciate your input."

"Thank you." John Bend rushed down the aisle quickly. He was dialing a number on his phone as he departed.

Attorney General Hopper then checked his list of advocate speakers and looked at Millie Jean. "It would seem to me that the second speaker should describe for us the exact location and amount of property that is being contested here today. Because Ranger Bend had an important commitment, his testimony was given first call. Now, let's begin at the beginning, shall we? Miss Millie Jean Marvel from the Clerk and Recorder Office of Peak County has consented to specifically outline the properties involved in this Eminent Domain case. Miss Marvel?"

Millie Jean pulled herself out of her chair and approached the bench. After sitting down, she threw a lethal stare at the Regime contingency. Her countenance emanated authority. Millie Jean Marvel was not someone to be easily intimidated. No one was going to tell her where those properties were located; her research was meticulous. She then opened her designated file and began to read. "These patented mining claims," she pronounced clearly, "are located...."

***

All HAPT Officers were out searching like blood hounds. The kill would possess some type of pattern for the officers. Libby was searching for cartridges near Buck's body. Marshall and Bill were searching to the west. The arid terrain would give them some clues on sniper location; it was only a matter of time. Jerry and his dog were circling east. Time was of the essence.

Tyler's nose inhaled deeply as he and Detective Jerry Neal inspected the sage and boulders. Jerry had, in his mind, drawn an imaginary line between Buck Jonquin's dead body and the outer perimeter. Whoever shot Buck in the back had to keep himself out of the line of fire and Marshall's vision. It just made sense. Jerry's position was farther out than the rest of the officers at this time. There was no doubt in his mind that this sniper had good aim.

Tyler stopped abruptly at a bush and smelled. He sat down in recognition of something. Jerry examined the bush closely and discovered that it looked like something had happened near the bush. Leaves were scattered on the nearby ground. That was interesting, he thought.

The K-9 then sniffed the air and circled farther out until he, again, sat down and looked at Jerry. Obviously, some other sign had surfaced. Jerry then inspected the area and stared down in disbelief at the tracks. It was like something out of the Old West; history was repeating itself, he reckoned. Yep howdy, the clues were there yelling for attention. "Hey! Over here!" he yelled.

The group gathered and stared down at the horse tracks. They were obviously fresh. "So our sniper rides a horse?" Libby asked somewhat shocked and intrigued.

"Yep. It is entirely possible," Jerry said as his eyes, once again, scanned the horizon. Let's report into the Command Center, then follow the horse tracks!"

He tapped transmit and waited.

"Captain Holly here. I hope you have found a lead. 10-4."

"Would you believe that our second sniper is on horseback?" Jerry announced.

"Nothing in this case surprises me anymore. Will change the BOLO details to include horse and trailer. 10-4."

"We're in pursuit. Have the other teams start heading due Northeast from their positions. We'll sweep this area in a full run. 10-4."

"10-4," Captain Jen replied.

***

"Thank you, Mr. Nathan Able for telling us about your interaction with the government officials and the events in Sourdough Gulch," AG Hopper announced. Nathan nodded at him. He figured now he was off the hook. He settled back in his chair in the gallery.

Attorney General Hopper took this occasion to summarize what the Zoning Committee had heard so far. "We now know that Nathan Abel has, at this time, quit claim deeded the Smoky Quartz Claim to his son, Jackson Abel. Miss Millie Jean Marvel has verified that the correct title transfer papers have, indeed, been filed. Please let the minutes reflect this change in ownership."

Attorney General Hopper paused to take a few notes before he moved on with the proceedings. "Another transfer of ownership has also been filed and verified. This is, of course, that all the claim owners have joined together and formed the Tiptop Wildlife Sanctuary. Am I correct?" The claim owners nodded.

The crowd murmured happily at this time. AG Hopper allowed them a few moments of talk before he continued, "We will now need each landowner to verify this action verbally. Hopper began:"

"Mr. Wally Hall?"

"You betcha," Wally said loudly and proudly.

"Mrs. Emma Keiser?"

"Yes," Emma said.

"Mr. Kevin Donner?"

"Yes, sir," Kevin declared.

"Mr. Jackson Abel?"

"Yes, sir," Jackson said.

"Let the minutes reflect that all of the claim owners have now, on record, verified their intentions to consolidate their properties into the Tiptop Wildlife Sanctuary. At this time I believe it would be appropriate to hear the details from the Tiptop Wildlife Sanctuary Representative, Mr. Kevin Donner. Are the claim owners in agreement that he can represent your views?"

"We are," was the resounding response.

***

"Are we ready to go?" asked Ranger John Bend.

"Thank you so much for reading my text and responding," Bix Bixler said. "Bernie and I aren't quite sure how to begin this search. We don't know the area that well."

"Well, Bix, it sounded like you were going to go with or without me. I think it's safer for you two to have the Forest Service with you. Don't you think?"

"I know you're right. Sorry that I came on so strong but, somehow, I just have this feeling that Frank really needs us. Intuition, I confess," Bix said.

"And you think that Buck dumped him somewhere up on one of these claims?" John eyed her closely.

"Yes," Bix stated.

"I wish we had more to go on," John said as he opened his truck door for the ladies and Simon.

"Me too," Bix mumbled.

Bernie Holden had been quiet up until now. She hoped that maybe there was something else in Frank's message to uncover. She asked as they left Tiptop and started toward the Freedom Mine, "Did you sense anything? Smell anything during the premonition?"

Ranger John Bend looked around at Bernie hesitantly, then he went with it also. "Yeah, like did you hear anything in the background, sense anything?"

"You know I did feel cold but that could just be caused by the whole premonition thing. It wasn't like he was talking to me. It was an image in the darkness…." Bix added.

"Close your eyes and see if you can remember anything else," Bernie prodded.

Ranger Bend nodded his encouragement. He

knew of stranger things that had happened during his life time. Why not? "Describe it. Tell me more," he added as the truck rolled over the dirt road.

Bix concentrated while holding Simon. Bernie and John rode silently giving her space. They were a mile from the Freedom Mine now. Dusk was settling over the mountains. John felt that this outing was probably a wild goose chase, but who knew? Logic hadn't been able to find Frank Mason. The police and HAPT were now so damn busy chasing the bad guys that Frank's disappearance was on the back burner.

John had read a police text during the meeting about the death of Buck Jonquin. He couldn't believe that another sniper had surfaced and on horseback! Of course this whole event had been crazy not to mention the predicament that Tiptop had gotten itself into. It just proved that ignorance was not bliss.

"It felt cold and moldy. Dark…and there was this strange echo." Bix mused. "Lots of silence though," she added.

John's mind brought forth some options. It had to be an enclosure of some sort. "I've got a few possibilities," he said. "Lets stop here at the mine. There's a hidden way to get in that most people don't know about. I bet Buck knew about it. We could see if there's any prints near the entrance." He slowed the truck down and crept around to the back.

***

The HAPT officers focused on Tyler moving

ahead now. He had the scent and it must have been strong. The horse was in a full gallop, Jerry calculated, from the length of the hoof strides. The horseback sniper was definitely traveling rapidly; the chase was on.

The sun was close to the top of the mountains; it would soon disappear and make their pursuit twice as difficult. The team moved swiftly climbing in elevation. Their boots thumped the dirt in unison; Tyler's pants accompanied their movement. The group found themselves suddenly back on the old mining road heading east. They could now move quickly. Their weapons were locked and loaded.

Jerry abruptly raised his arm and halted the team. He flipped on his radio and transmitted in a whisper, "We are now on the mining trail again heading east. I believe we are probably within a half a mile of our suspect. Be advised. 10-4." He flipped off the radio and they proceeded on this path.

Chief Marshall Tate was thankful that he was also a runner. He had not understood how physically fit this team was until now. His respect was growing with each stride; they moved at a very fast pace. He imagined that they might just be traveling as fast as that horse. Marshall glanced over at Libby who moved in tempo with ease. Thank heavens that he had started running with her in the mornings. The elevation was beginning to feel more comfortable for him now. Libby was a good trainer.

As they rounded a bend in the road, Jerry, suddenly smelled horse. It was faint but on the wind. They were now closer than half a mile. The team began to sense the upcoming confrontation. Detective Bill Smith checked his ammo quantity. He was now thankful that he had added some more brass this morning for the occasion. In the distance they heard a soft whinny.

"It won't be long now," Libby whispered.

***

"Therefore, it is the contention of the Personal Property Coalition that the terms of imminent domain are not valid in this situation. These landowners have joined together and created a trust that, in essence, donates these properties to the State of Colorado. It is their intent that the state will create the Tiptop Wildlife Sanctuary," Melanie Camp announced.

The spectators went wild with cheering and clapping. Attorney General Hopper banged the gavel to calm them down. He paused for their compliance. "Ladies and gentlemen, you must allow the speaker to talk without being quite so vocal. The audience repented.

"Therefore, this specific claim donation will benefit the community of Tiptop and also the public of America. Mr. Donner has informed us that there will be no admission fees; that all of the public, instate or out-of-state, will be allowed to use this refuge freely. This proposal meets all standards for public recreation. In fact foreign tourists will enjoy the benefits of this area and spend money in the United States. It will also meet the standard for water zoning."

"How so?" asked Attorney General Hopper.

"The ordinances that the state has grandfathered in about water ownership clarifies that all of Colorado utilizes the water as it simply passes through the state within its original flow. No alternatives in direction is needed or advised. And actually, Colorado law prohibits any disturbance of flow," Melanie Camp declared.

She then continued, "The Personal Property Coalition would have to contest in court any changes suggested by either Colorado or the existing Regime. Those proceedings could, of course, take years and the cost would be prohibitive," Melanie added. "This Zoning Committee would find themselves in the middle of any court dispute, and they would also share a proportion of the expense."

One of the Regime constituency stood and announced pompously, "Of course, the Capital Regime Government would be responsible for any court expense that would accrue in this case. We would not take it lightly and definitely would contest this case strenuously. The Zoning Committee would have our full financial backing."

"Thank you for clarifying the government's position, sir," Attorney General Hopper said. "It would seem now appropriate that we hear from the Tiptop Wildlife Sanctuary representative. Mr. Kevin Donner, are you ready?"

"Yes, sir," Kevin Donner said as he left his chair and brought forward the proposed contract.

"So please summarize for us the proposed contract with the State of Colorado for this Tiptop

Wildlife Sanctuary, Mr. Donner," AG Hopper requested. He eyed Kevin Donner with interest. So much policy was at stake, Hopper knew. Colorado would have its fair share of responsibility after this meeting. Court, might just be the Regime's best option, Hopper calculated. He hoped not, but one could never tell either way. One thing was for certain, Attorney General Hopper would have his hands full after these proceedings.

The audience leaned forward so that they could catch every word from Donner. The regulations would mean everything to them. It was their hope that the Regime could be stopped from stealing their environment, now and in the future. The evil concept that the rich and powerful could simply take over their properties and exclude them from these mountains was so incredibly scary. That any government takeover could reach the mountains to destroy their lives was simply unbelievable to them. Control of water supply was to control the country. Their minds tried to grasp that reality; it was so overwhelming and so wrong.

Kevin Donner stood up and cleared his throat. He believed that his actions today and the creation of the Wildlife Sanctuary Trust could be the most important public contribution of his lifetime. He felt his ancestors standing with him, determined and proud. To protect and preserve the environment was everything to America and the Donners. Kevin exhaled slowly, then began, "It is our intent that we will donate these claims to the State of Colorado to be used by all citizens and the natural wildlife. There shall be no fees to enter these properties and the federal government will not, at any time, be able to confiscate this land. If the Regime does make an attempt to control the water origins or quantity of water on these lands, the State of Colorado must prohibit their land grab."

One of the many Regime lawyers jumped to his feet and bleated, "We object to Mr. Donner's language! The Regime Government has every right to enact imminent domain. It is not a 'land grab!'" he huffed and puffed.

AG Hopper watched these lawyers closely. The speaker's face was bright red and his constituency nodded their heads in agreement. The spectators booed and jeered. Hopper allowed these reactions before he intervened. "Order. May I remind the Regime Constituency and the audience that this is not a court proceeding. We are simply meeting with the Zoning Committee of Tiptop. It is of the best interest of all participants to hear what Mr. Kevin Donner has to say and in his own words."

"Thank you, Mr. Hopper." Kevin smiled slightly and then proceeded, "We, the owners, have formed a trust for the control of this specific individual refuge. One of the stipulations for the State of Colorado is to uphold the ownership of the Wildlife Sanctuary Trust. The state must not relinquish these properties to any federal government entity without the intervention of all State and Supreme Court determinations." Kevin glanced at Jackson Abel who nodded.

He then continued reading their statement. "There will be no hunting allowed in this sanctuary. If the Regime should cancel the hunting regulations in this country and allow the privileged to 'kill at will' then the Wildlife Sanctuary Trust will still maintain these regulations of 'no kill.'"

Kevin then shifted his weight and proceeded to map out more details of the Trust. "If the day should arrive when the government decides to void all state law concerning ownership of property, then The Wildlife Sanctuary properties will be transferred to the Tiptop International Trust Fund Corporation in Sweden. This corporation will be regulated by a Swiss Bank of our choice. Under the Trust's stipulations, these claims will be exempt from any United State Government Regulations. If the Regime tries to intervene, then the proceedings will need to be done in an international court setting."

AG Hopper nodded. The gallery was given a few moments to rejoice before Hopper banged the gavel and brought them back to order. It was obvious that the tables had turned for the first time.

The Regime lawyers sat quietly at this juncture. They had become aware of the entirety of this litigation. Yes, they were in a little town in the mountains, but they had underestimated Kevin Donner and Jackson Abel's astute and well trained team. And, maybe even the State of Colorado to some extent, they pondered. Maybe this state would be more trouble than they had estimated when the war between the Regime and state rights began. They would have to watch Colorado very closely.

Unfortunately, these international ramifications had been totally unexpected, Lawyer-Number- One thought to himself. The world had intruded into their fascist plans once again. How many years would it take to get through an international courtroom? Too many, the lead lawyer surmised. Maybe it was better to wait until the big picture changed.

Donner's firewalls were, indeed, mounting up, the Regime Lawyer acknowledged. What else could this group of Denver lawyers have up their sleeves, he wondered? It might be more pertinent to wait until the government could destroy all state laws so that it wouldn't matter if this little shit of a town tried to stop them. All in due time.

"Shall I go on?" Kevin Donner inquired.

***

Officer Libby James could feel her heart pounding. It was not because of the run but because of the pursuit. Whoever was on horseback had all the answers to this case. They had to take the suspect alive, she knew. It was their last chance to get a confession from an active sniper. Any other participants would be swept up and sent East for the politicians to devour.

Libby's eyes began to survey the surrounding terrain. It possessed a great quantity of wild rose bushes and weathered wood. The area was expanding into a rather large meadow valley. She raised her arm to stop the team. "We need to get a group in front of him. The wind is blowing from the west so the horse might not pick up the scent."

Detective Jerry Neal saw the merit in her

strategy immediately. It was now or never, he calculated. It would be his judgment call as the designated leader.

As they had pursued the suspect today, Jerry had observed the pace of his runners. Chief Marshall Tate and Libby were the stronger pace setters. "Libby, take Marshall and head to the north now. Move in behind. Bill, Tyler and I will start making some noise. If our luck holds, the suspect will focus on us. Now, go!"

The group split up without any comments. Libby, with Marshall right behind her, headed north up the side of the valley meadow. They ran full out skipping from bush to wood trying to blend in as best they could. After 100 feet, Libby stopped and pointed at her boots then brought her index finger up to her lips. 'Quietly,' was the message. She began to focus on the ground ahead making sure that she missed cracking trigs and rustling leaves. They began to weave in their progress, avoiding noise as best they could.

Forty yards later, Marshall put his hand on Libby's shoulder to get her attention. He pointed down the valley where the man on horseback sat listening to the intentional noise being made by Bill and Jerry. Tyler, on command, was staying close to Jerry and occasionally told to bark.

Libby began to run with all her might. They needed to use this opportunity to get in back of the suspect. She glanced at the rider as they pulled ahead. Both horse and man, seemed to be fairly focused on the noise coming from the west.

Libby then began to angle their pursuit in

closer to the suspect's position. It had become weave and watch for them. Their approach had placed them some 20 yards above the suspect. They were closing in. Just another 10 yards closer and the trap would be set.

CHAPTER 27

COME TO JUSTICE

Bix closed her eyes and smelled the Freedom Mine for the first time. She had halted her progress after they had entered the hidden entrance. She allowed her senses to take control.

Bernie Holden and Ranger John Bend eyed her with interest. They remained silent and observant. There was a slight echo in the old tunnel but it was not really prevalent. In the background, they could hear water trickling down the walls. John switched on his flashlight and inspected the rock enclosure closely. "Did ya hear water in your premonition?" he asked Bix.

"No," she answered keeping Simon on his leash and close. How could she know that this tunnel wasn't the right place so quickly, Bix challenged herself? Yet, she knew. It wasn't a second guess; she knew for a fact. Even Simon knew that this wasn't the place. Premonitions, Bix scoffed, how real were they? She began to doubt herself. These days people manipulated facts to suit their convictions. Well, damn it, she knew this feeling was different; it had to be. This was not a pigheaded reaction, but something else… it was genuine, she decided. Yes, that was the word she was looking for: 'genuine and maybe authentic.' No hesitancy. Boom. It just happened even when it was inconvenient. "Let's go a little farther," she said, "but I have to say that this place doesn't feel right. It's just off, you know. Even the smell is off," she added.

"Hmmm," John murmured. "Let's go in from here. The mine does change somewhat," he added.

As they moved through the old entrance way, the tunnel did begin to open up. The walls were now plastered with cement and this actual mining area was much more modern. The recent search for crystals and minerals had changed the Freedom Mine considerably in the past years.

Old machinery was now parked along the sides like giant dinosaurs. These relics of the mining days had been well preserved in this tunnel. Bix had no doubt that these antique machines just might start with a little ether sprayed into their engines. Miners had tricks like that; they never quite left these historic mines completely closed down. New mining techniques or other mineral recoveries were always an option. The smell of machine oil and old metal became part of the ambience. Nevertheless, Bix knew that Frank was not being held in Freedom Mine.

"I can tell by your expression that we're

wasting our time," John said. He waited for Bix to nod. "Then let's go." He did give it one last chance, however. "Frank?" he yelled. "Are you there?"

They paused and concentrated; water dripped in response. They shut the door and went toward Ranger Bend's truck.

"There are maybe a couple more options, ladies. However, the police have already combed those areas, I assume. Guess it's worth a shot," he mumbled after looking at their disappointed faces.

"Look!" Bernie said pointing into the western sky. There, peeking out of the falling darkness on the horizon, was a small dancing light. It waved in the gentle wind. The illuminator glowed gently as if it were a soft candlelight. The specter drifted slightly like a kite on a string.

Hope, Bix thought. "It just might be the sign!" she declared.

"Let's go," John said as he opened the truck door. Simon was the first to jump in.

***

"Now, if the State of Colorado's public was to vote unwisely for the fascist opposition at the state level," Kevin Donner continued to read from the proposed contract, "the Wildlife Sanctuary Trust will immediately be turned over to the International Trust. It will not be included in any land grabs to promote fracking in Colorado state parks and monumental areas that would be ordained by either state or national entities."

The Regime lawyers just couldn't handle this

language; all eight of them leaped to their feet! "Mr. Hopper, this language is simply not acceptable even in a Zoning Committee Meeting! Mr. Donner has gone too far and we need to object in the most strenuous terms. This is pure slander and can't be allowed to stand!"

The spectators went wild. The audience booed the Regime Constituency. Donner's arguments were correctly stated for Tiptop. The public outrage was obvious.

Attorney General Hopper then banged his gavel again and waited for control. He, obviously, had a point to make about this interruption. "Sir, I'm not totally convinced that you are correct," stated AG Hopper. "As far as the insinuation of 'slander,' I need to clarify some information first before I rule. Has your party seized sacred lands in Utah? Did I not read that several areas have been government designated for fracking?" He stared at the Capital Regime Contingency waiting for their response. Their silence said volumes. Obviously, they were not prepared to contest this point. Donner's thorough contract was light years ahead of these bureaucrats. They would have to step up their case for the coming year.

Nevertheless, AG Hopper did relent somewhat as he continued, "I will grant you that Mr. Donner should have toned down his accusations about fascism. These terms are inappropriate for our proceedings. Having said that, I did state that this meeting needed to hear Mr. Donner's full statement. I would ask Mr. Donner then to tone down the rhetoric, please."

"Yes, sir, I can do that," Kevin replied with a slight smile.

"Do you have any more information to give us?" Hopper asked him?"

"We had one more stipulation to this contract, sir. Shall I go on?"

"Please," Hopper said.

"If the climate in this country would be controlled by the existing powers through the next election, and then, this existing government would relieve the states of all powers, and the international countries were blocked from owning any properties within our borders, then this sanctuary would revert back to our surviving families. These family members would then have to be vetted by the court of course. However, if all properties in this nation were to be then owned by the existing government, all bets are off and God help us all."

The audience remained silent. Most of them had not thought about this horrific scenario. What Donner was saying was a shock. The town knew that they had probably won this fight but what loomed ahead was a nightmare. Their fight for the country was just starting. Whether these mountain people wanted it or not, their path would lead to politics.

"Thank you, Mr. Donner. It would now be appropriate to hear from the Zoning Committee," Attorney General Hopper said. "Mr. Howard Page, I believe you are to represent the Zoning Committee? Is that correct?"

"Yes, sir, and it's Howie, sir," he clarified.

"So noted," AG Hopper stated for the record.

***

Officer Libby James and Chief Marshall Tate quickly closed the gap for capture. They stalked the rider and horse through the waxing dusk. Both officers had drawn their guns and were now hunting both man and horse. Libby could hardly breathe as she weaved closer through the shadows. Marshall had gone to the other side of the suspect The goal was to not be detected until they were close enough to stop any escape. Stop any gun fire; shut this getaway window.

Marshall signaled Libby that he would go in from the front and stand. Libby nodded then approached from the backside. She set her gun barrel on Jerome Walker's leg aiming up toward his body. Marshall directed his aim at the horse. He didn't like it but that was what this situation called for; he wasn't going to move no matter what happened at this juncture. If he had to fire then so be it. Maybe one warning shot could happen.

"You need to surrender and make no movements," Libby said softly. Her tone was confident and firm. She didn't yell so that the horse would become alarmed. The horse whinnied and nudged retired Sheriff Jerome Walker affectionately.

For a few seconds, Walker's mind entertained a thought about escape. His adrenalin surged then with a wise reaction, his shoulders slumped. This was not the time to get his horse shot and to stage his own death. There would be chances later, he judged.

"You have the right to remain silent…," Libby mouthed the familiar statement and held her position. "Do you understand these rights?" she finished.

There was a pause while Walker reviewed the circumstances. Reviewed his actions and then took responsibility for them. "Yes."

Libby removed Walker's Smith and Wesson revolver carefully. Marshall then pulled his 30-30 Winchester out of the saddle scabbard. "Dismount slowly, Mr. Walker," she said. "Very slowly."

Jerome did as asked with his hands up. The man was the consummate cowboy; riding the ranges right up to the end, Marshall concluded.

"Where's Officer Frank Mason being held?" Libby quickly asked as she proceeded to handcuff him. She waited while holding her breath afraid of his answer.

"That I don't know, young lady. Buck didn't get a chance to tell me. We was busy, you know? Somewhere where the sun don't shine is my guess."

Libby felt like a ton of rocks had fallen on her. It was hard to believe that Frank could be dead. She felt such sadness. Damn.

Marshall petted the horse and processed. How depressing was that? He led the animal to the old trailer some 12 feet from them so that he wouldn't knock the hell out of this old man right then and there. Son of a bitch had just smashed their hope with no regard whatsoever. He knew exactly how Libby felt and he hated it with a passion. Punching the old coot out would have felt so good. Was

Jerome Walker lying? Marshall, somehow, felt that he wasn't which made it even worse.

Marshall went ahead and contacted Jerry and Bill to come on in then radioed Captain Jen. He could hear her frustration and sadness when he told her about Frank. They still knew nothing. Marshall began to wonder how Walker with 35 years on the police force could show absolutely no remorse. Nothing. What could have made him turn, Marshall considered? Why the Regime and how could he have killed his friend?

Libby was also wondering at this juncture. She couldn't help but ask, "Why, Jerome? You didn't need to shoot Jonquin in the back. You could have arrested him?"

They knew, he assessed. Walker stared at her for a moment. Yup, there was a case to be made for him to lie and say he was helping with the arrest. It would be totally a fucking lie. Walker was tempted but it would go against his principles. He could slither out of the whole mess and hide under a rock, or he could tell the damn truth. He weighed the options for a few seconds.

Finally, he decided that there wasn't much time left to live in another lie. Maybe it is was now time to confess up. Age was taking its toll; he was going to meet his maker soon. Somewhere in a man's life, there had to be some dignity, Jerome Walker admitted to himself.

***

Howie Page had rehearsed what he was to

announce in this Zoning Committee meeting. The members had met an hour ago. Without Betsy Jonquin's opinions and the state present to support Tiptop, the Zoning Committee had wisely changed their minds. It was obvious that the Jonquins were going down, or at least Buck. All Howie knew was that the pro-Regime members were now second guessing their position or simply hiding safely. If they planned to remain residents of this county, they would have to rescind their vote. Capital Regime wasn't going to get its way today. Tiptop would side with Colorado.

Howie took a deep breath and then began to make history, "After reviewing all the evidence and listening to the public input and acknowledging the state's position, this committee is willing to rule for the State of Colorado." He did not even glance at the Regime Contingency; Howie Page stared directly at AG Hopper.

The audience cheered wildly and Attorney General Hopper applied his gavel. "Order, please," he waited.

Tiptop complied.

"Are you saying then that if the State of Colorado signs this sanctuary proposal, Mr. Page, these landowners will transfer their ownership to the State of Colorado? That this case of Eminent Domain will not be granted. That your committee will withdraw their objections and allow the contract to become law? Is that correct?"

"Yes, sir. We are in agreement," Howie beamed. The audience controlled their enthusiasm knowing that it was almost over for now.

"Therefore, as the Representative of the State of Colorado, I must inform you that we have accepted this agreement with pleasure. To have Colorado be able to acquire another sanctuary to preserve our heritage is certainly a monumental occasion. By the authority vested in me, I am very willing to sign this articulate and comprehensive proposal. The governor has given me permission to sign on this day."

Attorney General Hopper then stared at Kevin Donner and proceeded, "Mr. Donner, please submit your contract for the transfer of this land as described by Miss Milly Marvel's testimony. Let the record show that this sanctuary property, described here and transferred to the State of Colorado, is one and the same as described by Miss Melanie Camp in the Eminent Domain case and litigated by the Personal Property Coalition. These claims will now be consolidated and entitled Wildlife Sanctuary Trust, from this day forward." Attorney General Hopper signed the contract then banged the gavel for the final time.

The Tiptop residents sat silently for a few moments. Their minds began to process the success. The Eminent Domain case had been stopped by the town and their state. Their goal had been met.

Nathan Abel abruptly stood up and began to slowly clap; he was so proud of his son, Jackson. What a piece of legislation for Jackson and Kevin Donner to have created. His pride as a father was obvious. Tiptop supported and recognized this pride; they also stood as the applause began to spread throughout the room. It gained momentum as all the stress began to disappear.

Kevin Donner, Jackson Abel and Attorney General Hopper of the State of Colorado walked down the aisle shaking hands and smiling. It was a small victory but it was a win. The Tiptop residents so deserved this outcome. As the ex-claim owners left the courtroom, the residents followed to spread the word.

There, left to pick up after themselves, was the Regime Contingency. The room was silent and empty now. Their expressions said it all. The lawyers packed their legal papers. Lawyer-Suit-Number-One glanced at his team of seven and said, "All in due time, gentlemen. This fight is certainly not over. Delayed, yes, but not over." Their security men picked up the boxes and lugged them out of the courtroom. Eight angry white men followed.

***

The HAPT members looked to Libby who would ask the question, they calculated; her personality would demand it. Again, she voiced her question to Jerome Walker, "Why?" HAPT and Chief Marshall Tate listened. They deserved an answer for that at least.

The helicopter was on its way, and Jerome Walker's horse was in the trailer munching fresh hay, safe and sound. The area was quiet. All other police teams had been given the order to return to base. HAPT's order had been to stand down and wait for the transportation of this prisoner. Captain Jen Holly was flying in to take Walker back to

Breckenridge. It was over except for Walker's testimony.

"Why what?" retorted Jerome Walker staring coldly at Libby.

"Why did you shoot Buck Jonquin?" Libby ventured again.

"That's a simple one, young lady. He asked me to." Jerome stated. "We had a pact. If one of us got caught, the other one was to take him out."

"Did the government movement direct those orders?" Detective Bill Smith inquired. Bill was the politically oriented team member.

"Nope," Jerome said. "Buck and I have been friends for over twenty years. We believe the same things; we're on the same page. This doomed country just ain't going down the right path. The people need a military government. Strong authoritarian leaders to tell them what's right, not a bunch of shifty politicians."

"I thought that's what we've got right now," Detective Bill Smith responded. "An authoritarian crook."

"No we don't, young man, the real leaders are coming soon. All we got now is a majority of greedy men destroying our legal system. You'll see. The military will be forced to intervene. When all hell breaks loose, I'll be freed and called a hero. Ain't so, but that's what I'll be called in this here revolution. Won't make me ever feel good about killing Buck, but that's the way it is, and that's what he wanted," Jerome Walker confirmed sadly. "Now, I'm done answering your stupid questions."

Detective Bill Smith shook his head. This

delusional old man was scary as hell, he concluded. What a lose-lose situation Walker's picture painted. Angry old white men sitting around drinking beer and creating some hideous war ending, Bill concluded. Armageddon. Unbelievable, but unfortunately plausible if the country didn't vote for democracy. The public too often, he admitted, lived in some happy delusion lead by the enablers. Being aware and vigilant was crucial.

Bill made himself a wise promise at this moment. You don't simply pray to God to stop a revolution, you work and commit then pray to heaven for your success. Democracy was not a spectator sport, he knew. To vote meant everything, especially, this coming election.

The Police helicopter cut through the dark sky at that moment. The huge beacon spotlights illuminated the area while the powerful rotor threw dust with authority. Extreme noise filled their arid wilderness scene. It descended for a landing. Captain Jen Holly would take the suspect from here. Good. The HAPT Officers let out a sigh of relief that their mission to apprehend was over.

Detective Bill Smith couldn't help but think about Walker's testimony. It would wake up these mountain communities. Of course the newspapers would have a field day, telling and retelling the story from their own convoluted viewpoints. Spinning the truth until there was none. The balance between violence and order was becoming quite a job for everyone. The court system had won today. His neighbors had walked within the law and not against it like Buck and Jerome. Everyone had won today except Frank. Bill Smith couldn't help but keep hoping. That old guy had gotten out of a lot worse situations. Frank was a survivor and damn good friend, Bill realized.

CHAPTER 28

BEACON

It was that magical time of night when darkness replaced light and dimension surrendered depth. Bix held the beacon in her sight; she was afraid to look away. It had to be Frank's signal straight from his heart; his life, anchored to that one small rope. "Make it happen," Bix murmured softly. Simon, sensing her intensity, snuggled closer.

They were silent as the truck careened down the dirt road. Ranger John Bend could hardly believe what he was seeing. If it wasn't Frank, then who the hell was it? Tiptop was gathered at the rally. To assume it was a kid flying a kite tonight just didn't make sense.

Bernie sat in the co-pilot seat of the truck. She, also, was struck by this peculiar sight. The mountains possessed such power sometimes; it was incredible, she thought. This small light was a magnet pulling them. As they traveled closer to the vortex, they focused their energy. What would they

find, Bernie scrutinized? Frank alive and well she
hoped.

John brought the truck parallel to the light. He
parked it on the side of the road then turned on his
radio and began to broadcast. "This is Ranger John
Bend located three miles west of Freedom Mine on
the logging road. Bix and Bernie are with me. We
have spotted some sort of lighted signal south of my
parked truck. It could be a lantern marking Frank's
location. Be advised that we are on our way down
to the signal. Ambulance, stand by."

They threw on camping headlamps and
proceeded down the decline moving as quickly as
possible. Their headlamps flashed from ground to
distance; headlamp beams crossed as they glanced
at each other for direction. The ground was fairly
smooth with shrubs and sage sprinkled throughout.
Their progress set a fast pace.

Simon followed Bix cautiously; his nose up
sniffing the air. He thought their actions were
curious to say the least. Bix had put him on a leash
just to be safe. In one direction Simon began to
smell a familiar scent. He knew it from somewhere;
it was human. It was faint with a mixture of fear
present.

"I'm sure that the police have been in this area
recently," John mumbled as he avoided a rock in his
path. "I sure hope we'll find Frank this time."

"HAPT wasn't focused on a rescue when they
were here. Besides, Frank's signal couldn't be used
until dark," Bix said.

"I find it interesting that this light has appeared
during the exact date of the rally. You suppose he's

been keeping track of the days?" Bernie asked.

"Knowing Frank Mason, I have no doubt," Bix said as she halted to calculate the direction that they needed to go. Her hand then indicated a slight turn to the right. They moved quickly. The beacon was now almost straight above their heads. It couldn't be far!

Simon, suddenly, recognized the scent. It was Frank, his good friend, and he was in trouble! The little black schnoodle let out a frantic bark! Bix stopped and unleased him. Their tracking noise would have scared off any coyotes so Simon was safe. Besides, she could tell that they were so close.

Simon then disappeared into the underbrush. Whatever was ahead, he was determined to find it. His barks abruptly turned into yips as they approached the location. Their headlamps began to focus on the little dog. He was circling the entrance of the old cistern on Martin Keiser's property. His stubby tail was wagging as he circled around and around. His yips had turned to whimpers of impatience. His focus was now down in the bottom of that old cistern.

***

Captain Jen Holly leaped from the copter and ran toward her team. She bent low to avoid the churning rotors. Their circular motion sucked dirt and debris into the air increasing the noise level to an extreme roar. HAPT stood silently by waiting for the helicopter to shut down.

A few moments later, conversation was

possible. "We have secured the prisoner and he is ready for transport," Detective Jerry Neal said. "Glad to see you, Captain."

"And I am so glad to be here. Job well done, team," Jen said and saluted. It was all formality but so rewarding for them. There was nothing wrong with honoring success, she concluded. "Have you been able to take pictures and collect evidence here?" she asked.

"Just finished with all our evidence. We need to mark the area with crime scene tape, and we'll be done."

"Excellent," Jen said. "We'll need to leave Frank's truck on scene for now until the crime team can take fingerprints and comb the interior thoroughly."

"We figured as much," Bill said. "We collected all our weapons that need to be catalogued and placed them in the truck bed for now. Anything else?" he asked.

"I think that covers it," Captain Jen said.

Abruptly, Ranger John Bend's announcement came over the radio. The team stood still with their eyes glued to the ground as they listened. When the announcement ended, the officers found themselves in a group hug. Finally the pieces were coming together. Frank just might be found alive!

"What a relief," Captain Jen said. "Alive at least," she whispered realizing the importance of the moment. "Damn, I'd really like to be there." Her desire to be there with Frank suddenly became overwhelming.

The team comprehended how she felt. Captain

Jen Holly had been in the control center all this time. This Captain was used to being in the center of the action. Detective Jerry Neal could only imagine her feelings right now. Somehow, she needed to be there, he realized. His thoughts spun until he got an answer. There was an option; they could make it happen. "So how are you on horse back, Captain?"

"What?"

"We could have you saddled and ready to take off in five minutes. Just head down the logging trail until you get to Ranger Bend's truck then straight down the decline. That is, if you wouldn't mind letting the team here transport this suspect back to base?"

It took Captain Jen Holly two seconds to decide. "Saddle me up!"

"Secure the suspect into the helicopter, Libby," Jerry ordered. "Bill, help me get the horse out of the trailer and saddled. Follow me, Captain," Jerry said moving toward the trailer.

Captain Jen watched while Jerry backed the light tan quarter horse out of the old rusty trailer. The mare's white star blaze head markings and four white leg socks were beautiful, Jen decided. She moved slowly next to the horse and stroked her head; the quarter horse snuggled and whinnied softly. This mare was used to getting attention, Jen concluded. Even though Jerome Walker was arrested for killing his friend, he had obviously been good with horses. Did say something about the man, she comprehended. Captain Jen Holly adjusted the stirrup length then mounted the horse with ease.

Chief Marshall Tate decided to take a moment and watch Captain Jen ride into the sunset. How cool was that? Another thing that he did not know about the Captain; she had been an equestrian in her past. Captain Jen was riding to the rescue of her last missing team member. "Nice," Marshall murmured to himself. It was a fitting ending to say the least.

The team then resumed their own business. Marshall and Bill outlined the area with crime scene tape while Detective Jerry Neal activated the radio. Neal announced their intentions to all the forces listening. Libby heard the news on the radio in the copter as she handcuffed Walker securely in place.

This night would be remembered for a long time. The team was now assembled in the helicopter. They couldn't see the horse woman as they lifted off, but their imaginations focused on the image of a fellow officer charging down the lumber trail on horseback. Full out!

***

Bix stared down into the dark cistern and moved her lamplight around until she spotted the body of Frank. He seemed lifeless and still but from his arm, she could see that the rope was tied to his wrist! "Thank God," she whispered. "Frank? Wake up, buddy, and talk to us," Bix yelled.

There was a long pause as if time had taken a vacation. The quiet was deep. They became desperate to hear anything from him.

"Wake up, Frank," Bernie urged: a moan, a leg movement, a head looking up, anything to affirm life. "Come on Frank, move, damn it!" she demanded loudly.

Simon barked. He knew that Frank was breathing. He could hear him. "Bark," said Simon with a demanding presence. 'Wake up!' Simon stomped his paws on the ground and dislodged a rock from the cistern opening. The rock hit Frank's leg with a thud.

"Hey," Frank said in a weak voice. "What's happening. Am I dead?"

"Nope, you're alive and kicking," said Ranger John. His smile was contagious. Bix and Bernie could feel their mandatory smiles spreading.

" Frank, we are so relieved. Did Buck put you down there?" Bix asked.

"Yep, but it was more of a push. There wasn't anything gentle about my arrival. The fucker hit me on the head, and it was lights out. You got any water? God, I'm thirsty," Frank pleaded.

His request was met with a water bottle dropped close to his hand. He moved his arm until he could grab the water. Frank released the lantern from his wrist and opened the bottle.

The group then couldn't help but watch this beacon of light slowly drift away. It had been so important to them; they followed its last journey. The lantern danced in the breeze one last time before diving to earth.

Frank then opened the container of pure water and took his first real drink in days. He was lucid enough not to overdo. He leaned back and closed his eyes happily. The water tasted wonderful.

It was like saying goodbye to another world for

him now. His coma had been warm and comfortable yet so much had been at stake. To give up living wasn't a choice that Frank was willing to make, especially now . His eyes popped open!

"Get me out of here," he demanded!

***

Captain Jen Holly hadn't been on horseback since she was in her teens. She had worked at a stable back then and taken care of the horses. It felt so incredibly free to be riding, she realized. The rush was just what she needed. Some action!

Jen had conflicting opinions about her new position as Captain. The challenges were great but sometimes having to lead instead of being in on the action made her jealous. Somehow, she would have to reach a compromise.

Jerome Walker's horse was in good shape and moved easily along the road. The mare didn't seem to mind a new rider. That was good, Jen thought. They both watched for rocks and ruts and maneuvered easily. Captain Jen then saw, in the shadows, Ranger John Bend's truck. She reined in her horse and began to trot instead of gallop. Jen dismounted to make sure that she had found the right truck.

At that moment her eyes picked up on a movement in the sky. There, directly above her was the lantern. A short rope was dangling from it. It was free and drifting . Abruptly, the light went out and the lantern dropped to earth.

Jen's eyes stared into the darkness; the

journey down the decline would now be pitch dark. Fortunately, she had a small flashlight on her gun belt. One of those 'Captain decisions' she'd made when HAPT's uniforms were designed.

She decided to walk the horse down to the rescue site. Too many coyotes around to leave it tied to the truck was her thought. The ride had taken only five minutes. HAPT had been so close and yet so far away. Her eyes adjusted as she moved. About 50 feet down, Jen could hear voices and barks. She wasn't quite close enough to hear the conversation but she did pick up on the word, 'Frank.' "Yes," she whispered moving toward the noise.

"We need a rope," said John Bend. "Shit, there's one in the truck. Why didn't I think before we started down the damn hill?"

"I've got one," yelled Captain Jen Holly as she came into the clearing on horseback. She had mounted again when the area had cleared into a meadow.

Bernie couldn't believe her eyes. Jen to the rescue. How incredible and surreal, she thought.

Jen dismounted, secured the horse reins on a sturdy bush, then retrieved the rope from the saddle horn.

She began to straighten the rope as Frank yelled with more enthusiasm, "Ya got a rope?"

"Heck yes," Jen said while assessing Frank's position. He was 25 feet down in this cistern. Jen examined the shrubs and boulders near the opening. They would need to tie the rope securely for sure.

Ranger John Bend then proceeded to activate the radio again. "Ambulance needed at site. Please advise. Patient is talking and seems in good shape considering his possible concussion."

"Life Flight is on the way plus the ambulance. Please advise if the copter can land," Chief Marshall Tate inquired.

"Come on ahead. We're in a meadow and waiting," John affirmed.

"I'm going down," Captain Jen said. "Bernie, anchor the rope on that boulder for me."

"You bet," Bernie answered, moving into position.

"John and Bix, lower me down, please."

"Yup," John said. He and Bix positioned themselves for leverage. "Slowly," John said.

Jen had used the carabiner on her belt to secure the rope. Her boots backed down carefully on the cistern sides. She tried not to shower Frank with dirt as best as she could. Five minutes later, she found herself checking Frank's pulse. A little high but not bad at all.

"How'd you get here, Capt?" Frank asked.

"On horseback, thanks to Jerome Walker's steed.

"Walker help with the capture of Jonquin?" he asked.

"Long story, Frank. Right now let's concentrate on getting you out of here. Okay?"

"You bet ya," Frank answered letting himself finally relax. He would let these people take care of him now. If he had learned anything during this adventure, it was to let other people help. His body was weary and he was perfectly willing to let them haul him out of this damn hole.

He did reach out and retrieve the rock that good old Simon had hurled at him. His eyes twinkled as he realized that the rock was the crystal; the smoky quartz crystal that he had been eyeing for some time. He placed it, safely in his pocket. Frank would keep that crystal with him for good luck from now on.

The helicopter landed, the medical sled was lowered, a medic had attached an IV, and Frank was pulled out. It was over.

There hadn't been any time to say good bye, Miss Mouse realized. Her domicile had been besieged by a crowd of noisy humans. She hid and observed them. Her friend had departed wrapped like a burrito on a tray. Here one day and gone the next.

She now came out of her den, cautiously, after their departure. The hollow silence was new and unexpected; she suddenly felt lonely. He had plopped into her world and then he had left. Well, that was disconcerting.

Miss Mouse then saw that the humans had left their rope. It dangled before her. Her eyes traced the rope from her environment to the top, wondering. Well, why not, she concluded. Then Miss Mouse scurried up the rope and out into freedom.

CHAPTER 29

CONNECTIONS

Captain Jen Holly entered the interrogation room on the second day. Jerome Walker had given them answers about the crimes in Tiptop that he and Buck Jonquin had perpetrated. His answers seemed plausible to her.

Buck had murdered Martin Keiser on his own. Walker verified that he did have an alibi for that murder. He then confessed to starting the slide in Sourdough Gulch and driving Bart Gentry off the road. He claimed that he was supposed to only delay the rescue of Nathan Abel and Milt Gray. The goal was to keep Nathan away from the rally so that they wouldn't have to worry about his vote. "Bart Gentry just wouldn't stop his damn car," Jerome confessed. As far as Walker was concerned, Gentry was responsible for his own accident. Jerome, however, indicated that Buck had taken the shot at Kevin Donner and missed. He also added that it was Buck's idea to hide Frank. "Had nothing to do with that dumb move," Jerome verified.

Chief Marshall Tate was now trying to get Walker to tell him who was their Capital Regime contact. So far, Jerome had avoided answering. "Like I told you, we would just get orders by phone. Social introductions ain't necessary during a revolution. It was fucking obvious that the orders were coming from the top though," Jerome admitted. "I ain't incriminating no one. Don't want to get killed in prison." He shifted in his chair, tipped his cowboy hat back on his head and stared at Marshall.

"So you and Buck made a pact to shoot each other if there was a capture all on your own?" Marshall verified.

"How many times have I got to tell you that?" Walker grumbled in his crusty manner. "Take no prisoners was our pact. The Regime lawyers came to settle all the rest. Eventually, they'll get control cause you folks always talk and never take any fucking action. The money is going to control it all soon." His stare defied Marshall to take up the bait. Jerome shook his head, scratched his chin, and waited for the next question.

Marshall wasn't quite ready to let that go unanswered. "You do realize that you're the one sitting here ready to be shipped off to prison? Seems like an action to me," he said. "Was your pact only between you two? Were there more revolutionary members in Tiptop?" Marshall asked.

"I ain't saying," was Jerome's indignant answer. "Do your own damn job."

It was obvious that he was finished for now, Jen

354

Holly observed. Who knew what would happen during and after his trial, Jen thought. The courtroom rodeo was just beginning for this old cowboy. He had no idea. She found herself almost feeling sorry for him… almost.

Jerome's eyes then softened and landed on Captain Holly as if he had heard her thoughts. He had met her before and knew of her. Word was, that Captain Holly was a straight shooter. "I heard that you rode May in the gulch, and that you are boarding her. Wanted to thank you for that," he said. His stare was glued on Jen.

"Yes. Nice horse, Jerome. You've trained her well."

"A-yup I did. You want her?"

"Well I hadn't thought about owning a horse…."

"Give me a piece of damn paper and a pencil," he demanded of Marshall. Marshall complied.

They watched in silence as Jerome Walker quickly wrote a sentence on the paper and signed his name with a flourish. Jerome then confessed, "I don't have many possessions anymore that are worth shit, but my horse is an exception. Her quarter horse moniker is Miss Mayfield; she was named by her previous owner. Now when she gets stubborn, I call her that and the rest of the time, she's simply, May." He tossed the paper at Captain Jen and waited for her to pick it up. Captain Jen complied.

The deal was settled without a word just a nod from Jerome Walker. It struck Jen later as a cowboy thing, direct and simple. Jerome Walker was a revolutionist and a murderer but his cowboy mountain character was another thing, she acknowledged. The old guy had just gotten carried away by a corrupt movement that he didn't quite understand. How would it have played out if he hadn't been caught, Jen wondered? Would he have ever understood how important negotiations were in a democracy or would his prejudices overwhelm any chance for him to understand? And, who knew what prisoners felt about the newly formed government? Jerome Walker would get his chance to find out.

***

Some two weeks later, Bix Bixler and Bernie Holden sat happily at the restaurant waiting to be joined by the other ladies. They had selected one of the tables outside in the sun for the gathering. Fall might be spreading a chill toward evening but today was toasty. Their lunch date had been delayed until the media and the public settled down. Most issues were at least temporarily done. Not solved but heading in the right direction, Bix concluded.

Bernie would be heading back to North Dakota soon. Her family took care of the homestead these days, but she had been summoned by the clan. Matt Holden, her favorite nephew, was getting married. He had just finished college and was now taking his rightful place on the homestead. Bix had decided to drive up for the wedding next month.

Bix had always felt welcome in the Holden clan ever since their vacation in Buena Vista a couple years ago. It hadn't been much of a vacation what with the ugly events of fracking and Henry Holden's death. Even so, the family had been open to her help. She had camped on the outskirts of the park and suddenly found herself involved with the whole clan. Then she and Bernie found each other, and the Holdens adopted her without hesitation. Yep, she'd be there for Matt's wedding for sure; it was a special occasion.

Officer Libby James arrived for lunch first. Her red curly hair bounced as she gave Bix and Bernie hugs. "Good to see you. I am so glad to be included today. We'll have to make these lunches a tradition, don't you think?"

"Sounds like a plan to me," Bix said. "It does seem like we have a lot in common, doesn't it? Let's order some munchies while we're waiting for Jen to show up," she added.

"Is she going to be late?" Bernie asked Libby .

"Actually, she was maybe five minutes behind me. As long as Frank doesn't get an emergency call, she'll be here soon." Libby sat down and began to relax. She contentedly sighed, closed her eyes and enjoyed the warm sun. The HAPT office had been fairly quiet since the Tiptop case, Libby concluded. Kevin Donner and Jackson Able had taken the legal contract back down to their Denver offices. Any court proceedings wouldn't be scheduled for months. The Regime hadn't filed an appeal yet. Who knew, maybe it would all go away. Wishful thinking, Libby acknowledge.

"Speaking of Frank, how is he?" Bernie asked after deciding on the egg roll appetizers. Bix added chicken wings to that order.

"You know, he's back up to speed. I do think that he's a little more mellow these days," Libby added. "There is evidence that Frank has, indeed, come into his own. I like the change, actually," she admitted. "He seems to appreciate all of us more."

"Sounds good," Bix agreed. "How about a pitcher of ice tea all around?" Bix motioned to the waitress after the nods.

Captain Jen Holly parked and came down the sidewalk at that moment. She smiled, then waved and joined in a group hug. After she was seated, Jen glanced around the table. "I'm so happy to see you all, and glad that I could call this meeting," she stated then winked. "Has Libby told you her news yet? I can't believe that she hasn't simply exploded."

"No!" Bix and Bernie said together.

"I thought your adoption of Jerome Walker's horse was 'the' big news," Bernie emphasized the sentence correctly.

"Old news," Jen laughed. "Miss Mayfield has her own spacious stall now and expects me each morning before work. I know that she can tell time. No, I mean Libby's personal news." She leaned up in her chair and stared at Libby. Jen coaxed her once again, "The news about her and Marshall? Go ahead, Libby, while I apply a drumroll." The table rattled.

"Well, Marshall and I are engaged."

"Wonderful!" Bix yelped.

"When's the wedding?" Bernie asked. She'd have to be here for sure.

"Haven't decided the actual date but definitely

next summer. You'll be here, Bernie?" Libby asked.

"I wouldn't miss it for the world. That is, if Bix will have me?"

"I see no problem with that," Bix beamed.

"If she's busy," Jen said, " I've got a large rented stall that would be available. May does appreciate company. Just as long as you bring an apple and a brush," Jen joked.

"I'll keep that in mind. I am hoping that I might ride Miss Mayfield now and then if you wouldn't mind?" Bernie inquired.

"That would be terrific," Jen affirmed. "I was hoping that we could reach an agreement. She is an active filly."

They ordered their lunch , munched appetizers and sipped tea.

"So there is some other interesting news by the way," Jen said. "Did you hear that Bill's wife is thinking about running for mayor here in Frisco? What do you think, Bix?" Jen asked looking at her for a valued opinion.

"Off hand, I think it's a great idea. Bonnie is intelligent and thoughtful. Guess I'll need to campaign for her while Bernie is out of town. We all do need to get involved at the town level and the county, ladies. Good for Bill and Bonnie Smith. I like it. And, speaking about getting involved," Bix announced, "Melanie Camp from The Personal Property Coalition called this morning. Apparently, Kevin Donner and Jackson Able's Iminent Domain arguments are being used all over the country. There are state trusts springing up like bunny rabbits and the Regime is really frustrated. Courts seem to find the State of Colorado's adoption of the land sanctuary trust quite a compelling argument."

"Woot," Libby James said. "I like it when there's good news for the little guys. I'm tired of the rich bullies taking the media control. So, tell me some more good news," she pleaded while watching lunch being served.

"Well since you demand more good news, I do have one more tidbit," Jen offered as the waitress sat down her plate. She waited until they had privacy again. "Have you heard about Jerry Neal?"

"No! What?" said the group looking at her expectantly.

"Jerry has been asked by the State of Colorado to head a new police training project. He's going to offer training in K-9 and tracking techniques for the whole state," she announced. "He will have to resign from the Buena Vista Police Department. He won't have time to do it all," Jen added.

"Well, that is good news. Jerry is really talented. Is he still going to help HAPT occasionally?" Bix asked while cutting her salmon.

"Definitely. I have actually hired him on as Second in Command, Captain Jerry Neal working directly for HAPT. I think his leading the ground forces around Tiptop really made him think about his career," Jen revealed. "Jerry did an amazing job of commanding all the task forces pursuing Buck Jonquin. Our success was mostly because of his leadership. He now will be more active on our team. Since we are covering four counties instead of three, it makes good sense."

"And," Libby interrupted, "that is the news

from 'Chief' Jen Holly who was graciously promoted by all four counties by an unanimous vote!" A cheer sprung up from their table. The other diners paused and glanced at them just to make sure that it was good news. The group quietly concentrated on their lunch; the restaurant activity continued.

Libby finally broke the silence, "So, does Tyler then become Chief Shepherd of HAPT?" Libby asked with a grin. "Seems only fair to me. Maybe a badge on his collar?"

"We'll have to suggest that to Jerry," Jen said with a smile. "Maybe we could organize a celebration and give Tyler his promotion?" The lunch group nodded in agreement.

Jen then popped a pickle into her mouth before continuing, " Apparently, Jerry will recruit and establish the K-9 training school somewhere in Summit County. He will definitely find himself busy. Between the two positions, his talents will be utilized," she finished.

"Can you imagine not being able to use his talents during the McPherson Gulch Case and the Tiptop mess?" Bernie mused after taking a sip of tea. She was really glad that he wouldn't abandon HAPT at this point.

"Yeah," Libby chimed into the conversation. "Even good old Chief Carl Hagen in Leadville confessed that Neal's promotion should have happened sooner. For Hagen, that's quite a admission. He even admitted to me that he misses Frank over in Leadville now that HAPT is a permanent team. You don't suppose he and Frank will become friends, do you?"

"Times are a-changing," Bix added.

The group became silent as they finished lunch. Within their little part of the world, life was good today. The whole country needed help, but their community had survived.

"So has anybody been over to explore the Wildlife Sanctuary Trust yet?" Libby asked as the waitress cleared the table.

"Just the edge," Bix said. "Bernie and I went over to visit with Emma Keiser yesterday.

"How is she doing?" Jen asked.

"I think better now that the Regime has been stopped from taking the land. She has gotten permission to build a small monument for Martin on the property near her home. The Trust Fund also allows for Emma to live in their cabin for her lifetime. She believes that the agreement is fair," Bix finished.

"Also, the Friendship Mine will remain privately owned," Bernie added. "The owners have the right to open it up at anytime. They can even start tours of the old tunnels for the public if they want ," Bernie announced then concluded, "and most importantly, Tiptop can now make decisions about their own future. I like that." Once again, the group nodded in agreement.

They finished their financial transactions and tip discussion. As if there were no need for agreement, the ladies began to walk down the sidewalk toward the Frisco trails at the end of the street. They window shopped casually, and talked as they moved along Main Street.

The mountains surrounding Frisco guarded the peaceful environment allowing only sunshine and calm in today. Mount Royal stood at attention near them. Its steep slopes shared an amazing amount of history for tourists and locals alike. The old avalanche slides cut vast wrinkles on the face of this mountain. The complexion disclosed a history where a fiddler's concert had saved lives during an avalanche and a whisky distillery was built and hidden during the Prohibition Times. Even smelter relics remained from the Gold Rush. Mount Royal's history was all there waiting to be explored by enthusiastic hikers.

The ladies, however, sauntered across the bridge toward the trailhead. Their choice of paths today was the pleasant cement walkway that circled the town .

Libby, now, decided to introduce another topic into their conversation. She had been intrigued during the case by the appearance of the Smoky Quartz Crystals. The gems seemed to be a prize that she didn't quite understand. She figured it was a good time to find out. "So the mining for Smoky Quartz Crystals and other rhodochrosites will continue at the mine?" Libby then asked, "Why are they of value exactly?"

"Keep in mind that not all crystals come from that mine," Bix commented. "Martin Keiser was out hunting crystals to give to Emma when he was murdered; Frank found his crystal in the cistern wall. Apparently, one can hike the Wildlife Sanctuary and find them," Bix explained.

"Did you see Frank's Smoky Quartz Crystal?"

Jen asked now curious.

"Actually, I didn't. The rescue was so fast. He got pulled out and swept away in that helicopter."

"He showed it to me," Libby said. "Frank keeps it in his pocket. I just thought that it was interesting. Is it like a good luck charm?" she asked.

"I wouldn't call it a charm exactly. Crystals are known to interact with the earth powers. They're not like a rabbit's foot," Bix explained. "I have to ask why you want to know, Libby?"

Libby looked confused about that question.

Bix then clarified, "Sorry that I have to ask you, but I have gotten sick and tired of the scoffers. People who ask your opinion, listen, then say that they haven't heard that information, therefore, it is not real. Why did they ask in the first place becomes the question; to deny your information or refute it? Agenda, Libby, is important."

"Fair enough," Libby said. "I am simply curious. Please continue. I will not scoff."

Bix gathered her thoughts before she began, "You know what a Chakra is?"

"Not really," Libby admitted.

"Ancient philosophy says that there are seven Chakras or seven centers of spiritual power in the human body," Bix said then paused.

"And?" Bernie urged.

"Well, it is said that the healing energies of one of the seven Chakra is found within a Smoky Quartz Crystal. The brown color makes a connection with the natural energies of the world. Some people believe that it creates healing. Hence, your body interacts with the crystal. Actually, it is the national gem stone of Scotland. If I remember correctly, the Druids and Celts knew of the Smoky Quartz and would mine it. They made amulets out of it for protection."

"Sounds like one powerful force of nature," Jen said. "Do you think that people feel this energy?"

"Not sure but you might feel the effects and not realize it. America seems to believe in medicines as the only healing power. Maybe alternatives, like crystals, should be considered since they have existed longer than humans.

"Other entities," Bernie mused. "The Smoky Quartz does have a powerful legacy, doesn't it?"

"The Smoky Quartz Crystal is known as the actual stone of power," Bix thoughtfully continued. "It is suppose to ward off environmental and emotional stress. Druids named it the dark stone because of its forces. So to answer your question, Libby, no, a Smoky Quartz Crystal is not of financial value, but maybe we have been connected and protected by its power. Maybe this precious gem assisted us during our latest battles for justice. Believe what you like. "

THE END

**COLORADO
MOUNTAIN MYSTERY CAPER SERIES:**

**BOOKS CAN BE FOUND ON AMAZON AND
CREATESPACE.**

NOVELS:

THE RED QUEEN CAPER
THE WHITE GOLD CAPER
THE SMOKY QUARTZ CAPER

Simon Snoodle Publishing

ABOUT THE AUTHOR

The first book that I ever read on my own was a mystery. For some reason while other children were picking up the reading skills, I found myself having nothing but difficulty. The pages were simply blurs of words. The next summer, not to be outdone by my brother, I picked up one of my mother's adult paperback mysteries and faked it. I faked it until one day that summer, comprehension began. Heck with the children's books; I was hooked on mysteries forever!

For 34 years teaching became my profession, Drama and English. The interpretation of the written word motivated me into the educational field; I taught student levels 6th grade through College Prep. over the years. Eventually, retirement has blessed me. I now find the time to write mysteries and explore my favorite environment.

I followed my ancestors to Colorado and have spent 25 years in the mountains. The respect that I have for high elevation is incredible. I am addicted to hiking and being outdoors. Writing mysteries and hiking simply blended together into the Colorado Mountain Mystery Caper Series.

Janet McDermott

THE SMOKY QUARTZ CAPER